SUGAR ON THE BONES

ALSO BY JOE R. LANSDALE

THE HAP AND LEONARD NOVELS

OTHER NOVELS

SELECTED SHORT STORY COLLECTIONS

To Crystal

SUGAR ON THE BONES

A HAP AND LEONARD NOVEL

[signature: Joe Lansdale]

JOE LANSDALE

MULHOLLAND BOOKS

LITTLE, BROWN AND COMPANY
New York Boston London

Mulholland Books / Little, Brown and Company
Hachette Book Group
1290 Avenue of the Americas, New York, NY 10104
mulhollandbooks.com

First Edition: August 2024

Mulholland Books is an imprint of Little, Brown and Company, a division of Hachette Book Group, Inc. The Mulholland Books name and logo are trademarks of Hachette Book Group, Inc.

The publisher is not responsible for websites (or their content) that are not owned by the publisher.

The Hachette Speakers Bureau provides a wide range of authors for speaking events. To find out more, go to hachettespeakersbureau.com or email hachettespeakers @hbgusa.com.

Little, Brown and Company books may be purchased in bulk for business, educational, or promotional use. For information, please contact your local bookseller or the Hachette Book Group Special Markets Department at special.markets@hbgusa.com.

ISBN 9780316513296
LCCN [tk]

10 9 8 7 6 5 4 3 2 1

LSC-C

Printed in the United States of America

In memory of my brother Andrew Vachss. Warrior. Mystery.

Who holds the devil, let him hold him well,
He hardly will be caught a second time.

—Johann Wolfgang von Goethe, *Faust: Part 1*

SUGAR
ON THE
BONES

1

I could start this true story right in the middle of the bad business, as there certainly was plenty of that, much worse than we could have expected, and it came at us from an angle that damn near defied geometry.

I could do that, but I won't. Not just yet. We'll get there in time. I mean, it's clear in my head. I can still smell the gun smoke and I can still see Vanilla, her long blond hair under a black wool cap, wearing a headlamp, dressed in black, climbing up the rocks with a bow, a quiver of arrows, and a rifle strapped across her back. Jim Bob just below her, minus his cowboy hat, wearing a ski mask, a good coat, and hiking boots, his coat pushed back to show a black-handled Colt revolver nestled in its strap holster like a happy snake in its den. On his left side, in a special-made holster, he had a sawed-off ten-gauge, and woe unto whoever stepped in front of that little buddy.

Me and Leonard climbed behind them, me starting to feel a little weak with mountain sickness, with a slight tremble in the nerve that ran up my right leg, Leonard wearing a ridiculous wool hat with bear ears on it,

3

looking like he was doing fine, like he might decide to hang by one hand and drink a Dr Pepper with the other. If he'd had one on him, I wouldn't have put it past him.

Up we went, into the jaws of death.

And I'm not being melodramatic.

But I won't start there, as much as that memory clings.

Let's start at the place where it truly began for us. A time before it went utterly wet, dark, and dangerous.

* * *

Marvin Hanson said, "I've had enough. I'd rather drive a rusty nail through my dick and into a sinking boat surrounded by sharks than spend another day being a cop. I got the years in. I'm getting out while I'm young enough to waste some of my life properly. What's gone before just feels wasted."

"You're not that young," I said.

"And for heaven's sake, man," Leonard said, "just think. You got to know us. That's got to be a plus in your life. Right?"

"We are warm and fuzzy," I said.

"Like a tiger's butthole," Hanson said. "Nope. I'm finished. Put in the paperwork. Done, baby, done."

I said, "I guess Rachel is fine with this?"

"She's been wanting me to hang up my cop shoes for years. Knowing she's getting me away from you two is a capital reason as well. Wherever you guys tread, disaster follows, two times squared with shit-stained shoes."

"Sounds kind of shaky as math," Leonard said, "but you did talk a bit of Shakespeare there, so one might cancel out the other."

"That wasn't Shakespeare," Hanson said.

"But it sounded Shakespearean," Leonard said. "That's worth a few points."

"Rachel does hate us," I said.

"With a passion," Hanson said.

"You quit being a cop, then what you gonna do?" I asked. "Beg your wife for sex and not get any?"

"Already living that lack of pleasure, so nothing new. The kids are long grown and doing all right. My niece is spending a couple years behind bars, but word is she's learning the laundry trade and has made some friends. Rachel might not continue being as mean as a snake, now that I'm getting out of the cop business. Maybe I'll get me some once a month or so. May have you draw me some instructions on where what goes and how it's done, Hap. It's been a while."

Juvenile bullshit, but that was us. Old juveniles with bullshit.

We were sitting at a picnic table in mine and Brett's fenced-in back-yard. I had once been stabbed in that very yard and almost where I was now sitting in a chair. It was my birthday. The stabbing was not a present I had pined for. I nearly died. But I didn't. I'm pragmatic. It didn't bother me a bit now, sitting in that spot. I owned that space, not a bad memory. It was nice out, though the weather was starting to chill down a little, and in the next week or so I'd have to go for a heavier coat.

Hanson and Leonard were drinking beer, popping peanuts from a bowl. Me, I was having a glass of unsweet ice tea. Brett was out putting the sneak on a lady that was supposedly cheating on her wife. Gay marriage was start-ing to sound pretty much like any other marriage. I hasten to add: Except for mine. I was one happy dude in that department, and I got the impression that Brett felt the same.

"If I could retire, I'd want to be a dog," Leonard said. "I'd lie around all day and lick my balls in the shade. Course, could be bad for my back."

"And think about the strain of holding your leg up," I said.

"I actually hadn't considered that."

"Just looking out for you, brother."

Hanson took a swig of his beer, finished it off. "This is probably another reason to retire, so I can raise my level of conversation to a point higher than groundwater."

"Really," I said. "You retire, what you going to do? Got any real plans? Outside of getting some from the old lady now and then."

"We bought a place on Caddo Lake. I'm going to open a bait shop, maybe. Sell worms and minnows, beer and ice, fishing equipment, might rent some boats. You know, jack up the prices and tell them it's due to inflation."

"Wish you luck on that one," Leonard said.

"Who's taking over your spot at the cop shop?" I asked.

"I'd thought Manny. She was the natural choice, so they naturally chose someone else. David Justin. He's not from here. Brought in. Offered him better money than what I was making. He's not a bad cop, but he can be a number one asshole. He lacks my sweet disposition. He won't do you any favors, I can promise you that. As for Manny, she was born with the wrong equipment in her drawers. You know how the cop shop here is."

We did.

"Manny got screwed," Leonard said. "And not even by a friend."

"Yep, but she got a chief of police job somewhere else. I forget where it is. It's not far away. Still in East Texas. Oh, I remember. New Hope."

"Interesting," I said. "Chance moved there. They can be buds."

"Chance moved?" Hanson said.

"Along with Reba, who has become her ward, as Batman used to call Robin. Oh, and Buffy the Dog went with them, of course. Chance is starting her own investigative business."

"Chip off the old blockhead," Hanson said.

"I think she believes she's like Brett," I said.

"Word is, and I wouldn't say this to Manny, they were so desperate to have a chief at New Hope, they might have hired one of you jackasses, set you up with an online criminology course."

"That would be scraping the bottom of the barrel," I said. "They got Manny, they got the best they could get."

"Agreed," Hanson said, and made as if to get up, then hesitated.

"One last thing. Got something you might want to explore, make a little scratch, do me a favor. I wanted to catch Brett and talk to her too, since she's the smartest of the bunch, but give her my apologies. I'm only telling you because you're her employee and I'm picking up Rachel at her last day at work, then we're off to Caddo Lake in a moving van. When this town is in my rearview mirror I may shit with joy."

"That's a unique kind of celebration," Leonard said. "Will you wear a party hat?"

"Just tell Brett I'm sorry I didn't consult her first, but she can call me at Caddo Lake, she wants. Here's my number."

He gave us a white card with his name, phone number, and address on it.

"You could just write on a piece of paper with a pen," I said. "This is a waste of money."

"That may be right, but there it is. I got a pocketful, so need to use them up. Rachel's idea. Later we add something like 'I sell worms and minnows' to it. Again, tell Brett."

"We'll tell her," I said.

"Wouldn't want her to think I'd rather tell you two than her. I'd rather talk to her any day."

"We can understand that," Leonard said.

"Might want to get Jim Bob in on this one for backup."

"Oh, hell no," Leonard said.

"It's that kind of job?" I said. "Where we need Jim Bob? That sounds like more than I want to deal with right now. Maybe forever. Jim Bob is draining, and if he's needed, I'm sure the job will be draining too."

"I just thought of him as a help, since it might take a while, and the lady has money and wants to spend it to have this matter taken care of. You pass on it, you pass, but will you talk to her?"

"Who's her?" Leonard said.

"All I'm asking is do me this one last favor. I'm doing Rachel a favor. It's her who knows the woman. Name's Minnie. Minnie said she thought it might be a tough, maybe even dangerous job, didn't want to go to the police, hence my mention of Jim Bob. By the way, Rachel didn't want you to know the favor is for her. Hating you and all that."

"Understood," I said.

"All I know about the lady is she's big in community work and such. She and Rachel were in the same book club, and they are casually social. I guess you two came up somehow, and Rachel said Minnie called her and asked for help. Anyway, that's how you folks come into the picture."

"We've been pulling back lately on the muscle jobs," I said. "It's the muscle part. Mine hurt."

"You owe me," Hanson said.

"I like the way you said that, Hanson," Leonard said. "Little tremble in the voice, glisten to the eyes."

"There was no tremble and no glisten, so don't try and fuck with me. Here's her card. Name. Phone number."

"You got lots of cards," Leonard said.

"Remember, you owe me. Lots."

Indeed we did. I took the card and looked at it. It was unlike Hanson's personal card. It was glossy and white and had upraised gold letters on it.

Minnie Polson was the full name. The phone number and address were there too. I held the card so Leonard could look at it.

"We're on it," I said.

"You're on it," Leonard said. "Any possibility of having to be around Jim Bob and I might kill myself. More likely I'd kill him."

"Tomorrow," I said, smiling at Hanson.

"Don't count on it," Leonard said.

Hanson stood up. "Good enough. I've done my bit for Rachel. It's up to you."

He shook our hands, said, "So long, boys," and walked out of the garden and into the house. We followed. He went through the front door with a little wave, like the queen of England used to do.

He really did look happy for a change.

Like the poster boy for retirement and the possible renewal of regular sexual activity.

Of course, he would still need to locate a supply service for the worms and minnows.

2

Next day me and Brett went out to see Minnie Polson. Leonard, true to his word, did not get involved, even though we hadn't asked Jim Bob to do anything. As for the job, we didn't have any expectations, we were just doing a thing for a friend.

Minnie's house was out in the country. It was a big house with a long concrete driveway white as heaven's carpet. When we got out of the car you could hear and see little cameras spinning this way and that on the roof, at the windows, and just above the door.

The bottom-floor windows had cool-looking tan shutters on them. There were blue curtains hanging in the top-floor windows, except for one with a run of glass that was like the view shield of a spaceship. It was minus curtains, blinds, or shutters. I thought I saw movement up there, but then it was gone.

In the driveway, Brett said, looking at that big house, "If we take this job, boy, are we going to stick it to her."

I grinned at her. Like me and Leonard, she was more likely to do something for less than it was worth rather than bleed someone on price, but it was a cute thing to say.

Brett was looking cute, brown skirt, white top with a man's tie, brown suede boots. Her legs were long and nice and her face was nicer. She pushed her thick red hair back with one hand over her right ear, which caused her to look studious as well as cute. I hoped I too looked cute. I had on new blue jeans and had combed my hair with a comb that had four teeth in it.

We sauntered up the brick walkway that ran from the drive to the concrete-slab steps that led to a side door. We had been asked to use that door, not the front, and not the back. It was just under a carport that was big enough to house a couple of tanks, a bulldozer, and perhaps a trio of tricycles if you shoved them in tight.

Brett punched the doorbell, and rather quickly, Minnie opened it for us. For whatever reason, I had envisioned Minnie to be either an old lady or possibly a mouse. She was neither. She was small enough to be a mouse, though, about four feet tall, eighty pounds at the most. When she was younger, she would have made a perfect cat burglar. She looked fifty, tops. She was in good shape and had a pretty face, and her brown hair was shaved on one side of her head and swept up in front. It's a hairstyle that always makes me think they left the hairdresser's chair during an emergency.

She introduced herself as Minnie and let us know her pronouns were she/her.

"My pronoun is Brett," Brett said. "This is Hap. I'm not wearing any panties, and he has mine on."

"Oh," Minnie said.

"Fucking with you," Brett said.

Minnie's face wore inner conflict for a moment. I think her hand flexed to slam the door in our faces, but she didn't.

The interior decor was somewhere between discarded Buckingham palace goods and the stuff you might find on sale at Pier One. Minnie, for all the size and beauty of her property, seemed to be trimming her style.

She offered us a seat on an uncomfortable couch, one of the Pier One items, I assumed, and studied us carefully while we listened to the central air hum.

"Rachel recommended you," Minnie said.

"For what, exactly?" Brett asked.

"It's a bit complicated."

"We deal in complications," Brett said.

"I'm having second thoughts about hiring you, to be honest."

"That's all right," Brett said, "I'm having second thoughts about us being hired."

"I don't like that you made light of my pronoun announcement."

"Does my knowing your sexuality and gender matter that much?"

"It's progress."

"For you? I have a feeling you've done just fine without it. How about I be Brett, he is Hap, and you are Minnie, and we don't talk about your gender or who you prefer to fuck or how flexible you are on the matter. Because frankly, lady, I don't give a shit."

It went downhill rapidly after that. A few more words were exchanged, and a moment later we were standing on the carport steps with a slight breeze blowing our hair.

"Usually, it's Leonard that gets sideways," I said.

"I guess I'm making up for him not being here. Let's go home. I need to get this place out of sight and memory."

"For the record, I'm not really wearing your underpants," I said.

"Of course not, I made that up," she said. "But I wasn't kidding about me. I don't have any panties on. We get in the car, you want, you can have a peek."

3

Next day we were in the upstairs office of Brett Sawyer Investigations. The morning light was slicing through the blinds. Leonard, who had recently arrived, sat down and stretched his feet out on the ottoman while Brett explained why we hadn't taken on the Minnie job.

Leonard said, "You'd have thought I'd gone with you, way things turned out."

"I didn't like her," Brett said. "She's like those people that want you to know they drive a Prius because they're saving the environment, only with her, it's pronouns."

"We drive a Prius," I said.

"Not the point," Brett said. "We give a little to environmental causes and recycle, but I don't meet people with 'Hello, my name is Brett, I drive a Prius and recycle, and I'm a self-righteous asshole.' She just rubbed me wrong."

"I'm with you on that," Leonard said. "I never meet people and say, 'I'm Leonard, I'm queer as a three-dollar bill, and can I see your dick if you've got one?' Well, if I thought I might irritate someone I didn't like, I would. And calling a person 'they' confuses the dog shit out of me. It sounds like I'm speaking to someone possessed and in need of an exorcist."

Brett and Leonard looked at me.

"I'm riding the neutral wave on this one," I said. "Like some hamburger companies: Have it your way."

Leonard reached into his coat pocket and took out a folded newspaper, opened it, stretched it over his knees.

"Not to make an irritable morning any more irritable, but there's another reason I dropped in. Reading the town paper over coffee, all eight pages of it, I saw that Wilbur the Water-Skiing Squirrel is coming to town. There will be numerous performances, all out at the civic center."

"Didn't the squirrel have a different name last time he passed through?" I asked.

"Last time was maybe ten years ago," Leonard said. "He's been replaced."

"That sucks. I hope the old squirrel had a good retirement plan."

"Hap, his retirement plan was he died. Squirrels don't live that long. If he died in the bosom of a Southern family, they probably ate him with a side of greens."

"I know I would," I said.

"Me too, for that matter," Leonard said.

I had some bad memories about a particular squirrel from some years back, and it had nothing to do with water-skiing and everything to do with rabies. I decided from that point on to remain silent on the matter.

"That's your report?" Brett said. "The old squirrel retired and there's a new one? That's the irritable news? It wasn't like I had tickets to Wilbur's show and it was canceled."

"Nope. Something else. But I would like to point out — " Leonard held the newspaper up. "Wilbur got a front-page spread."

And there Wilbur was, on skis, clutching a handle on a rope, a little mechanical boat pulling him over the surface of an artificial pool. He had one leg lifted so a ski was out of the water. One of his tricks, I figured. His fur was damp. Wilbur looked intense. I wondered if he really wanted to do that.

"But the main thing I wanted to mention is on page two, minus any kind of picture and surrounded by store ads," Leonard said, putting the paper back on his lap, turning the page. "It's a news article that was trumped by Wilbur the Water-Skiing Squirrel. I remembered the name on the card Hanson gave you. Minnie Polson. I didn't know how that job worked out until this morning. But her/she, or she/her, got turned into a crispy critter last night."

"How's that?" Brett said.

"Got burned up. Her and her house and everything in it. Couldn't even save the mineral rights on that one, it burnt up so bad. Fireman, a Frank Bozeman, says here in the paper that…'had the fire been any hotter, Satan would have used a water hose on it.' Said he wouldn't rule out arson."

"Damn," Brett said.

That put a smell on things, and not the pleasant aroma of barbecue.

"According to the paper, and not fireman Bozeman, unofficial consensus is it was an accident," Leonard said. "Roast forgot in the oven, a wire-chewing rat, or something like that. But there hasn't been a true investigation yet."

I could see the color go out of Brett's face. "Doesn't mean her being burnt up has anything to do with the case she wanted us on," I said.

"But it could have," Brett said.

"And it might not," Leonard said. "It's not like you failed her on a job. Fact is, she never hired you. Didn't want to. Odds are it's just a coincidence."

"True enough," Brett said, nodding, but she didn't sound or look convinced.

4

_____

Lying in bed that night, feeling amorous, I reached over and put my arm across Brett's chest, my lips close to her ear.

"I'm not in the mood, baby," she said.

"That's all right," I said. "Could you get in the mood?"

"Nope. Not tonight."

"Could you pretend you're in the mood?"

"You mean service you even if I'm not wanting to?"

"Yeah. Something like that."

She laughed a little. "Really? I'm lying here feeling unromantic and kind of guilty, so no."

"Still thinking about Minnie?"

"Yeah. I mean, I didn't need to reply to her when she said 'she/her.' I could have just said, 'Hi, I'm Brett, this is Hap.' But — "

"You didn't."

"No. I didn't. Maybe I'm the one that's self-righteous."

"That doesn't sound like you."

"Don't start on me, Collins."

"Sorry. It's a hard road to walk because I'm on the side of everyone who has felt left out, and I'm on the side of those that don't fit in. Some things are hard to change with. We get locked into our own time periods. Thing is, things have gotten so PC that someone can find almost anything to condemn your whole life. It's hard to joke. It's difficult not to offend because so many folks want to be offended. But on the other hand, you got those who talk anti-PC, and to some extent I'm one, but they talk it so they can get by with saying awful racist, homophobic things. That said, I'm having a hard time keeping up with pronouns and, like you, find it unnecessary. But I accept there are others that find it important. I think the bottom line is how well we treat people. You and I both try. Leonard tries sometimes. Of course, to be fair, sometimes we shoot people."

"Are you trying to get a job as a professor? Because that sounded like academic gobbledygook."

"Sorry."

"Listen, in the morning, I say we investigate how Minnie died, just to find out if there's any question it might not have been an accident. I think that would make me feel better."

"All right."

"I think that would take care of things for me a little, you know, if it was an accident," Brett said. "A parakeet caught on fire and flew around the house starting the blaze, got caught up in the curtains or some such shit. She left something on the stove or was killed by spontaneous combustion."

"Or a meteor hit the house and started the fire. Maybe a cigar-smoking kangaroo stopped by, dropped his cigar in a trash can full of paper while trying to sell her tote bags."

"That would satisfy," Brett said.

"You feeling a little more in the mood now that you've got that off your attractive chest?"

"No. Good night."

"Is that final?"

"So final."

5

Come high morning the soft day turned on a sprinkle of rain that came down with the sun still bright and the street in front of the house slick-wet and shiny. Used to be, when it rained with the sun out, people would say the devil was beating his wife.

Brett and I had black coffee at the table on the narrow front porch. I ate some microwaved oatmeal sprinkled with some raisins so hard-dried that eating them was a bit like chewing warts. Brett had a piece of unbuttered raisin toast, which she ate like a truck driver. She looked so good with the wet sunlight against her face, it made the crummy oatmeal and the chewy raisins better. It was such a good face, and the life wrinkles around her eyes and mouth, so clear in the sun, just made her look all the better.

A short time later we drove over to the fire department and looked up the firefighter, Bozeman, who had been quoted in the newspaper, one that said it was an unnaturally hot fire.

The dispatcher told us where we could find him. We were allowed to go into one of the truck stalls looking for him. First firefighter we spoke to was him.

He was solid with weight-lifting muscles, and he seemed glad to see us, perhaps looking for something more interesting than washing dirt and bugs from the fire truck with a bucket of soap and water. There were two others helping. One had a hose. He looked like he wanted to spray us with it.

We walked with Bozeman over to the side of the stall to talk. We explained who we were and what we were doing. Asked him about his comments in the paper.

"Oh, that," Bozeman said. "I don't know. Let my big mouth write a check it can't cash. Chief didn't like I said that. Lot of people didn't like I said that. I don't know for sure it was an arson thing."

"But you thought it was?" Brett said.

Bozeman considered on that as if it were a multiplication problem. He pulled a tin of Beaver Chew snuff from his shirt pocket, opened it, pinched some out, and put it under his lower lip.

"I shouldn't have guessed," he said. "A guess is a guess, not a fact. Knowing is knowing, and I can't honestly say I know."

"What if we don't quote you," Brett said. "We're looking into Ms. Polson's death. Any lead might help us turn in the right direction."

Bozeman looked around again to assure himself there were no ninjas blended in with the walls or lurking under the fire truck.

He said, "I'm just telling you what it looked like from twenty years of experience. Arson investigators here in LaBorde, their training in fire investigation comes with a water hose and a Smokey Bear trading card."

"I'd like one of those," I said. "The card. I don't need a hose."

"You're saying you don't trust the investigator?" Brett said.

"Not saying that. I'm saying I don't know how skilled he is. Seems to be just waiting on retirement to me. Sees what's easy to see. Mind you, I don't know for sure what I think is true, but like I said, after you been doing this awhile, you develop a kind of instinct. It's like looking and seeing things you can't entirely point out to someone, but you see it, at least in your mind's eye, and you think it."

Bozeman paused to study the can of Beaver Chew he still held in his hand. "Damn, that fire investigator was the one told me to try this shit, to cut back on tobacco. Now I need some real snuff to get the donkey-butthole taste of this out of my mouth."

"That good, huh?" I said.

"It's mint and some such, and it tastes like mint and some such wrapped in sweaty underwear and seasoned with wet bullshit, not tobacco. I say that on speculation, not experience."

"And there's donkey butthole in there as well," I said, "and you suggest that on speculation too, I hope."

"Speculation," he said, and grinned some snuff at me.

"You were saying about the fire," Brett said.

Bozeman worked the Beaver Chew around in his mouth, made a face.

"Yeah," he said. "Way the house was burned. Hell, the color of the smoke. I think that fire was carefully and expertly set. Someone took their time. Dispatched the lady first, is my guess, then arranged it so her body and the house got blazed. It was all too perfect and too neat to have been an accident. Poor woman, she was mostly just a smoky memory. Found a melted watch on what looked like a burnt stick. That was her arm. I could smell an accelerant and what I thought was a strong bleach smell. Too strong for a single bottle of bleach to have been melted and spilled. I got a nose like a bloodhound. Accelerants can be in a house, stored in cans, in the garage and the like, and they'll have a scent. I mean, they would catch fire, explode maybe. But this was too even a smell, and it was throughout the ruins. In my mind, someone brought cleanup items and accelerants to the party.

"Another fire I was on, the investigator then had at least taken a course in fire investigation, said the heavy bleach smell indicated an intense cleanup before the fire. This one had similarities. You know, the arsonist bleaching out and burning up their DNA."

"What about the cameras?" Brett said. "We saw lots of those."

"None were found," Bozeman said. "May have burned up or been taken, can't say for sure."

"They catch the arsonist on the other fire?" Brett asked. "The one like it?"

"No, but they had a suspect. That was years ago. If it was the fellow they suspected back then, well, it wasn't him on this one. That guy turned up dead first day of deer season. Six weeks after the original fire. Someone shot him in the wild. To be specific, the head. Maybe a mistake, hunter thinking he saw a deer. Hell, maybe a deer did it. I don't know. But it can't be that guy. He's growing grass in a graveyard somewhere. Bullet that killed him, it was untraceable. No weapon to compare it to. Maybe that guy did start that first fire, was hired to do it, then the one hired him took care of him so there wouldn't be any talking. But that rules him out for this one. Talk to the current investigator. Jeffery Orwell. Might be he's smarter than I think, but if he is, that would put him on a level with a gopher. Don't say I said that. I'm in hot water already for speaking out of turn to the newspaper. And next thing I know, I'll be getting hate mail from gophers and lovers of gophers."

"Should we mention how much you hate the Beaver Chew?" I asked.

"Nope."

In the car, Brett driving, she said, "What do you think?"

"Bozeman could have something against the current investigator. But he sounded solid. Agree?"

"I do," she said. "We could talk to the current investigator, but until his findings are completely laid out, he's not going to chat us up. Bozeman, he wanted to talk. I think he'd have talked about the color of the sky if we had asked his opinion. Given us recipes for what groundhogs eat for Christmas dinner. He was chatty."

"I like them that way."

"Me too," Brett said.

"Seems to me, someone's got some thoughts on something, you give them space and time, they talk. Can't wait to talk. Can't shut them up."

"Are you telling me my business? Like I don't know that?"

"No. But like Bozeman, I'm chatty. Does this in any way affect my possibility of later romance?"

"It could," she said.

6

We drove out to what was once Minnie Polson's residence, saw what was left of it. I had never seen a house that burned up. Not a fragment of furniture, be it classy or be it cheap. Nothing was left but the burned dark ground and that smell Bozeman had mentioned.

Of course, I figured authorities had been through it, looked it over, but it was clear they couldn't have found much besides that melted watch, an item or two that would look at best like a Dalí painting. Poor ol' Minnie's arm wearing a melted watch. I wondered if a Timex might have survived where an expensive watch could not. Timex watches were like the cockroaches of watches. They could stand a hell of a lot. I was always thinking about puzzling things like that. It wasn't particularly useful, but I couldn't help myself.

"I don't know from arson," I said, "but Bozeman might be right."

We walked around the almost perfect square of blackness where once the house stood.

"Okay," Brett said. "I'm on the arson and murder train. Now I feel guilty all over again. Only more so. Maybe we could have prevented this had we taken the job."

"Might have burned it down because someone thought we had taken the job. Minnie didn't want the police in on it, and the question is why? Was it because it really wasn't a police matter, or was it something she didn't feel comfortable telling the police?"

"I know you're going to love this," Brett said. "But we need to talk to Rachel Hanson."

"Maybe you could do that?"

"You and me and Marvin are close, so both of us there is good. Leonard, maybe not. That helps us with Rachel, him not being there. We got to ask if she knows more about Minnie than she told Marvin, more than he told you and Leonard."

"If Hanson had known more, he'd have said. He wouldn't send us off to a parade without the parade float. Though he did mention bringing Jim Bob in on it. I think Minnie might have wanted some heavy arms to do a heavy job. But it might not have been the kind of job we wanted to do anyway. We are not thugs for hire. You and I aren't. Not so sure about Leonard."

"Rachel must know more or she wouldn't have asked Marvin to talk to you. This business has some serious flies on it."

"Pterodactyl size."

That's how me and Brett decided to drive out to Caddo Lake and find Rachel and Hanson and talk to them. I didn't look forward to it. Rachel blamed us for a lot of Hanson's mistakes, problems, not to mention injuries.

She wasn't entirely wrong, but neither was she entirely right. Hanson was his own man.

A light rain followed us for a while, then dried up about halfway to Caddo Lake. We stopped and had lunch at a little diner. It's often said that the out-of-the-way eateries, the little mom-and-pop places, are where you want to end up, that they have the best food. But the place we ate crapped on that myth. I should have asked to use their kitchen and cooked myself.

I can at least make an egg sandwich that doesn't taste like old grease and something yellow that ought to come with a stomach pump.

With my boiling stomach, on we went.

Around Caddo Lake the trees are thick and interwoven with moss. It's shadowy there. An alligator might crawl across the highway at any moment. You could almost believe all those tales of Bigfoot hiding out in the damp greenery.

Hanson's house was made of gray clapboard, but in a stylish way. It had a shimmering solar roof and was larger than I had anticipated. It was set on a high and large patch of land surrounded by trees on three sides. The open side allowed the driveway to reach it, and across from the driveway was the lake, shadowy green and rolling. It was an incredibly large lake, the only Texas lake not man-made.

There was a wood-slab dock that ran out over the water like an extended tongue. There were a couple of paint-peeling blue rowboats tied up to it. Out beside the house was a good-size building, and it was also made of gray clapboard, but not in a stylish way. It had gaps between the boards you could stick your arm through. It had seen better days, the last good one about 1945, and that early in the morning.

Hanson's and Rachel's cars were under the open carport, so that meant they were home. I'd been sort of hoping they wouldn't be.

On the porch, Brett knocked on the screen door.

A moment later Rachel opened the inside door, looked at us through the screen. Older than when I had seen her last, thinner, but nice-looking. She had the bones, you know. Kind that kept her features defined for a long time. I had good bones too, but mine had been broken quite a lot.

She still had the glare as well. The one that made me feel as if I might catch on fire.

"My mama taught me not to be rude," Rachel said, "but with you two, I could make an exception. Especially with you, Hap Collins."

"Understood," I said.

"I don't see Leonard. You and him are usually intertwined."

"He's twining somewhere else," I said.

"Marvin is out back, but I prefer you get in your car and head on your way, because every time you get him involved in something, it takes a piece out of him. And sometimes literally."

"Actually, "Brett said, "it's you we want to talk to. About Minnie."

Rachel lifted her eyebrows. "I didn't want to ask you people for a favor, but bad as I think you can be for folks, you can also be good, and this time I thought that might be the case."

"Minnie is dead," Brett said.

Rachel's knees bent slightly. She took a moment to rebuild herself, muscle by muscle, nerve by nerve, stacking her bones back the way they fit.

"I guess I messed up. I should have known you'd be bad instead of good for her. Jesus, what was I thinking?"

"It's not like that," Brett said. "She didn't hire us."

Rachel studied Brett's face, then opened the screen door and let us in just as Hanson opened the back screen door and stepped inside.

"Oh, shit," he said when he saw us.

It was heartwarming, way they were so glad to see us.

7

The living room was filled with moving boxes, but there was a couch and some chairs. We took seats, laid out what had happened, what was suspected by Bozeman.

When we finished, I said, "Hanson didn't tell us the score on Minnie, so we didn't know what we were there to see her about."

"I didn't know the all of it," Hanson said. "I was doing Rachel a favor."

Rachel reached over and put her hand on top of Hanson's. I liked seeing that, after all they had been through. Theirs was a relationship that had lived on the edge for years.

"It's kind of my fault," Brett said. "She got into the he/she stuff and it irritated me, for some reason."

"She is—was—trying to modernize her belief system," Rachel said. "For a long time, she didn't support her daughter, who is a lesbian. Minnie wouldn't accept it. Wouldn't admit that her daughter was gay. Until recently. Now she is—was—going overboard on the whole thing. Well, she was overboard for someone her age and ours, though if you look at it as changing with the times, maybe not so overboard."

"Do you know what it was she wanted to talk to us about?" Brett asked.

"She and I weren't really that close," Rachel said, "but I liked her. She called out of the blue, few days before we moved here, said she remembered me saying at a book-club meeting what assholes you and Leonard were, and Brett, I'm mixed on you. But I don't want to start trouble here. She said she remembered I said you folks were good at your job but dangerous at it too. I told her that Marvin knew you well and that I preferred he stay away from you. I was sharing too much, if you want to know the truth. Letting my mouth run. She said she needed someone that wasn't police because she didn't want to talk to police about it."

"All right," Brett said. "Did she tell you what she wanted to talk to us about?"

"I only know it had to do with her daughter. She said she was trying to cut things off at the pass. Thought there might be some danger. Thought the situation might require force."

"You should have told me all of it," Hanson said.

"If I did, I thought you'd be in the middle of it," Rachel said. "And I didn't know all of it either. I just knew from what she said it was the kind of job Hap and Leonard, and now Brett, get involved with. I wish I'd pushed to know more."

"Do you know where or how we can get in contact with her daughter?" Brett said.

"You're going to look into it?" Rachel asked.

"I want to at least investigate it a little," Brett said. "See if anything is lying on top and in plain sight, so to speak."

Rachel left the room and came back with a piece of paper she had written an address on. "This is all I know, and I'm not sure that's the exact address. I wrote it down the way I remembered. We had a book-club meeting at her daughter's house once. But this is the right street, and if that's not the house number, it's close. Her name is Alice Polson. Her girlfriend is... shit. What was it? Oh, Lilly. It's Lilly. I don't know her last name. Never met her. She wasn't with Alice when we had that meeting. That was before they were together, but Minnie mentioned her later. Said they were an item."

Brett looked at the address and passed it to me. It was in LaBorde. I knew the area, and I knew Brett did as well.

"We'll start there," Brett said.

8

Rachel seemed to have warmed to us a bit but not so much she wanted to chitchat and have tea and cookies or do pinkie swears and declare eternal friendship. She let Hanson guide us to the door and out onto the front porch without saying "Goodbye" or "Don't let the screen door hit you in the ass on the way out."

She was done with us.

"You know I'd like to help," Hanson said, "but I'm not a cop anymore. For that matter, I'm not anything anymore but a bait salesman, and so far, I'm not even that. Damn, every time I say that out loud, I feel like a failure, ending up at the end of my life peddling worms."

"You have yet to peddle your first worm," I said. "You don't know. You may find it soul-satisfying. It sounds pretty good to me."

"Does it?"

"Maybe not so bad," I said.

"You retire, you going into worms?" Hanson said.

"Probably not, but ask me when I decide to retire," I said. "By then, worms might look pretty good."

"Off the subject, but I want you to know, Chance is a hell of a young woman," Hanson said. "She and Manny came to visit, and the more I see and talk to her, the more I like her. Manny's no slouch either. She got screwed on the job at LaBorde."

I started to ask why Chance had come to see him but decided not to. She was out on her own, and if I asked, it might seem as if was checking up on her. Which I wanted to do but held my water in this case. She was going her own way, and I had to let her. Of course, she had talked me out of my Prius. In a few months I was going to give it to her, and Brett and I would buy a new car.

"We're proud of her," I said.

"And with good reason," he said.

When we drove past the spot where it had quit raining, it was as if a line had been drawn, and on the other side of it, it was still pouring. It drizzled on us all the way into LaBorde, making the streets slick as glass and the sky as gray as Methuselah's beard.

* * *

The next day, we drove over to the address Rachel gave us, but there was only an empty lot there, so she had to have been off a street number or two.

After we parked at the curb, there was nothing for it but to knock on doors and ask questions. It was a series of not-too-bad houses that had once been quite nice, but time had been brutal to the paint and shingles, and my guess was none of them were individually owned. They had the look of a slumlord nation about them.

We knocked a lot but got few answers. No one knew the name we gave them, no one had a clue, until finally we came to a door that was answered by a middle-aged man without a shirt, wearing flip-flops, shorts, and a tavern tumor. It was not a good look for him. The shorts were cut high and were off-white and pee-stained. There were ashes on his chest hair where his cigarette, which was stuck in his mouth like a pin in a map, was dripping burned cigarette paper and flecks of tobacco. It was a roll-your-own cigarette, and the smell from him and the house was so thick with burned tobacco and nicotine, I thought I might ought to have a lung cancer screening when we left out of there. There were also unidentifiable brown and purple smudges dangling in his chest hair next to the cigarette-ash deposits.

After we introduced ourselves, he said his name was Ronald Squire and he was just making a peanut butter and jelly sandwich and wanted to get on with it. He said he hated he was out of milk to go with it, but he was soldiering on.

This information identified the smudges in his chest hair. I was uncertain how you make a peanut butter and jelly sandwich and have it end up there, but Ronald knew how. I didn't give a damn if he had milk or not.

Brett asked him the main question, and he smiled at her. There were tobacco flecks on his teeth, but he seemed to think his smile was a winning expression. I could tell he was one of those guys that liked the ladies, even if they didn't like him back.

"Oh, the queer girls. Good lookers. Yeah. They lived here. I took over their lease. I lived next door then. Bigger place, this one, same money. Once in a while I'd see them kissing at the kitchen window. You know, get some curtains. Shit made me sick. One day they left out and no one saw them again, at least around here. When a rent sign went up, I jumped on that like it was a naked supermodel, if you know what I mean."

"I know what you mean," Brett said. I thought she might grab him by the throat and whip him with her shoe, but that moment passed. I think after our meeting with Minnie and her death shortly thereafter, Brett was being more cautious with her criticisms.

"Any idea where they went or do you know of anyone that might know?" I asked.

"Nope. Landlady damn sure didn't know where they went. She was pissed. She checked on them when the rent wasn't paid, and then she put up a For Rent sign. I think she had all their goods hauled to the dump. She said she didn't want to touch queer stuff."

"Being gay isn't contagious," I said.

"Yeah, well, how can you be sure of that? And there are those queer diseases. Tell you this, I was going to touch their crap, I'd want a fucking hazmat suit. Maybe a flamethrower."

He went back to the messy business of making a peanut butter and jelly sandwich with no milk to go with it.

We walked to the car. Brett said, "Just when you think the world is becoming more enlightened, you meet the Ronald Squires of the world."

"Or his landlady, if she's like he says."

"Yep."

"But since when did you think the world was becoming more enlightened?" I said.

"Valid point."

We decided to stop by Leonard's place and see if he was doing anything important like counting his coveted stash of vanilla cookies and Dr Peppers or possibly taking violin or opera lessons online.

There was also another reason.

Marvin Hanson was right. We didn't have a sympathetic chief of police to help us out anymore, but we did have Pookie, Leonard's boyfriend. He was a cop and might be able to assist us on a matter or two.

9

Leonard, wearing sweats and a shiny black head with razor cuts on it, let us into his and Pookie's place, which was toasty warm. The table had a couple of crumb-littered saucers on it, coffee cups by them.

"Just finishing up lunch?" I asked.

"That was from an early-morning breakfast," Leonard said. "We haven't had lunch yet. Pookie, he's in the shower. I was at the kitchen sink shaving my head."

"The kitchen sink?" Brett said.

"Yeah, Pookie has the bathroom all steamed up."

"Because you're balding, that's why the close cut, huh?" I asked.

"You ought to try it," he said, "all things considered."

"Honest reason we're here," I said, "is we're thinking, since we're all out of Hanson's help, Pookie might help us."

"Doesn't have the same access Hanson had."

"Has more than we have," Brett said.

"Fair enough. Coffee?"

We had some, waited for Pookie to finish with his shower. He came into the kitchen wearing a fluffy white bathrobe, steam from the bathroom trailing behind him. His pale, bald head gleamed. It didn't have any razor cuts. It never did.

"Thanks for telling me we have company, Leonard," he said.

"We have company," Leonard said.

Pookie sighed, took a place at the table.

"You two look like matching salt- and pepper shakers," I said.

"Pookie, they've come to suck up to you," Leonard said.

"We have a small problem," I said. "We'd like to know if two women we can't find might be listed as missing. Can you check on that for us?"

"That's easy," Pookie said, and wrote down their names and where they had lived. We only had Lilly's first name, of course, but it was a start.

"We also have a few other things," Brett said.

"How few?" Pookie said. He had the look of a man who felt like he might have stepped into quicksand after being told it was solid ground.

"There's a man that was a suspect in a past arson case, and he was shot and killed during deer season," I said. "Some time back. No one knows who shot him or if it was an accident or homicide. Perhaps you can find out who it was and see if there's anything about him as a suspect in an arson job. Also, there's the new arson investigator. We're curious about him. Name's Jeffery Orwell."

Pookie wrote it all down and went and got dressed for work. It was time for his shift. When he came out again, he was wearing a crisp uniform and highly polished shoes.

"I thought you made detective," Brett said.

"I did," Pookie said. "But I still got some of the old duties. Transition."

"Don't he look cute in that uniform?" Leonard said. "For a white guy."

Pookie looked like a large artillery shell wearing a uniform. "Cute" was not the term that came to my mind.

"See you when you come home," Leonard said.

"You know that's right," Pookie said.

"Keep the sausage warm," Leonard said.

"Always," Pookie said. He gave Leonard a kiss on his newly shaved head and went outside to his car.

"How nice, you seeing him as a sex object," I said.

"You know that's right," Leonard said.

"How have you two been?" Brett asked Leonard.

"Since yesterday? About the same."

Me and Leonard were so close, we usually knew exactly how the other was, but lately Leonard had been spending a lot more time with Pookie. I kind of felt like my buddy was being taken away from me. He once admitted that when Brett first came on the scene, he'd felt the same way.

"I'm stewing in domesticity," he said as he started loading the dishes from the table into the dishwasher.

"Is that a good thing or a bad thing?" I asked.

"I'm not sure."

"We like it for us," Brett said. "The domesticity, I mean. I don't think we're stewing much, though I have recipes."

"I know. And I like that you two like your domesticity, and I'm not saying I don't like it. I'm saying I don't know if I truly like it enough. Feels funny. I've had serious boyfriends before. But this is different. We're buying this place. Next thing you know, we'll have a dog. We're talking about marriage."

"I knew that," I said.

"That we were considering a dog?"

"No. That you were talking about marriage."

"But more than we were before. I think Pookie is obsessed with it. I don't know it matters."

"It doesn't in one way," Brett said. "But it is a sincere commitment. You're saying that you're going to make this work until the divorce."

"That's funny," Leonard said.

"You think you'll do it?" I said. "Make Pookie an honest man?"

"He thinks I will. He thinks he has me wrapped around his little finger. Or, more accurately, his dick."

"Does he?" I asked.

Leonard looked at me for a moment, said, "Can't say for sure. Probably. I've thought I was pretty much in love a time or two, but then Pookie came along. It's different. It's better. And that worries me some. I mean, I make this commitment, no more random fucking and no more being alone or just hanging with you guys. Course, not hanging with you guys might not be that bad."

"That's so sweet," Brett said.

"I am two hundred and ten pounds of solid, sweet brown sugar, baby."

"I'm thinking you might not be near that sweet," Brett said. "I know you, Leonard Pine."

"I'm thinking you might be about ten pounds heavier than that," I said. "Another thing I'm thinking, you're going to have a shaved head, you ought to let Pookie do the shaving. It might save you some blood."

10

Later that afternoon, I was at the office with Brett, just chilling. We got a call from Pookie. Brett thumbed the speaker on so we both could hear.

He confirmed that the two women had in fact been reported missing, and Minnie Polson was the one who had done the reporting. Neither woman had been found. Their landlady said they skipped out on the rent, left their goods. That last was stuff we knew, of course. But Minnie had made a point of saying she didn't want the police involved, so why had she reported them missing?

"Do you think they skipped out?" I asked.

"Possibly, but I think it would have been nice to have a look at the place before the landlady got rid of everything, brought a new renter in. I talked to him, by the way. The new renter. Good ol' Ronald. It was like speaking to a walking, talking cigarette."

"I know, right?" I said. "I can still smell it. I think it's in my hair."

"It's in my soul," Pookie said.

"Okay, so Minnie did talk to the police," Brett said. "Cops find out anything about the women, where they'd gone?"

"Word was that they went to Colorado for a vacation, and when they came back, Minnie said they were acting odd. Shortly thereafter, they disappeared. Acting odd before disappearing wasn't enough to get us police types to seriously investigate. A few questions were asked, and we moved on. We got things going on in the moment that are more pressing."

"Cats in trees?" I asked.

"That's nothing," Pookie said. "One shot and they're down, then you can kick the damn cat down a drain or something. No one will ever know. No, I'm kidding. Sometimes it takes two shots, even three. Shotguns make it easier, though.

"As for the missing women, thinking someone is acting odd and then they go missing isn't exactly enough to launch a major investigation. Think that's why Minnie asked you to investigate it. She maybe didn't want the police to know about her wanting to hire you, because she thought if she hired someone to search for them, the police would stop looking."

"She wanted to make sure she was doubled down on finding them," Brett said.

"My guess, yeah," Pookie said. "She probably had plans to hire someone else after you two bailed. Might have. I talked to the landlady. She is as pleasant as a heart attack, and not high on queers. Said she couldn't understand what a woman would find attractive about another woman's vagina. I can understand that. I like dicks. Still, I thought it best not to mention my orientation."

"I don't want to push too hard here," Brett said, "but anything on the man that was shot during deer hunting?"

"Nope. I looked. The real arsonist was found, and it wasn't that guy. Guy killed during deer season was probably shot by accident. Whoever did it went home without a deer but with a clear conscience, not knowing they'd popped someone off. The current fire investigator, by the way, doesn't seem like a bad guy, just dull. He wanted to talk about stamp collecting."

"Are the cops still looking for Alice and Lilly? A little? At all?"

"Officially they have their ears open, but unofficially, nope. I can only say I'll keep my ears and eyes open, see if anything turns up."

"All we could hope for," Brett said.

11

When we were through talking to Pookie, Brett said, "Minnie wanted a private investigator. We didn't work out. What's the next step?"

"What Pookie said. Hiring another investigator. She didn't seem all that knowledgeable about it, trying to hire us because she had heard of us from Rachel. I think she would've wanted someone else immediately. She would check for other private detectives hereabouts."

Brett lifted the lid on her laptop, began a search. "Probably she'd just go down the list."

Surprisingly, there were four private-investigator agencies in town, including ours. We knew a couple of them. One was owned by a nice lady who looked like everyone's grandma. All she did was divorce and security work, nothing else. She had been known to use a blackjack on some folks, and not that far in the past. I remember Manny used to call her Blackjack Jenny. Worked some tough divorces, I guess.

Next on the list was Pete Dawkins. Not one of our profession's finer

representatives; very likely to take any case he could get. He was always surviving somewhere between marginal success and living in his car, possibly
under an overpass. He was an old retired cop with a bad cough and a passion
for cigars. He had suit jackets with holes in them and he had mastered the
oily comb-over. I had crossed paths with him quite a few times. But not
lately. He liked Brett, but then, a lot of men did.

Brett called him on her cell, put it on speaker.

"Brett, honey," he said, "how's the ol' moneymaker shaking."

"Like a happy dog wagging its tail. How you been, Pete?"

"If I was any happier, I wouldn't be happy at all."

"Peachy. Listen, do you know a Minnie Polson?"

There was a pause long enough to have built the Tower of Babel with
prehistoric tools and a batch of monkeys.

"Why do you ask?" he said.

"I'm thinking she might have hired you, and I'm thinking you know
she's dead, being an alert investigator. I'm thinking too she may have paid
you up front, and now that she's dead, you still got that money, and it's
money for nothing. Am I right?"

"Maybe."

Nailed it. She had hired another PI, and one we knew.

"She tried to hire us," Brett said. "Didn't work out."

"She mentioned she didn't like you on account of you rained on her pronoun parade. Me, I'll go with she, he, it, them, that, and they if the money's
right."

"What I'm wondering is if you might have found out anything."

"I couldn't have predicted she'd die in a fire. I'm thinking, you know,
she doesn't need the money back, right? And it was a retainer. And now I'm
done with her business."

"I have no quarrel with you keeping the money," Brett said. "Not our
concern. But did you find anything? I know it hasn't been that long and she
was a client and all, but —"

"I can cut you off there, Brett. I never looked. Didn't have time. I was about to get right on it, and then there was the fire. My guess, her daughter ran off with her lover for whatever reason. Not exactly detective work, but my guess. Might have got into some financial binds and headed for the hills."

"They left their apartment full of their belongings."

"Yeah. Well, like I said, my client is dead, so I'm out."

"Nothing else?"

"Nope."

"Next question. We never got far enough with her to know what she really wanted. We only know what we know secondhand."

"She told me her daughter and her girlfriend went to Colorado for a vacation, some bump-pussy time or some such—pardon my French."

"I speak a little of that language myself," Brett said.

"Said when they came back, they were acting weird. Daughter asked Minnie for some money. Quite a bit of money. Minnie gave it to her, and before you could say 'Butt-fuck a rabbit in tennis shoes,' the women went missing. Cops didn't think much of it—that much I checked out. My guess is they took the money, went someplace with a sea breeze. What I got from Minnie was the daughter hadn't exactly been a huge success in life. Plans for her dog-grooming business went horribly awry when she groomed a poodle's ear right off its head with a sharp set of clippers and a yelp from the aggrieved dog."

"Ouch."

"That's what the dog said. Alice was, however, known for her excellent shampoos."

"Anything else?"

"Let's see. Minnie had fallen on hard times. Her husband recently left her, and it turns out he altered his will. Something happened to him, only thing she would have been left was a dick drawn on notebook paper. He managed to have their joint bank account shifted entirely to him. Has some good lawyers. Divorce isn't even final yet. Minnie had to sell some furniture, some other goods. But she had her own money too. She probably thought it was meager; most of us would think it was fine. Mr. Polson, Al, had quite a bit of insurance money on Minnie. And he had one big-ass amount on the house. Money, I suppose, that's up for grabs now that the house is a black spot on the ground and Minnie is dead.

"Rest of the money, according to someone I know that knows Al, the real stuff that's not in his bank account, stuff in stocks, this and that—his mistress is after it. Keep in mind, lot of this could be rumor. Listen, I know what you're thinking, that I'm a shit for keeping the retainer."

"Who would you give it back to?" Brett said.

"It isn't like it's making me wealthy. Enough to pay a month's rent and have a nice Happy Meal at McDonald's."

"Meal still come with a cookie?"

"Damn right."

"You maybe have the information on the insurance, the will, things like that?"

"Okay, maybe I do. Maybe I don't want to give up everything to an investigator my client didn't like."

"That doesn't sound like you at all," Brett said.

"Maybe I've grown some conscience as I've aged."

"I doubt that."

"Okay, she left some stuff with me. Might could give it to you if you'd let me take you to dinner."

"My husband doesn't let me date."

"You married that Hap guy?"

"Did indeed." Brett lifted her head and smiled at me.

"Guy like Hap," Pete said, "he made me think I might have chance. I mean, you know, in a storm, a dog or a badger."

"Which are you?"

"Whatever you want me to be, baby."

"How about we pass on the dinner date, but I slip you one hundred bucks for the information I need."

"Just as long as it isn't Monopoly money, you got a deal. Say tomorrow?"

"When tomorrow?"

"Anytime. I'm living at the office. You decide you want to give the hubby a night off, come by in the evening."

"Think I'm good on the night off, but I do have that crisp one-hundred-dollar bill I can bring you."

"Not quite as good as dinner with you, but better than having an elephant stand on my foot. See you."

When Brett put her phone away, I said, "I'd like to kick his ass."

"Now, now," Brett said, "jealousy is an ugly thing. Though a little bit of it, if it has to do with me, I like just fine."

12

_____

That night Brett did feel amorous, and we happily went at it for a while, finished up with both of us so satisfied, we did it again.

Details withheld.

We lay on our backs, sweaty, despite the air being cool. Outside it was even cooler, and rain was steadily coming down.

"I'm thinking perhaps this really isn't our case," I said, still breathing hard.

"Now there's some suave pillow talk."

"Minnie fired us. She hired someone else. She's dead. We won't get paid. And I'm feeling lazy lately."

"It's your age."

"Did I seem all that old a few moments ago?"

"I thought I heard your back creak just a little on that last round."

"That's due to job injuries," I said.

"Or age. But you know what, I had a bit of a foot spasm, and that might be age or maybe just a reflex from the thrill."

"The thrill, huh?"

"Thrill enough," she said. "I know we could let this go, but do you really want to?"

"Oh, hell, I can go again."

"No, I switched gears there. I mean the Minnie job."

That was disappointing.

"I want to want to let that go," I said.

"Whole thing bothers me. She asks for help. We bail. She hires an incompetent asshole instead of us."

"I'm fairly incompetent," I said.

"Ah, yes, but you have me as a boss, and I'm not."

"Touché."

"What I'm thinking is we see what Numb-Nuts Dawkins has for us, and if there's anything there, we dig in for a while," Brett said. "If nothing seems pursuable, we'll let it go."

"Will we? I know you. I know me. And when Leonard gets involved, and he will, none of us will let go."

"Okay, but here's the thing," Brett said. "Maybe we can at least find the daughter and her friend, even if we don't figure who killed Minnie."

"The daughter and friend are most likely dead."

"We don't know they're dead," Brett said.

"What do you think?"

She sighed. "They are possibly dead. Even likely dead. That's just surmising, though. Bottom line, is we don't know that. Finding them dead isn't as good as finding them alive, but it's finding them. Alice has a father who must care for her. She might be due some of that insurance money her father collected. He may not be a hundred percent shit. Might be some of the estate won't go to the mistress. I mean, there may be details within details. It was the wife he didn't care about."

"We don't know he cared about anyone. Another way to look at it is the father might be the suspect. Hell, the daughter could be the suspect. She knew there was insurance money. Could be why she and Lilly were acting weird. They had concocted a plan to kill good old Ma and burn the house down for the payout. Happens all the time."

"Does indeed," Brett said, "but if that's the situation, where is Alice? And where is her girlfriend? Inquiring minds want to know."

She was right. I wanted to know. Hell, I was like a mud cat, caught up in this business hook, line, and sinker. And it seemed like dirty business at that.

I was considering on this when Brett said, "Want to go another round?"

"Due to my age, before proceeding, perhaps I should stock up on provisions, get a canteen. Take a vitamin B shot."

"Naw. Come here. You'll be all right. My motto is 'If he dies, he dies.'"

13

Me and Brett went to the office bright and early in the morning. Leonard showed up, ready to work if there was work for him to do. There wasn't. At least nothing right then.

Brett was at her laptop, searching for as much as she could find on the Polson family, seeing if she could discover a hole we could crawl through to start our investigation.

She didn't seem to be finding much.

Me and Leonard sat around and drank coffee, talked, looked through the window at the rain, ordered lunch, and went to pick it up. Mexican food, our favorite. We ate at the office with Brett, talked some more, had more coffee, decaf this time, killing minutes and moments of our lives. We were waiting for business that didn't arrive as well as waiting until nightfall to visit Pete and pick up what he had, wondering if it would really be of help.

After a while, Leonard and I adjourned to different corners of the office and cracked open books we kept at the ready. I was reading a collection of Hemingway stories, and Leonard had an Elmer Kelton novel I had loaned him, *The Time It Never Rained*. Brett still had her laptop open, searching. Her thick red hair was pushed behind her ears and she was wearing some sporty glasses and an intense expression.

The day went by.

I had just finished, for I don't know how many times, Hemingway's story "The Battler" when I noticed the natural light was slipping away beyond the curtains. Night seemed to have come quickly, but that's because I had been lost in the stories.

I got up and switched on the lights. We took our leftovers from lunch out of the small office refrigerator and had a light and early supper.

Then we all went over to see Pete the fleabag private eye.

We got to the address. It was a dark spot where daylight and night-lights came carrying sticks and with a cautious attitude.

I got out with a walking cane I had stashed between the seats just in case I needed it. Place like this, one could never be certain. His office was on the top floor of a duplex. The bottom floor was boarded up and there were crickets singing in a patch of high grass near the front door, trying not to be too loud about it. Even they feared muggers.

It was me that went up first, then Brett and Leonard. There was a dull orange light on behind some nearly closed blinds, and the office door was cracked open. I turned and looked at the others. Leonard came over and stood beside me. Brett opened her small purse and took out a lady's gun, a .22 automatic. She held it down against her leg.

I leaned toward her ear, said, "Be sure not to shoot me in the back of the head, or anywhere else, for that matter."

"Francis Macomber," she said.

Having been reading Hemingway, I grinned.

Leonard, not one to fuck around, pulled a clasp knife from his pocket and popped it open. He put his toe to the door and gently nudged it wider. He slipped in quick as a ferret, quiet as a shadow, and I followed, left Brett leaning against the wall by the doorway.

Nothing bad happened. I could see Leonard gently bathed in the orange light on the other side of the office, which had a desk and two chairs, one of them for a prospective client. There were some paintings on the wall that looked like Pete might have light-fingered them from a cheap motel. The orange light was from one of those plug-in night-lights.

There was also a pullout couch in the room, and it was pulled out. There were stained white sheets on the couch—and lying on his back at an awkward angle across it was Pete. His heavily sprayed comb-over was flopped to one side of his head like an open trapdoor.

He wasn't catching a catnap or contemplating some problem requiring a meditative state. His eyes were open and one side of his mouth was lifted as if he were attempting an Elvis snarl. His skin was smooth without wrinkles, but the right side of his face was the color of an overripe eggplant. Blood was leaking out from under his head and was the obvious source of the stains on the sheets. He was wearing what had been a nice suit, especially for him, even a tie. He smelled of too much cologne, like he had been pickled in it. That was his style, though.

I slipped by Pete, used a Kleenex from my coat pocket to cover my hand, and quickly opened a door across the way, ready with my cane.

Darkness.

I reached inside, found a light switch, threw it using the back of my hand.

Porcelain from a sink and toilet winked the light back at me. There was a shower with a scummy plastic curtain pulled across it. I could hear water dripping. I touched the curtain with my cane and pushed it aside. The Creature from the Black Lagoon didn't leap out at me. There was just the leaking showerhead and a rusty ring around the floor drain.

I moseyed back into the main room. The kitchen was a hot plate near the desk, some Styrofoam cups, coffee makings—nothing of interest. The trash can was overflowing with takeout bags and boxes. He liked garlic in his Italian food. The smell from the can was enough to make my eyes water.

Brett glided into the room. She stood by the door, sticking her gun back inside her purse.

I glanced at Leonard, who was standing over Pete, looking down into his dead eyes.

"Living the dream," Leonard said. "Living the dream."

14

We searched around for any papers Pete might have prepared for Brett. We were careful to use Kleenex, which I provided from a pocket pack, for fingerprint protection so we could open and peek through drawers and so on. Pete didn't have much to look through.

In one desk drawer was a classic bottle of booze and an ancient revolver that looked as if it might be best used as a paperweight.

Brett sat at Pete's computer and, with a Kleenex-covered finger, popped a key or two. There was no password. The computer was ready to rock.

What it wasn't ready to do was reveal any files we might need. There were some nude women's photos, which I judiciously examined in case Pete had Photoshopped clues into their images. But nope. Nada.

Brett looked over her shoulder at me. "Have you memorized their proportions?"

"Just about," I said. "I could look at the blonde again."

"But you won't," she said.

She tapped more keys, found some information on stocks, something

Pete had obviously not been successful with. There were some odds and ends in the files, previous cases, some restaurants he had looked up, but we didn't have time to go through it. Hanging in an apartment with a dead boy without alerting the police could turn into something nasty hot-damn quick.

Leonard, still leaning over Pete, examined him carefully, said, "You know, I think he was beat to death. If he was shot or stabbed, I don't see the wound. Looks to me like someone clapped their hands over his ears hard, caused them to bleed. It didn't do his balance or thinking any good either. And that blow upside his face, that looks to have been done with a slap."

Leonard bent down and touched Pete's head with his elbow. It lolled to one side as if it might come off and roll along the sheets.

"And whoever did it broke his neck," Leonard said. "Might have been the slap done it, but if it was, that motherfucker had some juice behind it."

"That wasn't a very nice thing to do," I said. "I hate to say it, but I think now we call the police."

"Yep," Brett said. "Poor Pete. I feel sorry for him. About all he ever did was raise the temperature in a room."

"He's done with that," Leonard said. "He be chillin', stewing in cologne."

We went and sat in the car and Brett called the police.

It was a short wait. They showed up with sirens and lights, three cars full of cops with guns drawn. By the time they arrived, we were standing outside our car with our hands fully visible, being rained on. It was a light rain but cold as a well digger's ass just the same. Brett had placed her purse on top of the car because her gun was in it. I had returned my cane to the car. My story was I sometimes had a bad hip. This wasn't really a lie. Sometimes I did.

One man, not in uniform and without a gun, stepped out of the back of a police car into the rain. He opened an umbrella and started walking toward us. The cop lights strobed over him and showed his thick, dark hair to be tousled. He was handsome in a ragged kind of way, like a large Ken doll a pack of dogs had used as a chew toy.

He was wearing a brown pajama shirt, and the way his pants fit, I figured they were pulled over pajama bottoms. He had on house shoes, kind with the goofy animal heads. I wasn't sure which animal they were until he was closer. The back of the house shoes dragged dog tails in the mud.

Well, he had good taste in animals, even if they were imitations.

And that, brothers and sisters and those who identify as both or neither, was the last good thing I thought about him that night.

15

It was an easy guess that the guy with the umbrella was David Justin, the new chief of police, one who had taken Hanson's place. Probably trying to impress his cops by letting himself be pulled out of bed in the middle of the night to come to a call.

Still, not taking time to change clothes, carrying an umbrella in the rain, ruining his nice doggy house shoes — that was damn dedicated.

I figured it wouldn't last. Pretty soon he would be spending more time in his office instead of the field, and he would be slipping off to go home. Maybe I was thinking of me.

He stood in front of us and looked us over. "Who called in?"

Brett raised her hand as if in class.

"First, did you touch anything?"

"We were careful," Brett said.

"And your name?"

"Brett Sawyer," she said.

"Ah, thought that's what dispatch said. And you two must be the infamous Hap and Leonard."

"Infamous?" Leonard said.

"I know all about you," Justin said. "I know the previous chief indulged you. I will not."

"We found a body," I said. "We're not asking to be indulged, not asking for a loan or an extra helping of taters, just reporting a crime."

"I heard you had a smart mouth, Collins, but it's nowhere as smart as you think it is."

"That hurts," I said. Secretly, I suspected this was true.

"How you know he's Collins?" Leonard said. "I could be Collins."

"Because you're the black one."

"What?" Leonard said. "Motherfucker."

Leonard looked at me. I let my mouth fall open. He said, "My mama tried to tell me, but I wasn't having it."

"Enough," Justin said. "Let's not get off on the wrong foot." He said this as if he hadn't been the one who started it.

He signaled a lady cop over, had her take some notes on a pad. She stood under his umbrella to do it. She was new, black, professional-looking, but she trembled as she wrote. I assumed it was because she wanted to impress the chief. Maybe she was just cold.

As for us, we continued to stand in the rain, my and Brett's hair plastered to our heads, Leonard's bald head wet and slick. He had so many hats and yet had failed to have one with him. Except for a couple at the office, the rest were in his home.

We told what we had to tell. Kept it real but left some unnecessary details out, said how we were there to pick up some papers but there had been none to pick up.

"You touched things?" Justin said.

"I said we were careful," Brett said. "We been to crime scenes before."

Justin nodded slightly. "No doubt. Think what we'll do here is have our own look around. Not that we doubt your sincere detective work."

"We didn't do any," Brett said. "We found him dead, looked to see if the papers we wanted were on his desk, and then we called you. We'd done anything nefarious, we would have just left him where we found him and gone home."

Justin nodded. "You could have done that. Sure. But being good citizens, you called in."

"Goddamn right," Leonard said. "By the way, Pete looks like he got slapped to death."

A male cop who looked as if he might ought to back off the doughnuts and get a walking machine for something other than a coatrack came out of Pete's apartment and took the chief aside, along with the lady cop. We couldn't hear them well, but I assumed he was telling Justin what he had seen and found in the apartment.

When he finished, Justin and his assistant cop came back and stood in the same spot with the umbrella over their heads. The rain on the umbrella sounded as if someone was tapping his fingers rapidly.

"What we're going to do is, we're going to have you go to the police station to sit in a warm, dry interrogation room with some of our notoriously bad coffee, or so I'm told, and have you give your stories again, each of you, and then we'll probably ask again and offer you some more coffee, you want it. Maybe a little treat from the vending machine. I hear the little sugar-dusted doughnuts are to die for. You get pee breaks, and then we'll talk about things again. I want you to know, I'll do the interrogating. I so like that part. Because if you're lying to me, I will nose it out of you. The truth, I mean."

"Want to say right up front, I want you to be careful where that nose goes," Leonard said.

Justin turned his attention to Leonard. Justin didn't say anything, but he had chosen the wrong man to stare down. Leonard gave you the look—well, a stone statue's bowels might loosen.

Justin gave it up quick. He said, "You see, here's the thing, and I'm not saying it's the case, but you could have killed this guy and called in to make yourself seem innocent."

"That's not as bright an idea as it sounds," I said.

"We wouldn't do that," Leonard said. "We killed him, we'd have slunk off like coyotes with a dead baby in our teeth."

"All right," Justin said. "I'm going to split you up. You," he said, pointing at me. "You ride with Olivia."

The lady cop under Justin's umbrella said, "That's me."

"You ride with me," he said to Brett.

That figured.

He turned to Leonard. "And you, you drive the car in."

"It's my car," Brett said. "Leonard will ride with you. I'll drive it in."

"Okay," Justin said. I thought I noted some disappointment.

"Before you leave, you might want to call the landlord, say the shower needs fixing," I said. "It drips. A wipe-down of the shower curtain would be nice too. There's enough fungus on there to give the commode a yeast infection."

"I'll be sure and do that," Justin said.

"Oh," Leonard said, "and you have ruined the shit out of those nice house shoes."

"What I was thinking," I said.

"I got another pair," Justin said.

We ended up at the police station just as the rain slacked off.

16

———

Justin kept us late. I guess he had extra clothes in his office, because when he came into the interrogation room, he had on fresh clothes and tennis shoes.

We told him about Minnie. We told him about the missing women. We asked if he might look into it. He made no promises. We explained about us going to see Pete about information involving the matter of Minnie's missing daughter. We explained that part over and over.

Leonard said, "I'm going to tell you something, them sugared doughnuts ain't the shit, and for that vending machine, you need to get those little packs of vanilla cookies set up in there. Next to a vanilla wafer, they're the stuff. I could live off those sons of bitches, though a steak now and then and a glass of milk would be aces."

"I'll make a note of it," Justin said, "as I figure we might be seeing you again."

Finally, it was over with.

Me and Brett dropped Leonard off at the office, where his car was.

Inside his car, he shot me the finger, pushing it against the driver's-side glass. I shot him the finger back. By then, I was so tired I wasn't even sure I used the correct finger.

By the time we got home, I felt like I had been horse-fucked without benefit of lubricant and condom. Brett and me slept to the sound of the rain, and we slept late. I woke up feeling refreshed for a change.

We ate an early lunch, which included Brett's recent attempt at making a sponge cake for dessert; it tasted like an actual sponge. This was why I did most of the cooking and why the sponge cake lurked in plastic wrap in the back of the refrigerator like a mugger in a raincoat.

Brett went to the office. I put on my sweats, grabbed my bag, went to meet Leonard at the gym for our workout. I needed to keep the workouts up, because when I fell off, I couldn't drop twenty pounds in a couple of weeks and loosen my joints merely by stretching, as I once did. Those days were gone. Age is a bitch. Things hurt more, it takes longer to heal, and my dazzling good looks were a lot less dazzling these days.

I had noticed recently that kicking any higher than the midsection, which is really all you need, was difficult for me. These days, kicking high, it was like I had someone else's legs on loan and they didn't fit right.

When I got to the gym, Leonard was already in the bag room, hitting a heavy bag. He was hitting it the right way. He wasn't swinging it far out with his hits. His punches weren't shoves. They were penetrating.

I watched him hit as I strapped on bag gloves. I was both pleased and disappointed he wasn't missing a step. Someone got hit by a good punch of his, they might ought to have their will written out, along with funeral arrangements. The trick was not to let him catch you a solid one.

Leonard nodded at me. His face and shaved head were as sweaty as a whore's ass on Saturday night. We hit opposite sides of the bag until I was certain the bag was suffering and wanted a rest. I was taking out a lot of anger on that bag. I felt like Brett felt, though I hadn't told her that. I felt we had let Minnie down and that it was partly our fault she had hired a goober like Dawkins, and if I stretched that line of thinking far enough, I could consider that we had in a way caused a chain reaction of deaths — Minnie, Dawkins. And maybe by not helping Minnie when we could have, we caused the daughter and her girlfriend to be on the run or possibly dead. I didn't think that fit completely, as Alice and Lilly had already been missing, but I felt responsible, at least in that moment.

Fuck that bag. I hit it with a flurry. Then backed up, blasted out a long breath, started removing the bag gloves with trembling hands. I was quivering from head to toe. Moments like that, I knew I had touched that primal part of me; for all my philosophizing, at my core I was as ruthless and relentless as a bear with turpentine on its balls. I was, however, smaller, less hairy, and a little less dangerous. That dark part of me took some work to turn on, but I dreaded when the switch got flipped. It could happen so unexpectedly and so damn quick.

Leonard had also stopped, but he had waited for me to stop first. We went to another bag, one supported by a floor weight that was full of water. We practiced kicking.

Leonard was still kicking high, but as I said before, I felt like my legs were on loan from the Smithsonian. Still, when I kicked low, I was hitting hard.

After we tired of that, we did some light weights, then went into the boxing room, put on gloves, climbed through the ropes, and sparred a bit, all punches, no kicks, throws, takedowns, or locks.

We were for the most part evenly matched, though Leonard would disagree. Thing is, he was probably right in the sense that in a real situation, he could open a can of whip-ass and bad boogers quicker than I could and could dismiss all human concerns. That made him better in real situations. I guess maybe he was the one that was truly relentless.

He was also stronger, and that always matters. My hand-eye coordination was better. I could pick a target and hit it more accurately than he could, but though I had killed humans, I didn't really have a natural killer's instinct the way he did. I was about survival, and sometimes killing and surviving had to shake hands and get on with it. Still, once I opened the door, I could be nasty.

Me and Leonard went at it awhile, taking it slow, just keeping ourselves loose, our techniques sharp, practicing our control.

There were a couple of college-age kids watching, one black, one white. They were grinning. It was like we were an old-folks circus act or something. Old folks to them, anyway.

We finished sparring, and one of the kids, the white kid, who looked as if he had crawled out of a weight lifter's ass—his muscles had muscles—said, "Want to bounce around a little?"

"I'm okay," I said. I had come out of the ring and removed my mouthpiece and I was removing my gloves.

"I'm in," Leonard said. He had yet to take his gloves off. He was still inside the ring, leaning on the ropes.

"I won't go hard," the young man said.

"I will, though," Leonard said.

"All right," said the kid, and he grinned big, like a child who had found a forgotten candy bar in his coat pocket.

The kid had been watching us taking it easy. It was clear to me he thought he and his buddy were seeing us full throttle. His pal helped him put on some gloves. They laughed as they did it.

The kid climbed into the ring. "Don't worry," he said. "My buddy is ready to call 911, ask for an ambulance and a defibrillator."

"That's thoughtful," Leonard said, "because you just might need one."

The two of them touched gloves. Then the kid came out throwing jabs, and there wasn't anything soft about it. He was going for the gold. None of his punches were even close. Leonard moved his head, twisted his body, avoided them.

The kid started edging in, throwing well-learned combinations. He had something behind them but was mostly just punching air and slipping off Leonard's arms. It was all patterned combinations, and he didn't know how to create something different from what he knew. He could only use what he had memorized.

The kid dipped and started an uppercut, but when he brought it up,

Leonard was no longer there. He hit the kid with a cross and the kid staggered back, said, "Damn, old man, that was good."

"Wasn't it?" Leonard said. "Wait until you see the next one."

That's when Leonard sort of leaped at the kid like Jack Dempsey used to do and hit him hard on the side of the head with a left hook. The kid's body jumped and he did a backward bunny hop, then fell over and lay on the mat with one eye closed, his legs stretched out, ankles crossed, feet twitching. All those muscles he had might as well have been in a paper bag placed outside the ring.

"Jesus," said the other kid.

"Bring Jesus on," Leonard said. "I'll knock that fucker out too."

17

We got some smelling salts under the kid's nose and sat him up. He looked around as if experiencing the world for the first time.

"You're all right," I said.

"I don't feel all right," he said.

"Well, you will soon," I said.

"I didn't know he was like that," he said.

Leonard was out of the ring, pulling off his gloves. He said, "No, you didn't."

"You good at this too?" the kid asked me.

"Oh, yeah," Leonard answered for me. "He's good too." He looked at the other kid, who had grown silent. "You want to dance around a little?"

"No," said the kid. "I'm okay."

"Thought you might be," Leonard said.

We took a little time to talk with the kids. Ernie was the white kid, and Nemo was the black one. When I asked Nemo if he had heard of Little Nemo, he wanted to know if it was the fish in the animated cartoons.

"No," I said. "The Winsor McCay character."

He stared at me as if I were speaking in tongues.

"Look it up," I said.

We took a water break, then spent some time teaching the kids some moves. They took to it quickly. They both had talent, and now they had humility.

I told them, "Lesson number one: Don't underestimate your opponent, even if you're younger and stronger. You never know what you're getting hold of until you're gripping their tail, and that tail might belong to a tiger. In addition to that, just because we have skill and experience doesn't mean someone that doesn't know shit can't beat us. It can happen. Training and experience are on our side, but sometimes they take a day off."

They nodded.

"Here's another lesson," Leonard said. "You memorize patterns for a good reason, but if you think those patterns, those drills, are all you need, you'll find out soon enough they ain't. You found out today, Ernie. You got to change up, innovate, break your patterns apart, and use combinations that fit the moment, not just the patterns. And even then, you got to have a lot of left tit. Understood?"

They said they understood.

We wished them well, said we'd enjoy training with them in the future, they wanted it.

They said they did.

We showered, dressed, and me and Leonard left in separate cars, drove to the office.

Smart-ass kids.

18

———

At the office Brett sat smugly at her desk, hands behind her head, her chest thrust forward in what I can only call double triumph.

"What?" I said.

"Pete Dawkins came through," she said.

"Considering he's dead, that's some trick," Leonard said.

"Here," Brett said, and shoved a small stack of papers to our side of the desk. "Came in the mail. Pete had to have mailed it the day I talked to him, right after. It's not like it had to travel any great distance."

We took chairs and I pulled the pages over and looked at them.

It was the insurance information on the daughter, Alice. There were also some pages that were copies from a will. There were some handwritten notes from Pete that were addressed to Brett. I didn't study all of it.

There was a cover letter.

I HAVE AN UNCOMFORTABLE FEELING ABOUT ALL THIS, SO I'M GOING TO MAKE SURE I HAVE

NOTHING TO DO WITH IT ANYMORE. I'LL SEE
YOU TOMORROW NIGHT, BUT NOT FOR ANY
REAL REASON OTHER THAN I WOULD LIKE
TO SEE YOUR SMILING FACE. FORGIVE ME
FOR NOT CANCELING. SUPPER INVITATION IS
STILL OPEN. LEAVE HAP AT HOME. HERE IS ALL
I HAVE ON THE MATTER. YOU SHOULD HAVE
IT BY TOMORROW IF THE MAIL DOESN'T CRAP
OUT.

PETE

"Now, that's odd," I said.

"Someone maybe thought Pete knew more than he did, so they did him in," Brett said.

"That's not news," Leonard said. "We been thinking that ever since we found him pickled in his cologne."

"Yes," Brett said, "but it seems Pete might have been worried himself. And needed to be. He might have known more than he told us."

"What could he know about this that could get him killed?" Leonard said.

"What we don't know," Brett said.

I studied the pages. "The insurance is all for the daughter," I said.

"Yeah," Brett said. "There's another insurance policy Pete didn't mention when we talked. Might have held it back, might have forgot, or might not have thought it worth talking about over the phone. Husband gets nothing from that policy, but he does have one on his wife, where, if she dies, he gets a pretty good payout. Pete's notes say Minnie was contesting the policy, since she didn't agree to have it in the first place, or so she said. She was also trying to get a divorce. No surprise there. But she wanted a divorce payout, not just a pat on the ass and the house."

"Daughter might have wanted her mother's insurance money sooner rather than later," Leonard said. "Could be like that."

"It could be a lot of ways," Brett said. "The daughter's girlfriend, Lilly, might have done it, thinking she'd get money through Alice. Or maybe she and Alice teamed up to do Minnie in. Love can make you crazy. The husband could have done it to collect insurance money."

Brett picked up a pencil, tapped it on the desk.

"None of it feels quite right," she said. "Even though I know feeling isn't much of a barometer. I think Pete might have thought he wanted to pass on the runes, so to speak. Like in the M. R. James story. Fellow has these runes, and if he keeps them, he's killed by the curse, but if he can pass them to someone else, that person has to deal with the curse. We have been passed the runes."

"If Pete passed us a cursed runes," Leonard said, "it didn't keep the curse from taking him down as well."

"That's still a lot of guessing and not a lot of knowing," I said. "Was that information Pete got from Minnie worth killing him for? Doesn't seem like him knowing what's in these notes is reason to kill him. Kill him, nothing changes."

"I suspect they weren't so worried about this information but could have been more concerned about something they thought Pete might have known," Brett said.

I said, "If Alice and Lilly are alive and hiding and want to stay that way, would it be smart to come out of hiding to slap Pete around hard enough to kill him? Pete was a sturdy guy. I never saw him in action, but I've heard he was kind of a brawler. I doubt two young women would have been much of a challenge for him."

"For all we know, they might be professional wrestlers or mixed martial arts gals," Brett said. "And it could have been Alice's father or a hired killer."

"Got to consider the murders and disappearance of them girls might not be connected," Leonard said. "Pete had enemies. He was so nasty in his stinky dealings, dog shit would have been a deodorant."

Brett pushed her chair back and stood up.

"Let's find Mr. Polson, see how he smells."

19

My love of rain was sorely tested as we drove to the address that belonged to Mr. Polson. It came down steady and the wipers beat at it like a frightened bird.

Brett had to drive slow with her lights on. Even so, other cars passed us; we couldn't see them, even with their lights on, until they were nearly on top of us.

Nerve-racked, we arrived at the address. The rain decided to be cooperative and stopped dead.

When it did, Brett said, "Typical."

The place wasn't what I was expecting. There was no big, nice house or a vast expanse of lawn with a stone fountain. There was an open gate with a cattle guard in front of it and you could hear the water rushing beneath it. A barbwire fence ran in both directions from the cattle guard. It had wide strands that a cow could have gone through carrying an umbrella. The wire looked ready to fall over along with the posts that held it up.

There was double-wide mobile home that looked as if it had been rescued from a flood; I had seen a lot like that in the past few years. It sat unevenly on stained concrete blocks. There was a lot of dead yellow grass for a yard, and a cheap-ass carport was built out to the side of the mobile home.

In the carport was a Chevrolet from last century with gray filler spots where wreck damage had been repaired but never painted. The spots stood out dramatically against the faded mint green of the rest of the car. An old refrigerator lay on its side near the carport as if recently executed.

Brett parked out front of the mobile home. I got out and left them in the car, went up on a porch that looked less sturdy than the trapdoor of a hastily built gallows.

I knocked on the door. There was a burst of dog barks and snarls, and a man said, "Shut the fuck up, you morons."

Dog training at its best.

A moment later the door wedged open with the sound of water-warped wood, then the outside door, an aluminum framed one with tinted green glass instead of a screen, squeaked open a little.

I stepped back as the door was pushed wider, and there in all his glory was a man that looked as if he had been on a monthlong drunk and had maybe caught fire once or twice. His scalp was red and bald; his skin was all blistered. He wasn't wearing a shirt, and there were grease shines on his skin. He must have been kin to Ronald Squire, or maybe I was just having bad luck and was turning up shirtless folks.

He wore only boxer shorts, and they were not nice ones. There were holes that gave me a glimpse of a withered weenie and a nutsack so sad, it looked ready to fall off like an overripe fig.

Sight of it nearly blinded me. Or maybe I wished I would go blind.

"Hello," I said.

He'd had a shiny blue revolver behind his back, and now he pulled his hand around front and let me look at it. I don't know which frightened me more, view of his tired equipment or that pistol.

"I don't know who you are," he said, "but I don't owe you a goddamn thing."

"Not collecting."

"No? Wait, is that a woman in the car?"

"You can see her, and you have to ask?"

"Been so long since I saw a woman, I was trying to remember which one of us gives birth. And a colored boy."

"He isn't a boy, and 'colored' went out with bell-bottoms."

"Naw, bells are all right. I got a pair."

"Bells or balls?"

"Got a pair of each. As for the bell-bottoms, I'd need to lose about twenty pounds and shave my nuts real close before I could get in them. As for the darker fellow, I got no bother with that or whatever someone wants to call themselves. I grew up with folks who called them colored and were progressive in their day, I'll have you know. Term stuck with me. I did learn not to call Brazil nuts 'nigger toes,' though. An ass-whipping from a colored grocer set me straight on that. I didn't mean nothing by it, just ignorant and passionate for Brazil nuts. I was also ten."

"You are Mr. Polson, correct?"

"Bless your lucky fucking heart. You are looking right at him. Call me Al, though. Mr. Polson was my father, and he was a son of a bitch. Oh, all this red on me, the bumps. I'm not a leper and I don't have anything fucked up like radiation poisoning. Got an allergy to shellfish. Didn't always have it, snuck up on me in my later age. I do love me a crawdad, so sometimes I can't resist some boiled crawdads and dirty rice. This is my reward for enjoying them. I get where I have a bit of trouble breathing too. Told myself after this time, I'm giving them up. For me, they need a Twelve-Step program for leaving the mudbugs alone. Who the hell are you, anyway?"

I told him.

"So you're a detective?"

"That might be too high a bar, but I guess you could say that. I mean, there's mornings when I can't find breakfast by smell alone."

"You folks want to come in?"

I turned and waved to Leonard and Brett to get out and come on.

Al held the door open while we filed in.

Outside, the place was a mess, and Al had maintained a similar state inside—housekeeping by a wolverine. There was a Naugahyde couch that was riddled with rips and sagged in the middle. One armrest was gone. It needed to be shot and pulled out to lie beside the corpse of the refrigerator.

There was a big stuffed chair with a greasy sheen and three wooden chairs with blackened cushions that might have been rescued deck chairs from the *Titanic*. Two little yapping dogs ran around in circles as if they had some kind of brain disorders. Polson yelled at them to get out of there. They went through an open door and into the back room with only minor hesitation, and were quiet.

"They normally don't mind worth a damn," Polson said, "but sometimes they surprise me. They probably want something. Littler one, he got hit by a car once, never the same after. He's also prone to urinary complications. You folks want something to drink? I got water and whiskey. The water comes from a well that's got a dirt problem. Whiskey I'd have to pour in dirty cups. The ones got coffee stains in the bottom are your best bet. I keep them turned over so the flies don't get in them. The others, I wouldn't drink out of myself, and I got a stiff constitution on those matters."

Al was a gregarious motherfucker.

He seemed to notice suddenly he was wearing only his underwear.

"Well, now, lady, I apologize for being in my drawers. These are my holy pair, as I call them. You know, they got holes in them."

"Yep," Brett said. "I get the joke."

"I got some pants, but underwear I'm short on. This is not only my holy pair, it's my good pair. I'm going to put some pants on. We'll talk then. Whatever it is we're talking about."

"Thank you for that," Brett said. "The pants, primarily, but for talking with us as well."

Al went through a curtain at the back and disappeared.

Leonard and Brett looked at me. I shrugged.

Al wasn't in there long before he came out wearing loose khaki pants and a T-shirt, still barefoot.

We were still standing, so he motioned us to sit. Brett and Leonard sat on the couch. I sat in one of the chairs with black cushions.

Al sat in the big stuffed chair like the king of the garbage dump and surveyed us.

"So, what is it you want? Oh, decide about that whiskey?"

"We're gonna pass," Leonard said. "Scrumptious as it sounds."

"I get that. We could slug some right out of the bottle, though."

"No," Brett said, "that's fine. We're good. You should save that for some sort of special occasion."

"Christmas is coming," Leonard said.

"Won't last that long," Al said. "I ought to stretch it a bit, otherwise I got to break a piggy bank and drive that old wreck of a car to the liquor store. I really shouldn't complain. Car's all right. I need to pour a little gas in the carburetor to get it going from time to time, and I got the transmission wired up with a coat hanger. Same with the muffler. One day I started up the car and I thought it exploded, but it had just blown a dirt dauber nest out of the exhaust pipe. I ought to move it more. Keep it blown."

"Pouring gas into the carburetor sounds dangerous," I said.

"Well, you do fire the car up before you do it. I've had a couple of fires. Lost my eyebrows once in a flare-up. I looked constantly surprised until they grew back."

Brett stood up quickly. "There's something in the couch."

"Mice. I haven't the heart to kill the little fuckers. They don't bite. Me and them have an understanding."

"Me and them don't," Brett said.

By this time Leonard had stood up. "Feels like a lot of fucking mice."

"Fucking colony of them. There's enough they could start their own country. United Mice Land. Course, I doubt they'd govern well, being fucking mice, but then, who the hell governs well? What are you here for?"

"To discuss your wife and daughter."

"Oh," he said, and looked forlorn.

"Any idea what happened to them?" Leonard asked.

Leonard and Brett settled onto the remaining chairs. A mouse squeaked inside the couch, perhaps asking if they'd like to come back.

"Well, Minnie burned up, and Alice is gone. Hate that happened to Minnie. She could nag the balls off the Dalai Lama, but she was good-hearted. Loved the old bitch. Still, went off and left her for a floozy who spent most of my money; the rest I lost gambling. Oh, I got some put back, but I got to sell some stock and land to get myself right. I do, I'm in the green again. Just haven't been up to it. My floozy, Earline, drove my good car off, but hell, she earned it. As for Alice, well, that one keeps me awake at night. Filed a missing person report, but I might as well have started a trash fire in my yard and sent up smoke signals. I miss that girl. She's smart and sweet and pretty, and I love her. She has some of Minnie's nagging mouth, but I loved her too. Bet you're thinking I might have started that fire, am I right?"

"We're just looking into some things for Minnie," I said, not revealing we were on the job without having been hired.

"How's that?" he said.

"She asked us before she died," I said.

"And I'm one of the things you're looking into?"

"Our understanding is Minnie might have wanted more money than you wanted to give. In the divorce, I mean. And then there was the insurance policy, and the will we understood didn't give her much of anything."

"Hell, I didn't do Minnie right, and I know that. Got no excuse other than I wanted to spend my money on the floozy, that's all. Earline always dressed cheap and looked cheap, just the way I liked her. Looked like she worked as a pole dancer. Which she did, for a time. Went to a titty club and seen her and I lost my shit over her. Started giving her dollar bills, sticking them in her G-string. In a week those dollar bills turned into hundred-dollar bills and by then I was pussy-whipped from head to toe, and let me tell you, that leaves an emotional bruise. Sorry, lady. Bad habits. Learned to cuss from my mother. For years, I thought my name as a kid was You Goddamn Cunt. Thought my nickname was 'Shit-Face.'"

"What about Alice?" I asked. "You told the cops she was missing, and I'm assuming you haven't heard from her."

"I haven't. I also put in a report on her girlfriend, Lilly. I never met her, but I know Alice loved her. Told me how Lilly once rescued a baby possum from a swimming pool, gave it mouth-to-mouth, and nursed it back to health. She let it out one night, though, and next morning, there it was in the highway, a tire track across its back. But still, except for that getting-run-over part, a sweet story that says something about Lilly. I was supposed to meet her in a short time, but that didn't happen. And Minnie at first was all juiced up over Alice being queer. My take is any hole or pickle in a storm. Anyway, Minnie came around eventually. Hey. You know, you haven't even introduced yourselves. I've shown you my house and probably my balls, so I should at least know all your names."

We introduced ourselves.

When that was done, Al said, "Listen here. I still got a bit of stash, and I'll spend all of it, which would take about two days and one night, to find my daughter."

"Might take a bit longer," Leonard said.

"I'll have more before too long. Anything I can do to help, ask."

"Okay," Brett said. "We have questions."

20

First thing I want you to know," Polson said, "is I love my daughter. Hell, I loved Minnie. Should never have left her, acted like I did. But let me tell you, that young stuff makes an old man loony. And I do mean loony. It was like I had been hit in the head and turned into someone else. Met Earline, next thing I knew, I was eating healthy and losing weight and wiping my butt real good so as not to leave skid stains in my undies. Soon as we connected, all my common sense, suspect to begin with, went out the window on a suicide leap.

"Next thing, I left my wife and hurt my daughter's feelings, because even if her mother didn't accept her right away, Alice loved her mom and wanted me with her. She wouldn't even meet Earline.

"That girl I was so moon-eyed about, Earline, was only a couple years older than Alice. I was doing things with Earline I'd never done with Minnie or thought I wanted to do with anyone. Going into sex shops asking for a strap-on rubber dick, one of the large ones with knots on it, a box of edible panties in an assortment of flavors, chocolate primarily, asking if they had some made from pork products. Stocking up on incense candles. I got a prescription for Viagra, and believe me, I needed it. Couple months in, thought I might need a pecker transplant, and first time Earline strapped on that rubber weenie, sent it on an exploratory mission, it hurt so bad I could see Satan holding hands with the fucking pope. I started snorting cocaine with her. I was a different man. And some of that was good. Crazy part was I got to where I saw Earline in my dreams — without clothes, of course. I could make out her shape on a grilled cheese sandwich. Couldn't think about nothing but her. I could smell her when she wasn't even around. I could be in the grocery store at the fruit section, see a couple melons, and boom, I'm thinking of her titties. She had me pinched tight by the short-and-curlies. I was batshit-crazy. Cocaine wasn't shit compared to her.

"By the time the heat cooled, I realized I'd given her access to my bank account and signed over all manner of shit to her, and she'd taken a hike with all the clothes and shoes I bought her. Took the rubber dick with her, whole strap-on outfit. Left some of the panties. I ate the entire box over a couple days, tried to imagine her in them. They go good with coffee, by the way. But when it was over with her, it was over. She had a larger bank account somewhere and I had a smaller one. And that's all she wrote."

He reached into a drawer by the sink next to where he was sitting, pulled out a framed picture. He handed it to me. It was a photo of him looking a lot snappier, wearing a big white cowboy hat and snakeskin boots. He was with a woman way younger than him. She was indeed a knockout. Long blond hair, brown eyes that jumped out of the frame. A body by Sex and Lust with a side of Goddamn.

"Took this shot at a tractor pull," Al said. "See that? She's like a super-model with a truckload of Dallas Cowboys cheerleaders driven up her ass. Someone like that, be fair, wouldn't you slap your mama and steal her purse if she told you to?"

We didn't volunteer opinions. Leonard didn't mention he was queer. Brett sighed in that exasperated way women do when they realize they live on the same planet men live on.

"Next thing I knew, I was living in this fucked-up mobile home. Bought it with a loan. Let me tell you. I've done some work on this motherfucker. Used to smell like the bottom of the Trinity River. Got caught up in a flood. But good old Bob "We Tote the Note" Dowger fixed me up with this cracker box and threw in the furniture. Still looks like shit, but it's all about perspective. Picked it up for a song, and by then, a song was about all I had at the ready, besides my fucking sterling personality."

"Somewhere in this epic narrative," Leonard said, "I hope there's something to do with Minnie's death and your missing daughter and her girlfriend."

"I arrive where I'm going," he said, "but I admit, my thoughts sometimes travel by banana boat. Thing is, I was planning on trying to make up with Minnie. I missed her now that my gal friend had left me and skimmed me, and I will admit, Minnie had a little money left, and I didn't, not close at hand, anyway. Have to really jump through some hoops to sell my stock and such, way I got it all tied up, and the offshore money, well, you got to go snoopy on that, I'll tell you, otherwise you wake up in prison with a tattooed body builder that's way handsy and calls you baby. But it wasn't just the money. I'd get it eventually. I missed Minnie. I was hoping she'd take a foolish old man back. Of course, she got burned up before I could make my move. Left me with barbecued regrets."

"But you got some insurance out of that, right?" Brett said.

"I did. What I live on, and some of what I could give you for working for me. And I know that little financial miracle was the result of Minnie being cooked along with the house, but I didn't do it. Wouldn't do that. Already had this thing to worry about with Alice, her being gone, and then my wife was gone. Let me tell you, it's going to be some gloomy holidays coming up. Just me and those two fucked-up dogs."

"So, no idea where your daughter might be?" Brett said.

"None."

"Do you know where Lilly came from, what her last name is?" Brett said.

"I do not. Never met her. Minnie never met her and didn't want to for a long time. I think Alice was arranging a meet-and-greet for Minnie, then

75

me, but of course that never happened. Never even seen a photo of her. Alice said she was a stunner."

"You think Alice is alive?" Leonard asked.

"I have fears she might not be. I mean, I looked for her, told the law, but they didn't bother. Minnie hired a private eye. She told me that much. Right after that, she was dead. Wait. Was the private eye you guys?"

"No," I said. "Private eye she hired is dead."

"What the fuck? I was thinking he was out there beating the bushes, looking for Alice."

"Got killed in his office," I said. "Would have taken a tough person to do that. You look tough."

"Aw, come on. I want to find my daughter. That wouldn't help me find her. I didn't even know the private eye's name, just that Minnie hired one. We weren't exactly over-chatty. Just talked about Alice, as we both had her best interests in mind. Alice had gone off to Colorado, came back unhappy and nervous as a goat at a barbecue. Next thing I know, she and Lilly were gone, and then Minnie was dead. I called the cops several times. They are more likely to find Jimmy Hoffa and Amelia Earhart than Alice, because I don't believe they're looking. And let me repeat what I said before: I got a little money at hand, and I can get more later, though it might take some time. I can hire you to look for her, though you're already looking. Wait. Why is that? Minnie's dead, so you got no client."

"We were curious," Brett said. "Minnie and I had a misunderstanding, so she didn't actually hire us. I believe what happened to her was arson and murder."

"We're on the same page there, gorgeous," Al said. "I think Alice and Lilly brought something back with them from Colorado, some information that got them on someone's shit radar, and that led to Minnie. I think who-ever was bothered by what the girls knew figured they could get informa-tion from Minnie about Alice and Lilly. I'm pretty sure they got it. Everyone cracks eventually. Show me a pair of pliers and a wired-up car battery with jumper-cable snips on the end, hook 'em to my tits or my manly appliances, and I'll give you my life story and my parents' hereditary tree. So, may be too late for Alice and Lilly, but I'm hoping it isn't. Either way, I want to hire you."

"We'll look into Minnie's death and your daughter and Lilly's disappearance," Brett said. "But we don't want your money."

"We don't?" I said.

"Yeah," Leonard said, "I was thinking maybe we did."

"Not sure the insurance money you got is clean," Brett said. "Not sure I want the later money from a dodgy offshore deal."

"It's sizable moolah, but it's clean," Al said. "The insurance money is clean. What I got coming from other deals, it might have to visit some financial washaterias, but it'll be clean eventually."

"'Eventually' is the part that worries me," Brett said. "Since we're already on it, let us shake a few trees, see what's out there, what we can find."

"Can't ask for fairer than that," Al said. "Go, Cowboys."

21

As we were leaving, the dogs started up again, came running from the back room to bark us out and away. I could see them through the green glass inner door along with Al. It was as if I were seeing them through algae-thick water.

Al said, "Shut the fuck up, guys."

The dogs slowed their barking, but neither of them ceased entirely.

"Keep me in the loop, now," Al said, pushing the door open, stepping out on the porch, as we crossed the yard to the car.

The dogs kept barking but didn't leave the trailer.

"We'll get back to you," Brett said.

"Goddamn it, go to your room," Al said to the dogs.

The dogs finally stopped barking. Guess they had gone to their room, which, of course, had to be Al's room too. There weren't that many rooms in that place.

Brett drove us away from Al's bright mansion, sweet ride, and lovely pets. The rain had stopped for good and it was bright and cool. The streets had a snot-nose shine to them. The wipers were still beating, so Brett turned those off.

"That was surreal," Brett said. "I felt like I fell down a greased rabbit hole. A nasty one. He wasn't at all what I expected."

"I don't know what to think," I said. "He sounded loopy but sincere, making me wonder he might still have some of that cocaine in his sock drawer. That Earline girl certainly did his head in. But if we see him again, I think we ought to chip in, buy him some shorts."

"Something of real fucking quality," Leonard said. "Even festive. Soft, with a colorful pattern."

22

That night, while Brett slept, gently snoring, covered in a blanket, I sat propped up in bed with my pillows and the reading lamp on. I read some of an Owen King novel that was thick and good and was lost in it for quite some time. Thanks, Mr. King.

The light rain outside, the now and again rumble of thunder, the occasional flash of lightning seen through the curtained window that looked out over my side yard and the neighbor's roof top, was oddly comforting.

My eyes grew tired. I slipped in a bookmark, placed the book on my end table, and, with the light still on, continued to sit there, thinking.

The Polson family seemed to be undergoing a curse. Minnie incinerated along with her home. Alice and her girlfriend in the wind, possibly dead. Al Polson, having lost the bulk of his money to a hot woman, was living in a mobile home a homeless drug addict might reject. Living there with two angry dogs, a couch full of mice that were building their own civilization while their home provider lounged about with holes in his shorts, dangling balls, and a dirty glass full of whiskey.

I couldn't decide if I liked or disliked the guy. He seemed to be tuned into a station my radio didn't get without considerable static. The other thing was, I felt myself believing him, even feeling sorry for him, but if I turned out to be wrong about him, it wouldn't be the first time.

I ran all this business around and around in my head, finally played out with it, thought about other things, and finally nothing. I reached a meditative state, and contrary to what the yogis teach, I didn't feel any calmer or wiser.

The rain was still coming down, but the lightning and thunder had stopped.

I turned off my light and went to sleep. Early in the morning, I awoke feeling uncomfortable. I knew it was early because the clock on my nightstand, up against my lamp and book, told me so.

The discomfort I felt, along with having to pee, was a crawling snake of apprehension at the back of my neck. What was the cause? Had I heard something in my sleep? A noise?

I got up and went to the bathroom, but my unease remained. The feeling that something was wrong was so intense, I quietly opened my nightstand drawer and took the .22 automatic out of it. The gun was as light as a ham sandwich minus the mustard and lettuce. I didn't really like the damn things, but in my line of work, one had need of such now and again. I was also an unerring shot, and my ability with one was hard for me to explain. I had never really trained much with guns and never went to the gun range. I could just do it. I was especially good with a long gun, and with a handgun I was better than the average bear, even if the bear had armed response training and a steady paw.

I was wearing only boxer shorts, but unlike Al Polson's, mine were clean and intact. I took the time to put the pistol aside and pull on pants. If a booger was going to get me, I didn't want it to take me away wearing only my drawers. I picked up the gun again and, using caution, slowly opened the bedroom door and went barefoot into the hall and onto the stairway landing.

I looked down into the living room, but it was just a room full of shadows. The outside light from the street helped me see a little better than I might have, but it didn't help me see anything that mattered.

I was starting to feel foolish. Still, my skin felt colder than the night warranted. The hair on the back of my neck was standing up straight, and goose bumps traveled along my arms and felt like icy pimples.

I walked softly along the landing, looking into the living room from different angles. I could see the opening to the dining room and kitchen, but I couldn't see inside. An elephant could have been in there sitting at the table drinking a glass of water and eating peanuts, and from that angle I wouldn't have seen it. It would have the edge on me if I came down and went in there. It would have what Leonard and I called the elephant of surprise.

I stood on the landing by the stair railing and listened intently. A car went by on the road outside, beaming lights and splashing rainwater, and then it was gone.

I heard a light mouselike squeak from the kitchen area, and then it was silent. That squeak would have come from the spot just in front of the sink. I had been meaning to hire someone handy to pull up the old linoleum there and see what was going on, fix the floor and replace the linoleum with tile.

I didn't dwell long on my needed home repairs. I started silently downstairs.

23

There was a light from the carport coming through the garage. We left it on a lot of the time. The light came through the kitchen window and outlined a man sitting at the table. He was a small man dressed in black. His head was shaved. That seemed all the fashion these days. There was a stony stillness to him.

On the table was an empty saucer with a small glass beside it. Next to it was a large silver automatic. His right hand was close to it.

Even in bad light I recognized him. He was the man Leonard and I called Kung Fu Bobby. We were not close, but we had a history. He had handed me and Leonard our asses in every physical encounter we'd had with him. He was a well-trained martial artist and deadly. That big gun on my kitchen table made him even more deadly.

I was pointing my pistol right at him. I felt certain I had him. If he made a move, I figured I could ruin his day, but he had fooled me a few times before.

"Drop in for a snack?" I asked.

"Found some vanilla cookies under the cabinet, had a glass of milk. I suppose I should say thank you."

"You shouldn't be in my house," I said. "And you damn sure shouldn't have eaten those cookies. I keep them for my friend when he drops by."

"The black man."

"The man," I said.

He smiled at me. "I was about to go upstairs and wake you," he said.

"Were you?"

"I was. But I could hear you up there on the landing."

"You have good ears."

"Training. I didn't know about the squeaky place in front of the sink. I was stepping light, but it still squeaked. I was putting the cookie bag back. Being polite, except you're missing four cookies. I'm not here to harm you, by the way."

"I could shoot your eye out and pop you twice more before you hit the floor."

"I know that. And I know last time you spared me. You could have shot me. I saw how you could shoot. But you let me run away."

"Shooting you in the back would have been a highlight that night. What makes you think I missed you on purpose? Wind might have kicked up. You don't know."

"You could have knocked my head off even at that distance. You didn't. I owe you one. I pay personal debts."

"That's sweet," I said, "but how could you possibly pay me back a life? Stock tips? The hell with it, fellow. Thanks for coming by."

"I owe you, but I don't owe you forever. I'll tell you once, then I'm gone, and if you're lucky, you'll never see me again. I'm letting go of a lot of scratch, doing this. Because now I'm out, I'll keep going and not come back. Not for this thing, anyway. Something else, who knows? But here's your lifesaving tip. This business with the Polson family—let it go. It won't turn out well. And you best keep your guard up if you don't let it go. Even if you do, you might still want to keep one eye open for a while. This is more than you and your friend and your wife can handle."

"You know a lot about me," I said.

"I do."

"You warn me but don't tell me what it's about? What kind of warning is that?"

"Kind you're getting. I don't usually talk this much about what I'm involved with. I don't normally talk this much about anything. I will tell you simply that I don't know all the details, as that's on a need-to-know basis. I'm hired help, but I know enough to know you're just about to put your dick in a buzz saw. Lots of lines of business going on here, and not all of them know about the others, at least not fully. Yet they crisscross. I got enough puzzle pieces in front of me to make out the general design, if not the whole of it. More important, I don't like owing a debt, and when you showed up in this, I decided it was time for me to pay it."

"I never charged you," I said.

"In your own way, you did. I don't have a ton of scruples about what I do, but I have what you might call personal convictions. But that's all you get for pulling your shot to the left."

"It was to the right," I said.

"Was it?"

"Yep."

"I been thinking all this time it was to the left."

He knew exactly to which side I had pulled. My guess was he was making sure I had indeed pulled as he expected. I had just confirmed that for him.

Kung Fu Bobby stood up slowly, leaving the gun on the table.

"Did you slap Pete, the private eye, to death? Splashing hands and all that?" I asked.

He gave me a faint smile, and that was all the answer I was going to get.

"I'm going now, before my employer realizes I'm gone and not coming back. Consider yourself paid in full. And if I see you again, there's a good chance I'm coming to kill you. I don't foresee such a thing, but in my business, who knows? Sometimes the money is too good to pass up. They may want to hire me back, and if the money is right, I might want to come back.

They won't be able to find me, but they can leave a message, and they offer me enough, I might sign back on. I'm worth a lot, you see. So who knows."

"Yeah. Who knows?"

"You stay out of it, back off, you and yours may be just fine. Otherwise, what can I say?"

"Yeah, what can you say?"

He kept his eyes on me as he picked up his gun, gripping it at the barrel with his thumb and forefinger.

"Putting it away," he said, adjusting it in his hand and tucking it under his coat.

I never let my gun move away from him. I tracked him as he went through the kitchen door and outside. I stood in the open door and watched him go. He didn't look back.

Kung Fu Bobby walked away casually, turned right at our garage, and disappeared in front of it.

I walked outside in my bare feet, crossed the patch of wet grass that led to the garage, and looked around the corner, the gun still ready. He was nowhere to be seen. It was as if it had all been a dream.

24

Somehow, the sunlight that came through our kitchen window seemed damp. The kitchen table had a streak of light on it that made the wood polish shine as if just wiped with water. It made Leonard's head shine as well. His skull looked a bit like dark mahogany, which might account for his ability to take a punch.

"The son of a bitch," Leonard said. "I told you sparing him was a bad idea. I knew that's what you did. You don't ever miss."

"Now and again," I said.

"And he got into my cookies, and that right there is the goddamn ticket to hell."

"I know. I'm sorry. I think he ate six or seven of them. Okay, I ate a few, so he probably ate four."

"Really, boys," Brett said. "Cookies. The worry here is he got through our locks like they were smoke, and there's nothing on the security cameras. He knocked them out somehow."

"He's a ninja," I said.

"He could have killed us in our sleep," Brett said. "Because of him, we know there's certainly more to this business than just arson, murder, and insurance fraud."

"It sounds deep and packed with shit," Leonard said. "As for Kung Fu Bobby, I can't stand a thief or a skulker, and he's both. Maybe he's just trying to get us out of the picture without having to get messy. If he doesn't have to kill us, that's easier for him."

"I don't think he minds getting messy," I said. "I don't think he cares about it being easy either."

"Who the hell hired him?" Leonard said. "What is this all about? And this is your fault, Hap."

"My fault?"

"Remember I didn't want to get involved in this goddamn business? Remember that?"

"Vaguely," I said.

"Vaguely!"

"I thought deep down in your little black heart, you truly did want to be involved if me and Brett were."

"That's playing dirty pool, Hap, putting yourself and Brett into something you knew I'd get into eventually."

"That's ridiculous," I said.

"Boys," Brett said, "that will be enough. Hap, you did use your friendship to get Leonard into this. Leonard, even if Hap played you, you wanted to be played."

"Did I?" Leonard said.

"You were not going to leave it to us no matter what, and you know it," she said. "You are playing the victim, and I think it has to do with your pending nuptials. It's made you cranky and a little uncertain."

"The wedding isn't set," Leonard said.

"Oh, yes, it is, and you know it is," Brett said. "And another thing—you are not obligated to stay in this with us."

"That hurts," Leonard said, and he did indeed look hurt. "How can you say that to me?"

"I say it as your friend, and I think Hap would say the same thing to you as his brother. Friendship or not, we don't want you doing anything you don't want to do. Don't want you involved in anything you don't want to be involved in, despite a long friendship."

Leonard looked as if he had just suffered an injury.

"I don't think that at all," I said. "I was purposely trying to manipulate you. And that little speech Brett gave? She's playing you about as good as we play one another."

"Damn, Hap," Brett said.

"Hell, you know I'm with you two," Leonard said. "And maybe me thinking about getting married is making me feel like I won't be able to be part of things like this anymore."

"I think that might be some of it, but my guess is having a solid relationship scares you," Brett said. "You've had some that didn't turn out well."

"I have you two," Leonard said.

"Yeah," Brett said, "but marriage is different. I love you Leonard, but mine and Hap's relationship is a whole different thing."

Leonard nodded. "I get that."

The air was pregnant with unspoken thoughts. In my case it was because I couldn't think of anything to say.

And then, surprisingly, a profound question came to me. One might say the pregnant pause delivered a curious baby. "What do we do now?"

Okay. Not that profound.

"You boys do what you always do, due to your lack of investigative skills," Brett said.

"Shake trees till something falls out, even if it's a gorilla," Leonard said.

"That's right," Brett said.

"Yeah," I said, "we can do that."

25

Later that morning, we were all in the office, Brett looking at her laptop, searching for things related to Minnie and her husband, Al. Me and Leonard were trying to figure out whose tree we wanted to shake for gorillas when one of the gorillas came by to see us.

Chief Justin. He was all spiffy and sharp. Wore a blue suit with a blue-and-white-striped tie lying smooth and flat against his silver-white shirt. His shoes were not the house shoes with the dog tails. They were polished black shoes with heels high enough to add an inch of height. His dark hair was combed so smooth and was so product-shiny, I could see myself in it if the light hit it right.

He looked around, perhaps surveying for dust, standing there with his gray overcoat thrown over his arm. He said, "So this is how the toy cops live."

"No," Leonard said. "We work here. Live elsewhere. Would you like a view of the stairs as you tumble down them?"

"Threatening a cop isn't a good idea," Justin said.

"Insulting a man that is still letting his coffee soak in isn't such a smart idea neither," Leonard said.

"Let's call a truce, okay?" Justin said. "I might have something for you and may have a few questions, and you could have a few answers if you're willing to share."

"Okay," Brett said. "Let's hear it."

Justin carefully draped his overcoat over the back of the client chair and sat, pulling up his pants legs a little as he did. He looked like he was posing for a magazine shoot.

"I been thinking about the fire where Minnie Polson's body was found. I thought about it enough to have an independent investigator look it over. She agrees with you that it was arson, and that it's most likely a cover-up for murder. Not that murder can be proved with what's left of Minnie. But that's part of the reason the investigator thinks it was murder. As she put it, the body was professionally burned. Whoever did that knew how to burn the house so completely, no evidence was left. Not to mention the body that became primarily smoke and charcoal."

"Okay," Brett said. "Thanks for looking into it."

"Now that I've confirmed something for you, let me ask you a question. That night at the private investigator's office, did you pick something up there, something we didn't find on you or in your car? In other words, were you lying to me?"

"Told you we went there to pick up some information but we couldn't find it," I said. "Not like we took the place apart after we found Pete dead to see if he had hidden it in the walls, written it in code on a fast-food wrapper. Remember, we called the cops."

"That you did."

Brett said, "In the spirit of cooperation, I'll tell you this. We didn't pick anything up, but Pete mailed something to us that came the next day, after he was killed. He was just trying to get me to drop by that night. He didn't know I was bringing my husband and Leonard. Pete had a fantasy that, given the right opportunity, me and him might click."

"I bet a lot of men have that fantasy," Justin said.

"Lot of women too," Leonard said.

"That's true," Brett said. "It's a burden I've learned to live with."

"So," Justin said. "You going to share?"

"Yes," Brett said. She opened her desk drawer, took out the papers Pete had sent us, and slid them across the desk to Justin.

While Justin read the materials, I turned on the coffee machine and made myself a cup. I had a rice cake, and it was almost as good as Styrofoam. When Justin finished reading, I asked if he'd like some coffee. He wouldn't like. Leonard, on the other hand, had another cup, along with some vanilla cookies he kept locked up in the small table that supported the coffee machine. Brett already had coffee in her cup, so my barista duties were done.

"Not much here," Justin said.

"No," Brett said. "Not much. But I think it might be the tip of some horrible iceberg attached to a whale."

"I feel the same," Justin said. "Once upon a time I dealt with something, and it has bothered me for years, because I was never able to solve it. I was on the police in Tyler then. Not a chief, but a homicide detective. There was a paramilitary group. Small group, very right wing. Made Atilla the Hun seem like a peaceful diplomat. I consider myself conservative, but these people were anarchists, didn't like any form of government. To them, government was a handout and they were against it. They thought everything was socialist, even free ink pens at the bank."

"Well, come my time," I said, "I'll be glad to take my Social Security and Medicare. And I like a free pen now and then."

Leonard wasn't in total agreement with my point of view, but all he did was make a kind of grunting noise. I think, as he was now in his fifties, he could see sixty-five down the road, coming near and coming fast. Age kicks in, going to work gets harder, retirement starts to seem inviting, and Social Security, Medicare, a rocking chair, and the latest issue of *AARP* magazine begin to look pretty good.

"This group, back then," Justin said, "there weren't many of them. Johnny Joe Capps was their leader. Things weren't as crazy then as now, but

I could see it coming. People radicalized by fear, constant twenty-four-hour news telling us how the world was going to hell in a flaming handbasket. Assholes convincing people there were pedophile rings in pizza shops, that there were cabals of liberal, socialist politicians and Hollywood actors that drank blood and could turn into lizards. Johnny Joe Capps decided that a small group of workers for the Democratic Party had plans to use something, a drug, a goddamn space ray, I don't know, but according to him, they had something to turn everyone into a lizard. I kid you not."

"What kind of lizard?" Leonard asked.

"I don't know," Justin said. "A lizard. Human-size gecko, maybe. Komodo dragon. A space lizard from Neptune. I don't know. Who gives a damn what kind of lizard?"

"Just curious," Leonard said. "I was hoping for a Gila monster in Bermuda shorts."

"Let him tell it," Brett said.

"Back then, this ridiculous stuff was starting to surface. Who would think that nutballs would embrace ideas like that on a large scale? Kind of a forerunner of QAnon. It's like these folks had a disease and it was something you could catch and spread.

"Thing was, though, I don't think Johnny Joe Capps believed that business at all. He was a manipulator. People tired of worrying about illegal aliens crossing the border to take all the jobs away from brain surgeons, needed some other ignorant idea to grasp onto. How bored and angry do you have to be in life to hook up with this stuff? Thing is, some of Johnny Joe's group, a paramilitary bunch, kidnapped four men and two women from Democrat headquarters, took them out, and tortured them, looking for them to confess and turn into lizards. They would probably have confessed to anything after what was done to them. And I bet they tried hard to turn into lizards. I know I would have. In the end, the group killed them, burned them up in a car, did it so well they couldn't find a germ left over. But one of the idiots involved in this, couple days later, woke up, realized no one had turned into a lizard.

"He confessed. Said he thought he was helping save the world, one lizard at a time. Said he was riled by Johnny Joe, and next thing he knew, he was invading Democrat headquarters in full daylight, kidnapping victims. One of them was a teenage mom, just old enough to vote. She'd dropped by for registration papers. The others were nice community members. Closest they'd been to lizards was a terrarium.

"The culprits were brought in, all except Johnny Joe Capps, who couldn't be found. Case went to trial, and now, get this: This was a slam-dunk case. But the jury, a couple of them, bought the killers' bullshit. Said it couldn't be proven otherwise, so there was doubt. The judge, not buying the possibility of lizard folk from outer space, declared a mistrial."

"That's wild," I said.

"Yeah, here's something wilder. Next trial, they were acquitted, even with one of the group admitting to the atrocity. Lawyer discredited him, and rumor was, there was a sympathetic judge."

"Insane," Brett said.

"Nothing is about common sense anymore, and lies, not to mention stupid belief systems, are common currency."

"Nothing on Johnny Joe?"

"Johnny Joe Capps was like Manson, had others do his dirty work. And he was still gone. No one could find him. Didn't even know if Johnny Joe Capps was his real name."

Justin paused for effect.

"Now I have some guesswork I want to lay out for you. See what you think."

26

By this time Justin had decided coffee would be fine, and I went back to my barista duties.

Justin sipped his coffee and asked for milk, anything to maybe stun the taste a little, or so I presumed. My barista skills were mixed.

"I don't think one person is responsible for every nutty thing goes on out there, but I do think Johnny Joe Capps, or whatever his real name is, has a lot to answer for. You see, one thing I didn't mention was the bunch that killed those people, and a plethora of like-minded folks not directly involved, had given their life's savings to Johnny Joe."

"Now it comes into focus," Leonard said.

"Obviously he's a con man, but he's a unique one," Justin said. "He runs wildly different cons. I can't prove this, but I have a description of Johnny Joe from that witness's confession, and it recalled an earlier con where the man running it fit the same description. He was selling insurance policies that promised everything. If you checked on their website, you could see all the wonderful payouts they had for you should you encounter ill fate. They asked for a year's payment up front, and if you did that, you were in for half price for the rest of your life. Of course, after they spent a year setting up shop in various towns and cities, running a heavy ad campaign, all the insurance checks were cashed, and the amount of money was sizable—"

"And Johnny Joe was gone and so was his insurance company," Brett said.

"Correct. Snooping around I found out about other things of interest, like a driveway-paving business. It was an oil spray, not a real asphalt job, and looked good until it rained or the heat broke it up or car tires pulled it up. Guy running that sold door-to-door, stopping at houses offering what he could do, giving them a card. Lot of people bought into it. He convinced them he'd invented a new kind of asphalt mix. He could hit a bunch of driveways in one day by having several workers who did the spraying in different locations. Asphalters, or fake asphalters, only took checks.

"Interesting thing is, a few years back, guy bought some property and the place had a well with an electric pump. The well gave up sludgy, dark water that smelled. Owner had it checked out. They discovered the well had been filled with bodies."

"I remember that," Leonard said. "Someplace in the country near No Enterprise."

"That's the one. It took them a while to identify all the bodies, but they were all known criminals, small-time folks from Texas and Oklahoma. I don't know it for a fact, but I think what they found was Johnny Joe's asphalt crew. The address had been rented by Specialty Asphalt Services, which is no longer listed anywhere. People in the well were probably paid in bullets instead of money. They had been machined-gunned, if we want to use the old-style vernacular."

"Cuts down on overhead," Leonard said.

"There was also a girl by this time, nice-looking young lady—stunning, several of the duped said. Thing was, she so classically beautiful you couldn't really nail her down as far as a description went. Like those starlets Hollywood cranks out that seem to look so much alike. She had dark hair sometimes, blond others. Unnatural-looking eyes. Large and purple. It's a rare sort of thing, and some say there is no such thing, but then, look at photos of Elizabeth Taylor. Guess, she wanted, she could cover it up with tinted contacts or sunglasses. Purple Eyes went around with Johnny Joe and would take calls on her cell phone. Johnny Joe's talking someone up, trying to make a sale, and her phone would ring. She'd step off a little to the side and she's thanking people out loud for their kind words about the asphalt work. Yes. They were adding jobs to their list, and if their son, uncle, brother, whatever, wanted some work done, they'd try hard to squeeze him in. But they were almost completely booked. It was all theater that made the business seem solid and in demand. Made people want to get on the list.

"Purple Eyes may have been Johnny Joe's daughter, his girlfriend, what have you. There were no female bodies in that well, so she may still be with him. Course, he could have killed her at some other point. Don't know. But here's the connection to your case.

"Yesterday, Al Polson came to the station to refresh that he'd reported his daughter missing. Said his wife had also reported her missing. Said he had talked with you three and that he had hired you."

"Kind of," Brett said.

"Al was a bit on the goofy side. I checked things out after he left and saw, as he said, Alice's mother, Minnie, had filed a missing person report as well. There had been a preliminary investigation, but they hadn't turned up much other than they couldn't find her. Al Polson mentioned the part about how her mother hadn't accepted her sexual orientation right away. Minnie might have sung a new tune later, but maybe the old tune still had too much reverberation for Alice, so she and her girlfriend decided to take a hike, get away. Maybe Alice decided she doesn't like her mother and wants money from insurance and the will. The girl she's with, Lilly, could be the catalyst for arson and murder."

"These are all things we've considered," Brett said. "Nothing new there."

"I know, but I have to put it out there for you to understand the connection I'm getting at. Then there's the private eye you went to see, him being murdered. Coroner said he was beat to death but in a sophisticated manner.

Whoever did it knew exactly what they were doing, where to hit, and they hit hard."

I immediately thought of Kung Fu Bobby, but I didn't bother to mention it. He was already on my shit list, but now I was putting another mark by his name. And another beside my own for purposely missing that rifle shot.

"Lot of things suggest that all this business ties together," Justin said. "Just the other day, a young woman saying she was Alice claimed the insurance money from Minnie. She then went to Minnie's lawyer's office and requested money from the will, as it was set up for a quick payout. I suppose that was because Minnie didn't want her husband contesting the will, maybe ending up with the money. Both were sizable payouts, and those checks were cashed immediately. I just found this bit out.

"Since the LaBorde investigator concluded the fire was accidental, Alice didn't have any trouble getting the money. This was before my investigators called it arson. When I asked the insurance lady about Alice, how she went about acquiring the payout, she said she had a driver's license, credit cards, and even a passport to prove who she was. I asked what Alice looked like. She said she was a tall, beautiful blonde, perfect skin white as porcelain. She was well turned out, wore sunglasses. Figured she was maybe thirty years old. The lawyer gave a similar description, with one addition. He said that when Alice signed for the money from the will, when she put her head down to write, her sunglasses fell off. As she put them back on, he noticed her eyes seemed unnatural; spooky, he said. Beautiful and bright. Violet, he called them. Said he had never seen eyes like that, thought maybe it was the light."

"I'm going to guess and say it wasn't Alice that picked up the money," Brett said.

"Doesn't seem that way," Justin said. "I've seen photos of Alice, and she's a nice-looking lady but doesn't fit this knockout description. And her eyes are green, and she's four foot eleven with shoes on and standing on a brick."

"Beginning to think," Leonard said, "that Lilly might have a lot to answer for. Insurance, the will, who knows what all? That's a lot of money, a lot of sugar on the bones of poor Minnie."

"And my thought is Minnie isn't the only one," Brett said. "I bet Purple Eyes has licked a lot of sugar off a lot of bones."

"I think you're right," Justin said. "Now you know what I know, and I know what you know, and in the end, I'm not sure either of us knows that much."

"Tell you one damn thing," Leonard said. "I know now to watch for those damn lizards."

"You know that's right," I said. "Damn pizza-eating reptiles."

27

Brett and I were sitting on our front porch at the little table there. It was dark except for streetlights, but there weren't many of those where we lived. The sky was clear, so we could easily see the moon, a cheesy slice of gold. Now and again, a car would drive by.

We had eaten an early supper and were enjoying the night air. We had been sitting there for some time. The air smelled damp, but there was no rain.

"Your instinct was right," I said. "This stuff with Minnie, all of it is screwy, and it isn't just about a bad divorce, an angry child, and pronoun trouble."

"When Lilly, or whatever her name is, collected the money in Alice's name, the reason she wore sunglasses was to keep from wearing colored contacts. She would have had to have done that all along, otherwise she would be too noticeable. I know, for me, I need a break from contacts now and then. The sunglasses went along with her break."

"And what about the real Alice?"

"I'm sure I'm thinking what you're thinking."

"Dead."

"Yes," Brett said.

"Could still be Alice and Lilly that did it. That's not out of the running."

"I think it is. If Alice was in on it, she would have picked up the money herself, wouldn't have needed a fake passport, license, and so on."

"Yeah, of course."

"What really gets me is how perfectly Minnie was burned up, except for her arm. That's odd to me."

"Is it odd enough you've developed an opinion?" I asked. "I smell an opinion."

"What if Minnie didn't die in the fire? What if her arm was chopped off and left to convince the cops she died there?"

"What would be the point of taking Minnie with them, and with an arm cut off? I'm sure she wouldn't have been doing too well, bleeding all over the place. She would be just as dead if they left her there. Think it's a lot more likely she was burned up and for whatever reason only her arm survived."

"Just a feeling I have, justified by nothing," Brett said. "You know, this purple- or violet-eye thing. Got curious and looked it up. Some of what I read is certainly myth. It's always women, most of the material says. Some say men can have purple eyes, but they aren't born that way—in time their eyes turn purple. Women with purple eyes are said to be nearly always Caucasian and have perfect white skin. Their skin won't tan or sunburn, no matter how much time they spend in the sun. They have perfect body shapes, appear much younger than they are, and it's said they live for a very long time. Some claim they stop aging when they reach middle age, can live up to a hundred and fifty years in perfect health, though that's obviously a bit of blanket stretching. They have strong constitutions and are rarely ill, don't even catch colds. Another curiosity is they don't have armpit or pubic hair. Just hair on the head, eyebrows. Otherwise, they are smooth as a lotion-soaked-baby's butt. They don't gain weight no matter what they eat. Don't need to exercise to keep their muscles toned. They don't have menstrual cycles. And my favorite — they don't need to go to the bathroom much. Very little excrement, and what's there doesn't smell."

"Superwoman," I said. "Can she fly and does she have super-strength and X-ray vision?"

"Purple-eyed women were thought to be witches in the old days. That might not have turned out well for them. Otherwise, purple eyes go along with a lot of positive traits, even if only part of the story is true."

"And maybe they just have purple eyes and have to suffer with the same sunburn, hairy armpits, stinky shit, and short lives as the rest of us. Elizabeth Taylor, who may actually have had purple eyes, gained weight and didn't die ancient."

"Yeah, I know," Brett said. "But it's sort of interesting to consider there might be people out there that are unlike the rest of us."

"The products of alien insemination."

"That sounds right," she said. "Or a mad scientist who really likes the color purple and wants everyone to have that color eyes. Maybe it's just the lizard people that have purple eyes. Damn, I'm exhausted and silly. Going to bed. You coming?"

"In a bit," I said. "Too soon for me. I'm going to sort my brain out a little."

"Don't hurt yourself."

"I'll try not to."

Brett stood up, leaned over, kissed me on the forehead, and went away.

I sat there longer than I'd planned. I thought about how there were people wanting to conform so badly, they would embrace ridiculous things to be part of a club. It reminded me of the homogenous fifties. Everyone on the same page. Dad at work, mother dressed to the nines while cooking dinner, pearls around her neck, waiting for her man to come home and admire her ass and have a nice meal with the family. Children in church, everyone dressing tight and right and thinking the same thoughts about the glory of God and the perfection of country. We seemed to be back in those conformity days, only now it was worse. Lizard people indeed. Right-wing dumbasses, left-wing do-gooders gone off their nuts trying to make everyone talk and act the same. Both sides needed a good hosing. Common sense needed a turn at the table.

I looked at the sky, one of my favorite pastimes. I saw red blinking lights. A jet coming from somewhere going somewhere.

My guess was it was going to land in Shreveport, as it was heading in that direction, though the way planes could be rerouted, I couldn't say for sure. It might be making a giant circle. It might be a plane full of purple-eyed folks heading to a purple-eyed people convention. They could arrive and over drinks talk about how little they needed to poop and weren't the rest of those stinky poopers a funny lot.

I went inside and locked up, looked in the kitchen, half expecting to see Kung Fu Bobby sitting at the table eating Leonard's vanilla cookies. But now with purple eyes that glowed in the dark.

Nope. Nothing.

28

Come morning, Brett drove to the office with a mug of coffee and her pistol. I took the spare car, met Leonard at the gym. He looked like he had been run over by a bulldozer.

"You look like hell," I said.

"Pookie kept me up. He has this whole new sexual thing going, and he wanted to try it. It was exhausting. I finally faked an orgasm and went to sleep. He mentions doing that business again, they'll find what's left of him out behind Walmart in a cardboard box."

We worked the bag, did some light ring sparring. We hadn't been going that long when Nemo and Ernie showed up at the base of the elevated ring.

"We thought you might train us," Nemo said.

"How'd you know we were here?" Leonard said. "Seems like more than a coincidence."

"We know the owner, asked him to call us if you guys came in so we could get down here."

"Yeah, well," Leonard said, "that shows some will, but it isn't dedication.

Not yet. You know the fundamentals, but you don't really know how to use them. Why don't you work the bags a bit, get warmed up, let me and Hap finish up here, then we'll take you guys on for a little while."

"That sounds great," Ernie said.

Little later we were all in the ring. I said, "My turn this time. Nemo, how about you be my sparring partner?"

"Yes, sir," Nemo said.

Leonard and Ernie helped us put on our gloves, then they stepped through the ropes and stood outside them on the platform.

"Don't be a sitting duck," I said. "Don't drag your back leg. You'll find your style in time, once you've had more experience. But one note to always keep in mind is always protect yourself. Combinations are good. They win fights, but they need to be used directly against an opponent, not just you standing there and throwing them and hoping whoever you're fighting jumps into your punches. Bobbing and weaving is good. Leonard will teach you some of that. He's better than I am at it."

"Hap don't need it," Leonard said from outside the ring. "Unless it's me hitting, he don't get hit that much."

"I move," I said, "but constant bobbing and weaving wears me out. That's another thing. Get older, you have to accept some things change. But you can change too, rely on different strategies and techniques. I pad punches away, ride them off my arms, duck and move my head a little. Fact is, I do good against bobbers and weavers, though Leonard is an exception. Little tip: You bob your head, never bob it back to the same spot where you started. Opponent may be throwing where you were, and he might just find you if you put yourself in the same place."

We began moving around the ring, throwing a few exploratory blows. Nemo was pretty good, but he was getting cocky.

He picked up the pace and started punching harder. I heard Leonard say to Ernie, "Your boy is about to be schooled."

I moved quick, got into the middle of him, looped a right over his left arm, caught him upside the head with a left. I hit him with an uppercut to the midsection with the same left. That made him step back. I hit before he got too far back, a good right, but I didn't put all the bricks behind it. Still, he went down.

While he lay on the mat, I started taking off my gloves.

"I will say this," I said, "both of you got balls, but in the end, brains are better, though balls, or heart — what Leonard calls left tit — are worthy accessories. Also, I broke it up by hitting high and low with the same hand. Not just lefts and rights."

Nemo was sitting up. Leonard and Ernie had entered the ring. Ernie was taking off Nemo's gloves.

"You know," said Leonard, "you remind me of me and Hap. But without the skills, experience, and common sense."

"You had me until 'common sense,'" I said.

Leonard grinned at me. "We got it, we just don't use it enough."

We spent another hour with the boys, showing them how to slip, how to shuffle, how to put their hips into their shots.

They went to the shower, and me and Leonard sat on a bench.

"They could be pretty good," he said.

"Could be."

"Should we train them?"

"We know some stuff, but you know well as I do that boxing is an auxiliary to us," I said.

"Our boxing is all right."

"Maybe even quite good, but they want it, we can teach them the Shen Chuan stuff, Thai boxing, things we've picked up here and there. Real self-defense, not just the ring stuff. Might be fun. You know. Passing it on."

Leonard said, "Time for you to pass it on. You know you're not getting any younger, Hap."

"Look who's talking. You nearly got killed having sex. Faking an orgasm, man. That's low."

"I am a little ashamed."

29

So that night I'm lying in bed, trying to go sleep, listening to Brett snoring little pig snorts, and I'm thinking on this and that, and one thing I'm thinking about is Kung Fu Bobby's warning.

I didn't feel too nervous for any of us, as we hadn't yet poked back into the Polson business after hearing from Justin. We had talked to Al, but that didn't seem like enough to put us on their radar. Maybe we weren't on their radar at all. I wasn't sure there was any way anyone on the dark side of the fence would know we had spoken to Justin or Al.

In the end, summing it up, what we had right then was a lot of speculation about the possible involvement of Johnny Joe Capps or whatever his current name was, the possible connection to a purple-eyed woman, the weirdness of Al Polson, the fraudulent attainment of estate and insurance money, and the ever-constant question of where exactly was Alice Polson.

Those questions might not all be linked, none of them might be linked, but though I could accept a lot more coincidence than a cop, some things just smelled of connection. I was beginning to feel there was a conspiracy here, a group trying to accomplish who knew what, but certainly they weren't working for world peace.

I hated conspiracy theories, and yet here I was, beginning to believe one.

On top of that, Kung Fu Bobby's warning about not knowing what we were getting into kept echoing in my memory.

I thought it might be a good idea to consider once again letting this business lie still and have the cops do the work. Problem was, they weren't doing the work, and even Justin had come to us, hoping, I'm sure, we would do things that a police chief couldn't.

Small crimes are simple and simply motivated, and when you get right down to it, complex crimes are simply motivated.

The big motivation is power. Even burglary is power. You want items, but it has to do with the power over others, feeling smarter because you can climb through a window, rifle through someone's closets and drawers, and take whatever you can carry, owning parts of them in the form of salable or usable talismans.

Money comes from the theft, so that's certainly a part of it, especially if you're in need of drugs, and the monkey is chattering in your ear. Still, I knew of an East Texas thief who would steal anything, and seemingly without consideration of its value. Not being the brightest star in the firmament, he once stole a skip loader, dug a hole with it, drove it inside, climbed out, and spent four days covering it by tossing dirt with a shovel. He said he just liked stealing, but he only bothered to sell small things he had stolen. The rest, like the skip loader, was just a buzz. That's still power.

But this bunch—for bunch I thought them to be—were in it for the power and money, and they were looking for serious money. Johnny Joe had taken money as a cult leader, had had his followers commit foolish murders that showed him just how much power he had over willful idiots. Then he was an asphalt salesman who peddled bullshit instead of real asphalt, and when it came time to pay his workers, they ended up unpaid, shot, and tossed in a well. Now he was stealing insurance money and payouts from wills with the assistance of a purple-eyed beauty who just might have shit that didn't stink. And no telling what all else he had going.

The whole enterprise, if connected as I suspected, had a mythic feel to it. It was so outside the law that it was a law unto itself.

I started to doze, and then it hit me.

I sat up in bed.

"Naw, couldn't be," I said to the room.

Brett continued to snore, but I was now wide awake.

I crept downstairs to the kitchen, poured myself a glass of milk, found my stash of animal crackers, sat at the table, and ate them.

Oh, yeah, I thought. It could be. It damn sure could be.

It took me a while to feel that I could go back to sleep, but finally I thought I could, and I did. Drifting off, I felt I had punctured a part of this mystery and let some of the air out of it.

30

When morning came, I didn't tell Brett what I'd thought last night, which then had seemed as real to me as the rising of the sun.

Now, soaked in the sober light of day, I could see my idea was a little foolish.

After coffee and a sausage and egg biscuit, I caught up with Leonard at his place, having left Brett to go to the office and take care of a job that required little more than paperwork and a discussion with her client.

Leonard was wearing a black cowboy hat today. He said, "Okay, where we going? You said be ready, but you didn't say why. Should I have brought a big stick?"

"I'm holding off on the why, but the who is Al. I'm not sure I have anything more than wishful thinking going on, but I want to see how wishful I feel about it when we meet up with him."

"We're going to see that nut again?"

"He's part of this case, like it or not."

It was a clear, cold day, but it was warm in the car, and we listened to

SUGAR ON THE BONES

some music as we cruised. I had downloaded some John Prine, and that was
our soundtrack for the moment. Leonard had me play "Sam Stone" three
times. I didn't mind.

When we got to Al's land, the mobile home had its front door and glass
backup door open, and out beside it, not too far from the carport, a massive
white yurt was going up.

Next to the yurt was a crew of workmen digging a hole for a septic
tank with backhoes and such. A big concrete septic tank was on the back of
a large truck bed fastened to a cab. Near that was an enormous forklift and
about a half dozen men with thermos cups, sipping and considering. I guess
to get a job like that done, you had to have someone to drive the backhoe
and six more to hold the ground down.

"Big as that tank is, Al must plan on shitting a lot," Leonard said.

In the carport, Al had the hood up on his Chevy and was tinkering with
the engine. There was a straw cowboy hat on top of the car, and the car's
windows were rolled down, and inside on the back seat were the two dogs.
They were barking at the machinery, and us.

We parked and walked over to the Chevy and Al. The sound of the digging machines was brain-shaking. Up close to the Chevy for the first time, I
saw the tires were bald enough, a severe word might pop them.

When we came up to Al, he didn't look surprised. His face was less
red, and the spots on his head were almost gone. He had on a blue shirt
and, thankfully, pants—new jeans—and he was sporting a pair of work
boots that looked as if now was the first time the soles had ever touched the
ground.

He said, "Hang on, boys, I got to hold my mouth just right and push my
balls to the left to get this fucker to work. Goddamn, dogs, shut up, will
you?"

They shut up and lay down on the car seat.

Al was shaking a fuel line with a pair of pliers. "I think it's got some shit
clogged up in it," he said. "Hope it ain't no dirt dauber's nest."

"They'd be some damn small dirt daubers," Leonard said.

"Well, I need to take the lid off the carburetor, check in there."

"So how would dirt daubers get the top off?" Leonard said.

"Nature is a peculiar thing," Al said. "I'm of the opinion that insects have certain instincts that allow them to vibrate at a frequency that lets them travel through walls. You know, blending atoms and all that shit. They could easily travel through a fuel line or into a carburetor. Bet a lot of insects do it, otherwise where do roaches come from?"

"Sounds like a *Flash* comic," I said. "The Flash vibrated through walls."

"Where I got the idea," Al said. "I thought it made a lot of sense."

That didn't surprise me.

"What's with the yurt?" Leonard said.

"I come into some money yesterday. Was able to sell a small amount of stock I had forgotten about, picked up enough dough to get me a better pad. Having been in my current abode, you can understand my reasoning."

"Skin looks pretty cleared up," I said.

"Got the right medicine, and maybe I got a little less anxiety, which wasn't helping matters."

"I got a question for you, Al: Did your girlfriend, Earline, wear contacts?"

"What?"

"It's a less complicated question than do dirt daubers walk through walls," I said. "Believe me, I ask it with a purpose, has to do with the case concerning your wife and daughter."

Al lifted his head out from under the car hood, paused to tap the fuel line a solid blow, wiped his hands on a rag, and looked at me.

"Yeah, she wore contacts. I saw her little case, and she had couple bottles of that juice you use to grease them up so they slide in. Said she had the kind of contacts she could sleep in. I remember that. I didn't know there was such a thing. Me, I've had cataract surgery, got some lenses put in. I got twenty-twenty vision now, though, late at night, I'm still comfortable with Walmart glasses. Seems like my eyes get tired by the end of the day."

Al could be said to have problems with all kinds of focus, not just vision.

"What color were her eyes?" I asked.

"Jesus, man. What color are your old ladies' eyes, and by the way, where is that good-looking woman? I wouldn't mind looking at her every day."

"Al, come on," I said. "What color were Earline's eyes?"

"Brown," he said.

"Got to ask," Leonard said to me. "I too am a little confused, brother. What does the color of her eyes and if she wore contacts got to do with our case, or most anything? Why not ask Al his opinion on Attila the Hun?"

"Treated a little harshly by history," Al said.

"It was a figure of speech," Leonard said.

"He did slaughter a lot of humans and animals, but he could throw a party," Al said.

"Al, talking to you is like trying to teach ants how to shop for shoes," I said.

"Why would they shop for shoes?" Al said.

"To put on their little feet," Leonard said.

"Here's the lede I've been burying," I said. "I'm thinking your girlfriend Earline was also your daughter's girlfriend Lilly."

31

That's absurd," Al said.

He said it so sharply, the dogs started barking, but after Al yelled at them, they shut up again, though one of them did a low growl for a short time, just to let us know he was only being polite and wasn't intimidated.

Here was a guy who believed dirt daubers could travel through fuel lines and pass through walls as molecules based on old *Flash* comic-book reasoning telling me my idea was absurd.

Of course, he might have been right.

Leonard said, "Well, that certainly isn't what I expected."

"Think about it, Al," I said. "You don't have but the one photo of her, like she's avoiding the camera. Not something good-looking women tend to do. And the one picture you have is not great. It's in shadow. You can tell even from that that she was looker, but what you can't tell is the coloring of her skin. I think she knew exactly what she was doing, not letting her picture be taken clearly. I'm betting she had pale, porcelain-white skin."

"She did," Al said. "I generally go for darker meat, but she wore it well. So what?"

"When she collected the insurance money and the money from your wife's will, she was described that way. Pale-skinned. The general description fits. She had brown eyes in license and passport photos, but when she picked up the money from the will, her sunglasses slipped, and I'm guessing she didn't have on contacts. She had purple eyes."

"I don't think I can buy that," Al said. "Who the fuck has purple eyes?"

"She sucks you dry, or nearly dry, and when there's nothing to suck, she hits the road," I said. "Next thing you know, your wife is dead and her home burned to the ground. And if you buy my premise, Purple Eyes collected the money that was meant for your daughter, Alice. She's calling herself Alice now and has identification to fit the claim. She knew all about that money. I think your family was picked, and not at random. And Earline, or Lilly, isn't alone in all this."

Leonard had been mulling this over, and from the look on his face, I could tell he was starting to embrace the idea. "I got a question," he said. "Al, ever have asphalt put on your drive?"

"What?"

"The house you and Minnie shared, one that's burned down."

Al thought a moment. "Minnie got duped, had it done. Said some guy sold her on the idea. Showed up at the door selling asphalt, then sprayed the drive with oil or some such, and by the time she realized it was just an oil spray, he had her check cashed and was gone. She had the drive done up then in concrete."

"Was there a woman with the asphalt salesman?" I asked.

"Minnie didn't mention one," Al said. "I never saw the guy."

"Okay," I said. "I'm going to guess when they saw the house Minnie was living in, that's when they realized there was real money there, and they went into research mode. I don't think they made the kind of play they made at random."

"You say 'they,'" Al said. "You're talking about this fast-talking oil-spray salesman and my girlfriend, saying they worked together to skin us. That Earline and Lilly were the same person, fucking both father and daughter?"

"It's possible," I said.

"I can't imagine being fooled like that," Al said.

"No one can, until they are," I said. "What you were thinking was 'Here's a hot woman interested in me, and I'm going for it,' and your common sense went out the window with a brick tied on its tail."

"Yeah, there was that whole buying-a-rubber-dick business," Al said. "No doubt she had my nose open."

"She used your biology against you," I said. "Here you are, thinking you're making out big time——"

"Oh, I was."

"Okay," I said. "But she planted the hook deep down in the gullet, made sure you paid for the pleasure of her company. Did you go to that men's club regularly, the one where Earline was wrapping her leg around a pole?"

"I did. I have a thing for women wearing little to no clothes. Jesus probably wouldn't approve, but then again, He never met Earline."

"Was Earline a pole dancer at the club when you first started going there?" Leonard said.

"No. She came along later...ah, fuck. She got a job there to play me."

"Looks that way, pal," Leonard said.

"They're dangerous in a big way," I said. "And I think, right now, they got an even larger scam going on. Don't know what it is, but I think they need the money they got from you and Minnie to make it happen. Takes money to make money. And you can be assured they're not using the money they've made to build an orphanage. And you can bet that you and Alice and Minnie aren't the only ones that have been skinned or will be skinned."

Al looked at Leonard. "What about you? You're thinking the same, aren't you?"

"Starting to get my head around the idea," Leonard said. "My main surprise is Hap figured it out."

32

One thing wrong with your idea," Al said. "I did take photos of her, and I have a whole drawerful of them. Old-school photography, with film and a camera. I used to do that a lot. Kind of a hobby."

"Can we see the photos?"

Al moved his lips around as if that helped him think. "Wait here, I'll go get them. There are some nudes of her, and I'd rather not show them. Main reason, I'm in them, minus an outfit."

Al started walking away. The dogs barked, leaped out of the car window, and trotted after him.

"He has those photos, and they're good," I said, "that can help us figure a few things out by showing them around. To the insurance lady, the will lawyer."

About five minutes later, Al and the dogs came back. Al didn't have anything in his hands. Coat pocket, perhaps? He lifted the dogs up and set them through the car window onto the back seat.

"Gone," he said. "She must have taken them. Now that I think about it, Rap, she never liked the photo idea."

"Hap," I said.

"I was sure you said Rap the other day."

"No, I usually get my name right," I said. "So, no photos."

"Little scamp," he said. "Damn, was I really duped that bad?"

"Having been duped by an ex-wife, I know how you feel."

"Thing is, during sex, I would yell out my Transcendental Meditation mantra. So I gave that up to her too. Took my money, my mantra, and my self-respect and murdered my wife, maybe my daughter."

Leonard said, "Old-school photography with film, you said."

"Yep."

"Did you keep the negatives?"

"Looked. Gone as well. I'm starting to feel like a big braying jackass. Therapist I'm going to hasn't helped me a bit when it comes to not repeating the same mistakes over and over. Shit, she's got me punching a pillow to let out my angry. I'm not angry, I'm fucking stupid. Earline wasn't my first mistress, but wasn't none of the others worth leaving my wife for. I thought Earline was different."

"We got that one photo you showed us," Leonard said. "And it may not be the best, but that fellow who ended up in Alice and Lilly's apartment saw the girls. Right?"

"Right."

"What we do is, we take that phone photo, and you ought to send us a copy of it so we'll have it," I said, "and we go over and see this fellow, show it to him. Maybe he can say if it's Lilly as well as Earline."

"Let's do that," Al said.

"You don't have to go with us," I said. "We're working for you now. No need to get your checkbook, though. I could be way off on this business."

Al picked his straw cowboy hat off the top of the Chevy, put it on, pushed it back off his forehead a little with a poke of his finger.

"Let's find out," he said.

33

Not exactly sure how we got talked into it, but we rode over to Ron's apartment, formerly the address of the missing women, Alice and Lilly, in Al's Chevrolet. It smelled like mold inside and the back seat sagged a little.

Leonard got the front passenger seat, and I got the back. The two dogs sat on either side of me until one nodded off due to bark exhaustion and curled up in my lap. I scratched him behind his ears. I didn't know a dog could purr like a kitten.

The Chevrolet, for all its damp smell and a suspicion of dirt daubers in the carburetor, hummed along without so much as a muffler burp. The brake pads could have used replacing, though. Every time Al hit the brake, they groaned like a constipated man with a cork in his ass. Those bald tires were held together by Al's optimism more than rubber.

We made it to the apartment without blowing a tire or the brakes going out and sending us darting into traffic or causing us to ride fast and hard into the wall of a house or business. Al, of course, had known right where to go. He had been there before there was a Lilly to visit his daughter, Alice.

The brakes made with one last moan and seemed as if they might play out but didn't. Al parked at the curb and we got out. Al made sure the windows were partly rolled down for the dogs, the weather being cool but not too cool. He said to them, "Now, you little shits stay put."

"Unless they have car keys," Leonard said, "I don't think they're going anywhere."

"With them, you can't be certain," Al said.

In Al's universe, where insects could pass through walls by vibrating atoms, perhaps dogs could drive cars. If they did, I hoped they'd stop somewhere to get the brakes fixed, maybe purchase some new tires.

We knocked at Ronald's door with some assurance he was home because the TV was on. Though there are some folks who leave them on so burglars might think the same.

I doubted Ronald had anything a burglar would want, unless it was peanut butter and jelly without milk. I imagined Ronald ate straight from the jar sometimes, sticking a fork in, licking it clean, and repeating. Brett didn't know it, but I did that from time to time.

Ronald answered the door. Cigarette smoke rolled out of the apartment like a poison cloud. He had on a shirt and it appeared devoid of peanut butter and jelly.

"You again," he said, looking right at me.

"Yep. I'm back. Feared you might be at work."

"I got a bad back. I get a little check for it. Disability."

Leonard said, "Funny, you don't look disabled."

I rushed in with "Hey, we got a photo. We want you to confirm or deny that it's one of the girls lived here."

"Why you asking that?"

"'Cause she's missing," I said.

Al was watching Ronald like a hungry, soaring hawk watches a rat, waiting for it to slip out from under a bush and expose itself.

Al took out his phone, pulled up the photo, held it for Ronald to see.

"That ain't such a good picture," Ronald said, "but a bad picture of her would make an excellent picture of some runway model look like a loser in a dog show."

"So it is a photo of one of the girls?" Leonard said.

"They were both pretty ripe, you know what I mean, but that one there, damn."

"You're certain she's one of the girls lived here?" Al said.

"I am. I was always pissed they were on the queer team. Wasted ass, you ask me. Me and them could have had some parties."

"Have you ever been thrown down the stairs?" Al said.

"What?" Ronald said. "No. I don't have any stairs."

"Maybe we can find some," Al said.

"Take it easy, Al," I said.

It was too late. Al grabbed Ronald and pulled him out of the doorway, lifted him off his feet like he wasn't more than a sack of flour, tossed him down the three front steps, and bounced him onto the lawn. "How's your back now?" Al said.

Ronald got up quicker than I would have expected for a guy collecting a disability check. I guess his back only hurt when he picked up his "little check" for it.

"You about to get you some now, buddy," Ronald said.

This turned out not to be true. Ronald started up the steps and Al dough-popped him, short and sweet, right on the jaw. Ronald was knocked off the steps and back into the yard. He was unconscious this time.

"I think we ought to leave," I said.

Heading back to the car, Leonard said, "Those weren't stairs, Al. Those were steps."

"I know," Al said. "I had to make the best of it, all things considered."

34

We tooled along in the Chevy at a fearsome speed with the air turning misty, the windshield beaded with rain.

"Shit," Al said. "Me and my daughter were both fucking her, and she was fucking us in more ways than one. I'm going to have to stop."

He pulled the car over, got out, and puked on someone's lawn. We got out with him. The dogs watched from inside the car, their heads poking out a half-rolled-down window. They looked concerned.

Leonard held Al's straw hat while he continued to puke.

"Jesus," Al said, and went back to throwing up.

When he was empty of vomit, he sat on the curb in the rain and said, "Alice is dead, isn't she? I mean really dead, not just suspected to be."

"Can't say for sure," I said.

"Damn Lilly. She conned me and my baby both. And now she's gotten rid of her. Shit. Why didn't she get rid of me? I wonder. I'd have been easy. Wouldn't have suspected for a moment."

"Let's get back in the car," Leonard said, and handed Al his hat.

We did that, but Al asked me to drive. He got in back with the dogs. They reared up on their hind legs and licked the rain and tears off his face.

I started the car, cruised away from the curb. "Why didn't she kill me?" Al said again. "Why not? Hell, I wish she had."

"Didn't need to," Leonard said. "Had to kill Minnie for the insurance money. As for Alice, we don't know she's dead. They could still be together. Alice might not even know the con is on."

"You know that's not right," Al said. "Alice is dead. I can feel it in the pit of my stomach. Soon as that asshole back there identified Earline, I felt it. It come over me. My spirit went out into the wilderness carried by wings, touched my sweet Alice's spirit, and I knew she was dead. That goddamn Earline, whatever the hell her name really is. I'm going to see that bitch dead as the Pleistocene, and I'm going to burn her up like she did Minnie, along with that rubber dick."

"Don't get ahead of yourself," I said. "We don't know for sure about Alice, spirit travels aside. Besides, you don't really know where that rubber dick ended up."

"I know you think I'm full of it," Al said. "But I'm telling you, soon as I knew Earline was Lilly, I felt little Alice's spirit tremble. I don't even have the bullshit comfort of heaven, thinking Saint Michael's giving her wings. Spirits I believe in are all emotional responses."

We didn't know exactly what to do with Al right then. I suggested taking him back to the yurt construction, but he didn't want that. We rode around for a while in the rain, then ended up at my house, in the kitchen. Leonard made Al some coffee and gave him some of my animal crackers, but I noted he didn't offer any of his cookies.

I left the two of them in the kitchen and went upstairs for privacy and called Brett at the office. I laid out all that had occurred.

"That was some nifty thinking," Brett said. "Figuring out Earline and Lilly were the same."

"Sometimes I amaze even myself."

"But not often."

"No. Not often."

Brett laughed. She had a throaty laugh, which was just one of the many reasons I adored her. That laugh was sexy, wise, and downright heartwarming.

"I think we ought to tell Justin about this," she said.

"Reckon so. I'm not quite sure what to do with Al. He's eating all my animal crackers."

"I leave that solution to you," Brett said. "I know. Let me call Justin, see if he can come by the office, and you can bring Al with you."

"Al's threatening to kill Earline. Maybe he doesn't really mean it, though I think he does. Not sure Justin needs to hear his threats."

"Al should be here with us if I can get Justin to come by. Al can vouch for who is who. Might not want to mention he threw Ronald out in the yard."

"And knocked him out."

"Yeah. Might let that slide too."

I went back to the kitchen. Al had pulled his chair close to Leonard and was crying. Leonard had his arm around him. I know Leonard hated that kind of business, but like me, he had no idea what to do.

Al cried for a while. Leonard said "There, there" a lot. We sat and waited for Al to get finished.

In time Al let out with a loud sigh, took a deep breath, and stopped crying. Leonard gave him a box of Kleenex.

Al plucked one from the box and wiped his eyes. He did the sighing thing again.

"Just learning how to share my emotions," Al said. "My therapist told me I needed to do that, not keep it inside, not some macho shit about being able to take on anything without showing how I really feel. That and punching a pillow. I do feel better. I feel like a weenie for doing it, but I do feel a lot better inside. We all have something to cry about, and we can cry together. You can go first, Leonard. What do you have to cry about?"

"I'm going to stay in my macho-bullshit frame for now," Leonard said.

"I'm good," I said. "I start that business, I'll never stop crying."

35

After we convinced Al he didn't need one of our pillows to take with him to punch, we went over to the office in the Chevy.

Justin was there with Brett. Al told what he knew and how I had been right about Earline, Lilly, and Purple Eyes all being the same person. For that matter, Purple Eyes had also briefly been Alice, as Justin suspected.

Al suggested we all cry together but didn't find any takers.

When it was all spoke out, we told Justin goodbye and left Brett at the office, and Al drove us to his place and to my car, grinding the brakes mercilessly until we were able to come to a full stop under the carport.

We sat in the Chevy for a moment. The workers were gone. The big septic tank was no longer visible. The large hole in the ground had been covered. The rain was coming down in a constant drizzle.

"Shitters can be used now," Al said.

"Those are magic words," Leonard said.

"You want to use one of them?" Al said. "You can be first."

"No," Leonard said. "I leave that supreme honor to you."

"I'm having the trailer dragged off to the back of the lot," Al said. "I'm leaving it and the couch to the mice. I'll probably put some goodies in there now and then for them. You know. Loaf of bread. Froot Loops strewn about. I understand they love a good cardboard toilet-paper roll. I can save those up for them."

"Mouse Nation," I said.

"Even now they're writing their constitution," Leonard said.

"I hope so," Al said, and he still looked weepy.

Before another bout of crying started and we all began feeling bad over Alice again, we got out of Al's car with quick suggestions about brake pads and new tires.

We climbed into my car and I started the engine. We watched Al get out of his car and go inside the yurt. He walked like a man crossing a battle-field full of familial dead.

"Poor guy, he's had a rough day," Leonard said. "And he is kind of crazy."

"Hard to disagree," I said, and started us home.

It was still raining.

The rain had tried my patience. I no longer felt happy to have it. I wanted it to go away.

Until I would want it back again.

* * *

I called Brett and set up supper at Leonard's house. We were going to have one of Leonard's specialties: Delivery.

He picked pizza.

Me, Brett, Leonard, and Pookie sat in the kitchen, sharing a pizza the size of a flying saucer, sucking on Dr Peppers. I had yet to talk Leonard into stocking the diet version, as the original was so sweet it made my back teeth ache. I would have preferred ice tea.

Though I had told Brett about what we had found out during our visit with Al, we put Pookie in the loop as well.

"Al sounds like a hot mess," Pookie said.

"He's old-fashioned and modern at the same time," I said. "Chauvinist and liberal-minded about women while thinking about their titties."

"I think most heterosexual men think about titties," Brett said. "That's not the problem. The problem is when they think only about titties. I really wouldn't like it if they didn't think about them at all. Far as my own man goes, anyway. Of course, it's my titties I prefer he think about, not stray or random titties."

"It's not just titties Hap thinks about," Leonard said. "Ol' brother Hap is a kind of knight in rusty armor. He's a rescuer of women, children, animals—men too. Al, I think he's just wounded. He may have been born wounded. But I should add that Hap does like titties."

"What's acceptable for men to think about and say has changed," I said. "We just haven't all caught up to it. Al being a prime example. I think he lives confused."

"I don't give a shit," Leonard said. "I'll talk about dicks if I want to. He can talk about what he wants to talk about. I get tired of listening, I'll quit listening. Shit, who isn't confused these days?"

"It's Leonard's gentle way and shy expressions about sex and relationships, the nature of the world, that first drew me to him," Pookie said, and batted his eyes.

Leonard let out a laugh.

"If we can't talk straight, even if some of what we talk about isn't delicate, then what kind of relationship do any of us have?" I said. "And Al. What about that poor bastard?"

"We all know Al is one wee-wee shy of a specimen," Leonard said, "and there's only so much Earth-to-Al communication we can manage with him. Being around him is tiring. But I do feel for the old fart."

"Unless we can find Lilly or figure out what happened to Alice, we're still lost in the wilderness," Brett said.

"True that, baby," I said. "By the way, you'll be happy to know Al has had a yurt built and is leaving the mobile home to the couch mice."

"That's so sweet," Brett said. "Kind of nutty, but sweet. It's nice to think of those rascals living their best life in a mobile-home couch. Though you can bet, in time, they'll be eyeing Al's yurt."

36

Old-timers, and that includes me and Leonard, still refer to it as the "old tuberculosis hospital." Its hospital days are long gone, its former patients either deceased from the disease, cured, or naturally obliterated by the relentless march of time and age.

The former hospital is down deep in what is now shaded woods not far from the banks of the Trinity River. I don't know how Leonard came to know of it, but I had been there because, when I was a teenager, I had relatives—an aunt, an uncle, and a cousin, Benny, lost to me now—who lived not far from the Trinity River and the hospital, and I'd go with my mom and dad to visit them.

Like the Sabine, the Trinity is a muddy, twisting river, but for me it always lacked the magic of the Sabine. Perhaps that was because I grew up not far from the banks of the Sabine and spent time on its waters and in the woods that bordered it.

I learned from Benny the joys of peanut butter, slab cheese, and onion sandwiches as an afternoon snack. Now and again, when I can't sleep at night and I'm thinking about the old days, I put one of those sandwiches together and sit out on my porch and eat it. It's as if I'm capturing escaped memories by way of my mouth.

On one of those long-ago visits, me and Benny, as teenagers do, decided to leave the elders to their reminiscing and memories and set out to create some of our own.

We both enjoyed fishing, so we gathered cane poles, dug some worms, took Benny's single-shot sixteen-gauge for snakes and such, and drove down to the Trinity in Benny's old pickup. It had been bought cheap and rattled like a rattlesnake.

We parked under the river bridge on a sandbar that stuck out into the shallow water. The bar was short and thick and shadowed by the bridge.

We took our goods and hiked along the edge of the river. When the trees encroached, we went up a deer trail Benny knew, one that finally broke open, and in a slate of bright sunlight, we could see the old hospital. Most of its windows were long gone, looking like empty eyes. Trees at the back of it dropped broken limbs on its solid roof. What had once been a long, wide road of concrete out front was cracked open by nature, and pushing through the cracks were green and brown weeds. Concrete might be tough, but nature was tougher.

We put aside our poles and tackle box and explored the place, me carrying a flashlight and Benny his sixteen-gauge.

It was creepy in there. Instead of a place where kindly medical staff helped people recover, it seemed a place of unimaginable horrors, scalpels, hooks, and chain saws.

At least, that's how my imagination ran. Inside there were old gurneys and rooms that had fragments of collapsed furniture along with rusty bedsprings. In some cases, there were mattresses stained dark from rain blown through empty window frames.

In one room, a chicken snake, what some call a rat snake, thick as my wrist and five to six feet long, squirmed out from under a leaf-dotted mattress and disappeared through a hole in the wall that seemed too small to accommodate its size.

It was no threat, so Benny didn't shoot it. They are aggressive snakes, but not poisonous. They keep the rat population at bay.

The hallways and most of the rooms were piled with damp leaves and trash from those who had camped there in the past. It wasn't too far from the train tracks that had once run over a rail bridge next to the overpass we parked under.

Hobos, killers, and adventurers had no doubt passed this way and walked these abandoned halls. There was a smell of sweet rot and sour defecation, both human and animal. Its combined stench was so heavy, it was hard to breathe. Who knows how many germs I inhaled that are now nesting in my body waiting to infect me with tubercular contagions? Probably none, but I was the kind of guy who thought about those things.

After our exploration of the abandoned hospital, we went down to the river to fish, far less exciting than our grand tour of that abandoned building.

Until the old hospital came up, I had nearly forgotten about it because it wasn't a memory I needed. Now the memory was intense again and no longer a teenager's make-believe palace of horrors. It was something far worse than I could ever have imagined. The horrors were peculiar and real and, from my viewpoint, almost surreal.

37

Let's color this story orange for a while. The same color as a convict's onesie. Don't tell me that Texas prisoners don't wear orange or onesies, because I don't care. This is my take on a true story told by Chief Justin. I thought I'd add my own color and fashion design.

Okay. Let's put inside that onesie a convict named Peter Jenkins, called Pooter by his loved ones and "that son of a bitch" by a wide variety of people who had lost lawn mowers, jewelry, guns, and, in one case, a small space heater to his thieving hands. He even stole a set of false teeth and tried to pawn them along with some gold bracelets with a name etched inside. That's what got him caught the first time; the pawnbroker said, "Wait a minute. Let me check something," and walked off to the back of the shop.

What he checked was his cell phone. He quietly called 911, and as Pooter was watching the pawnbroker slowly and laboriously write up his pawning of the false teeth, the cops came through the door.

The pawnbroker wouldn't have taken the false teeth if they had come directly from Pooter's mouth, but writing them up was a good way to stall.

The happy ending of this story is the false teeth were returned to their rightful gummy owner, and the jewelry now clanks on a wrist somewhere.

Pooter was a nice-looking lad and did well enough in prison. There he went by the name Petey Baby or Vacuum Suck. He gave a lot of rough boys some satisfaction in return for protection, chocolate bars, and cigarettes.

One bright morning, on trash duty, Pooter decided his life as the prison poke wasn't as satisfying as one might think, and it led to a lot of raw-ass problems. So when a garbage truck went out, he managed to roll under it, grip something beneath, and ride away with it.

He dropped out from under the truck when it slowed for a stop sign, rolled his ass into traffic, barely avoiding being hit, and headed across a pasture, where he tore his onesie climbing through a barbwire fence.

Pooter stole a Pontiac Firebird out of a yard a short time after, hot-wired it, and drove it north; he ran out of gas just as he reached the end of Angelina County.

He ran on foot over that old rail bridge, the one next to the river bridge beneath which Benny and I had parked his pickup so long ago.

Pooter hadn't gone far when the hounds started baying. Someone had reported the car theft, and a highway patrolman had noted it fleeing north.

As fate would have it, the patrolman's vehicle encountered a broken bottle in the highway that left the officer parked beside the road with a blown-out tire and a pissed-off attitude. But good old cell phones can beat an elderly Pontiac Firebird on its best day.

Law enforcement in Nacogdoches County got word. The abandoned Firebird was found, and that's when the private-sector hounds were called in. These hounds were good ones, bloodhounds, shepherds, Malinois, and a handful of mixed dogs that could trace their lineage back to the first mean-ass wolf that ever gleefully ate a human being and shit his remains off a cliff.

The dogs were right on him, and then they weren't. Dog handlers couldn't figure it. Could Pooter fly? Where had he gone? It was as if he reached a spot not far from the end of the old railroad bridge and jumped off into a hole into another dimension.

Pooter was gone for two days before he was returned to his former life as a prison romantic with an extended sentence and a bit of prison-hospital time. And he had a story to tell.

He had been kidnapped, he said. The only thing missing from his story was aliens who wanted to check out his innards with surgical tools and get a stool sample, because who wouldn't want that?

He'd caught a ride. There he was, in his prison garb, standing beside the road near the railway bridge, and a car stops for him.

What we have here is a great bit of luck.

But not for Pooter, as he'd first thought. It was luck for the driver and his companion. After the car stopped, the window came down, and a man with close-cut gray hair said, "Hop in," and considering the baying of the hounds was in Pooter's ears, he did. Got in the back seat of the car and thought he was caught up in a heavenly chariot. That he was about to do an Ezekiel, witness the spinning of wheels within wheels and be off to heaven, maybe with a quick stop at the Burger King drive-through before arrival.

The car was a bronze Porsche, as inconspicuous as a shaved rat in lace panties. But Pooter said the good part, the thing that made him so happy, was that in the car was, not one of his prison mates with the hairy eyeball, a thin smile, and a bulge in his pants, but something that fit his heterosexual dreams.

A beautiful woman sitting in the back seat with him, short dress, legs that invited examination. "A goddess," he said, "with purple eyes so dark and deep, they were like wishing wells."

She smiled, Pooter said, and she had the nicest set of teeth he had ever seen. Just before he made a short prayer to thank God, whom he envisioned as the Baby Jesus, Purple Eyes' hand flashed. Pooter saw a needle, then it was sticking in his arm and she was pushing the hypodermic plunger.

Pooter said the woman turned to colorful goo, and he went sailing out into the heavens, and they were neither black nor blue but instead a swirl of colors, the stars all green and yellow, the moon a wheel of cheese.

Next thing he knew he was waking up groggy with a headache. There was a strong light overhead, and he blinked against it. He was strapped down, feeling drained, lying naked on a table. Standing over him was a thin, bald man wearing scrubs, a mask, and surgical gloves and holding a scalpel in his hand.

The man in scrubs said, "Better pop him again. He's coming around. Can't have squirming."

Pooter turned his head as someone on the other side of the table moved. It was the woman again, the goddess with the hypodermic needle and the brilliant smile. She gave him another shot. He turned his head to see Scrubs Guy lean over him with a scalpel, and behind him was the gray-haired man, watching intently. Next thing Pooter knew, his head was full of colors again, and then he was waking up on the slab, no longer strapped, feeling pain in his belly.

Pooter lay there awhile, trying to remember which end of himself was up. Finally got his brain working well enough to slide off the table, hold on to an IV rack, and place his bare feet on a freezer-cold floor.

He touched the side of his belly. It was cut open. If not for the medical tape stretched over it, it would have been a gaping red mouth of a wound.

Moments later, the hounds and their masters and a bunch of law enforcement folks were charging into the room.

They had come back to that location to see if Pooter might be found, and the dogs had picked up his scent where he had been taken from the Porsche and hauled in for a stripping of parts.

"I'm glad as hell to see you guys," Pooter said.

He didn't realize he was in the old tuberculosis hospital and that harvesting of his organs and skin had been halted when the sound of men and dogs coming along the riverside trail was heard.

38

We were all in Justin's office, him telling us that story, the one I embellished just now.

"So they got Pooter in a hospital with devices pumping and wheezing, tubes poked into him. Ironically, he is not on the top of the list to get a kidney transplant, even if one of his is gone. He can do all right with one."

"I thought organ theft like that was a myth," I said.

"Apparently not. These folks came prepared. Had a medical professional, or at least a veterinarian. I'm sure, had the dogs and trackers not found them, scaring the harvesters off, all that would have been left of Pooter was a wet spot on the gurney. Pooter told the law to tell Butch back at the pen that he'd be home soon with a jar of Vaseline.

"And you know what? That isn't even the half of it. That old hospital, it was stuffed with trash, but there were a handful of clean rooms. There was an electric generator, lights, operating tables, and a couple of empty organ carriers. You know, those things that look like ice chests and, well, are?"

We all nodded like those bobbing toy dogs you see on car dashes.

"They set that place up quick, did what they did, and left when the law closed in. Not sure how long they were there, but it took them very little time to take organs out of people. There's big money in that. If someone can't get on the list for a kidney, or if the wait is too long, they can illegally get one through back channels for a serious bill of cash money. It's not like those organ pirates take a check or pay taxes.

"There was blood all over that place. There were stacks of human bones and charred clothes. That old hospital is full of DNA, and hopefully some of it will be identifiable. By this afternoon, we might know something about who was there, a way to catch Johnny Joe by knowing his real name, and perhaps there's something in there that will nail Purple Eyes down as well. It's a waiting and wishing game.

"I don't know how they found the place, but the money Purple Eyes stole from the Polson family was most likely their seed money for the operation. You know the old saying: Takes money to make money."

"Thanks for sharing," Brett said.

"We're working together, right?"

"Kind of," Brett said.

Justin smiled. "That sounds a bit tenuous. I'm thinking you can stay on this and go places me and the law can't go. And because you are concerned citizens, you will come to me with information, just in case I can solve this without letting you take the law into your own hands."

I thought he would very much let us take the law into our own hands if we could rid him of a problem like Johnny Joe and Purple Eyes. And I could understand that. I could also understand he couldn't come right out and say that.

39

Over the next few days, we all hung out at the office and looked through internet records and files. Once you chucked out the obvious bits that didn't fit, you found there were a lot of bits that might fit.

Insurance scams discovered after the fact—it began to look like the organ gang was behind them. Had an Empire of Greed going on. You could start to see a pattern. Recognize their methodology.

Scams like the asphalt-spray business. Insurance scams where people who weren't dead were reported as dead. And then there were those that turned up dead. Traps were laid, but Johnny Joe and Purple Eyes were always a step ahead of the law.

"Somehow they always knew," Brett said.

"Luck?" Leonard said.

"Could be," Brett said. "But looking all this over, there were a few common denominators. Certain lawyers and insurance agents are connected to all this. They're a bit too much of a constant not to be part of the arrangement."

"Okay," Leonard said. "I'll bite."

"I think the body harvesting is something they came up with because you can grab someone off the street—it doesn't require a lot of planning and finagling. You got the money for the doctor or vet, the generator for lights, and so on, you're in business. And you make so much from it, if you need to, you can leave equipment behind."

"I'm surprised this really goes on," I said.

"There was this guy I read about, Lee Cruceta," Brett said. "Made deals with morticians, traveled to funeral homes. Someone was to be cremated, in forty-five minutes, he or his flunkies could remove the skin and organs from a corpse. Even corneas and cartilage, collagen for plastic surgery. Stuff went in picnic coolers, and body parts were exchanged for money.

"If it wasn't cremation, they'd saw off the legs at the hips and take the ligaments from them. This way, the corpse could still be shown in the casket. But the internal organs and the legs were bagged up and gone.

"In case someone was suspicious, Cruceta's team had signed releases for the people whose bodies they harvested. Thing was, they were forged, but no one asked questions. Proceeds from one body was often over eighty thousand dollars."

"One of those a year, and you're living okay," Leonard said.

"They were doing a lot more than one a year," Brett said. "But they got caught. Johnny Joe has taken it a step up. He nabs live people if he has to. Money on the hoof. Or the shoe, if you prefer."

"Like saying car parts come from wrecked cars when they're from new ones," I said.

"Right," Brett said. "Johnny Joe and Purple Eyes are an industry. They and their compatriots could be making millions."

"Can't imagine there are people that low," I said.

"You can't imagine it because at heart you are so stupidly sweet," Leonard said. "But I can imagine it. I always can."

40

You act like you're waiting on the rest of your order," Brett said, "but pussy is a one-course meal. It doesn't come with ketchup and fries, a soft drink."

"Sorry," I said, and worked my way up from between her legs to lie beside her in bed. "All this murder and such has got my tongue tangled up. It's not that it isn't fun down there, but I think I'm wasting mouthfuls."

"You do feel a bit like a damp paper towel."

"Just can't get that stuff about Pooter, all of it, out of my mind. Okay I ask for a cunnilingus rain check? My mind is adrift and my tongue is tired."

"Truthfully, I'm not feeling all that sprightly either. It reminds me, though, back in high school, parking with this boy on our local Humpers Hill—"

"I don't want to hear this."

"Boy I was dating, I mean, he was down there working it, and then I discovered he had false front teeth. They were loose and came out, and there I was, two teeth in my adventure zone."

"I said I didn't want to hear it."

"He let me keep the teeth," she said. "He thought he needed to be refitted with a better pair. I was sympathetic, but that was our last date. I couldn't look at him without thinking of a young Gabby Hayes. Later, he got the teeth replaced, but by then there was no going back. You, on the other hand, may return to the fork in the road at a later date."

"Was this toothy event when you were Sweet Potato Queen?"

"It was. I still got the teeth somewhere."

"Ah, shit. Not really?"

She laughed. "No, not really, but I had them for some years, then them and my arrowhead collection got lost somehow. Listen here, hon. I'm pretty rattled myself. I think Kung Fu Bobby being in our house has something to do with it. That creepy shit about Pooter. They know where we live, and they have resources."

"Yep, I'm down there in the land of goodness, and I can't but think the bedroom door is going to swing open, and there will be Kung Fu Bobby."

"With the rest of your order," she said.

"More like with a shotgun, or he'll slap me to death like I think he did Pete. Course, Kung Fu said he was out, and I believe him, but he also said if there was enough money he might come back."

"He got past our locks and cameras, sat in our kitchen, ate cookies, and drank milk. He might have peed in our toilet."

We hugged up, and when I awoke in the morning, we had rolled in opposite directions and had our butts pressed together.

I got out of bed carefully, went down to make breakfast. I was about halfway finished with flipping pancakes off the griddle and was about to make our coffee when my cell buzzed.

There was a text from Hanson. It said: Come see me. I have something for you. From a future worm salesman. Rachel is gone for most of the day. And you can pick up that tackle box I told you about.

I got Brett up and we ate breakfast. I showed her the text.

"Thinking I may drive over to Caddo Lake," I said. "See Hanson."

"All right, but I'm not going. I'm taking a brain-rest day. I won't be staying here or hanging at the office. I'm going to go to Rusk and take that old steam train ride. I may go to Tyler from there and shop like a real girl. Probably see if Chance and Reba will meet me in Rusk at the train. We can take the ride, then all go into Tyler, have lunch, and go to the stores. I plan to fulfill all expectations of women shopping. I'm going to be like a goddamn advertisement for it."

"I'll see what Leonard is up to. I could call Hanson, see if he'll tell me what he has to tell me over the phone, but I think he actually wants company. And I want to pick up that tackle box he promised us some time back. As anglers, me and Leonard aren't very sophisticated, but us just having that box full of flies and ties will make fish tremble in fear."

"That's showing them," Brett said. "Goddamn stupid fish."

41

Brett called Chance, made plans to meet her and Reba in Rusk to ride the train. They would then drive in separate cars to Tyler, take a run at Dallas, have an overnight thingamajig for the ladies. It wasn't a bad way for Brett to get her mind off organ harvesters and a purple-eyed woman.

Leonard picked me up in Pookie's truck. It was black and shiny as a wet rock and the windshield had a crack in it from flipped-up gravel. I never had a car with an uncracked windshield for long. Gravel was always the culprit. It was good to see it wasn't just me.

Leonard was wearing new jeans, red cowboy boots, a blue Western shirt, a black leather vest, and a black cowboy hat. His fleece-lined Western-style leather jacket was tossed over the middle of the seat.

I had on some bland clothes and some dirt-stained tennis shoes. But I had combed my hair and was wearing my blue-jean jacket with the Sun Records symbol on the back. I have a blue-jean jacket with Batman on the back, but it seemed like a music kind of day, not one for stalking the Joker.

"This is a long drive," Leonard said. "Hanson better have something more than that fishing tackle box. Like a lunch."

"Then we might have to be around Rachel," I said.

"Yikes. That's right. Maybe just the tackle box, tickets to Six Flags that we can trade for money, and a custom-fitted silver cock ring."

"Actually, he said Rachel would be gone most of the day."

"That's good."

"We are terrible people," I said.

"Don't you know it," Leonard said.

We listened to Roy Orbison and Postmodern Jukebox on the way over, stopped once at a station to pee and buy bottles of water. After that we quit listening to music and solved some world problems. I did, anyway. Leonard had terrible ideas.

Truth was, long drive or not, I felt like Brett did—I wanted to get away from all that murder and weird monkey-ass business we'd been looking into. I think the bottom line for Hanson was he wanted to see someone from the old days.

He'd been gone only a short time and was already looking for diversion, so I had a feeling the worm business hadn't turned out to be his heart's desire.

When we rolled up in front of Hanson's house, the day was as gray and sad-looking as an orphan's Christmas.

Hanson came out on the porch with a steaming cup of coffee in his hand. He looked happy to see us, and when we got out of the truck, Leonard slipping on his coat, Hanson smiled and yelled for us to come on in and have some coffee.

I thought Rachel might have had Hanson set a trap for us: We go inside, she jumps out with a hatchet, puts us down, chops us up, our remains to be used for Hanson's bait business. It would save money on worms.

We didn't get axed, but we did have some very good coffee and some cinnamon rolls.

"I thought we might go out in the boat," Hanson said. "I got one. I mean a new one. It's got a motor and a roof on it and everything."

"Damn," Leonard said. "Retirement has made you a big dog."

"You know that's right," Hanson said. "But I called you over to give you some information that I could have given you on the phone, but then how would you have seen my boat and felt envious?"

"Phone photos," Leonard said.

"Not the same," Hanson said. "This has to do not only with my cool boat but with the Minnie business."

"I thought you were out of law enforcement," I said.

"Things still drift my way. And sometimes I call a few friends at the LaBorde cop shop and they give me some information that I kind of ask for."

"Kind of ask for, huh?" Leonard said.

"Come on, boys. Let's ride the waves."

42

There were no waves. At Hanson's private dock, we climbed on board what proved to be a decent-size boat with bolted-down swivel deck chairs of the sort that gave one the impression that one was going shark fishing. A tarp was stretched over the back of the deck so the rain that was falling wasn't falling on us.

Hanson carried out the tackle box from inside the wheelhouse. He set it on the deck. It was old, large, silver-colored, and designed to lock tight and float. Leonard opened it. It was full of all manner of cool lures and handcrafted flies. There were also fishing knives and a pocketknife that was sometimes called a Swiss Army knife. There was a flashlight, a twelve-gauge flare gun, and some flares.

"Wait," Leonard said. "We can't take this tackle box. No inflatable raft."

That got a bit of a laugh.

We examined the box's contents for a while, thanked Hanson, and put the box back in the wheelhouse for the time being.

Hanson fired up the boat as I removed the dock line. He eased the boat out smoothly and we cruised under a rumbling gray sky, went bumping out onto the vast lake that was well spotted with a flooded cypress forest, hanging vines and wads of moss. The trees and vines were so constant, they made little alleyways along which the boat traveled. There were stumps and little islands in the lake along with all the trees. This made me hope Hanson's boat credentials hadn't come from a box of Cap'n Crunch.

We found a comfortable place in the water near a mass of rising cypress trees and anchored beneath their thin gray shadows. I looked out over the lake, eyeballed it through the cracks in the trees and hanging vines. There were thick growths of trees on the faraway shore. In that forest all manner of animals roamed. According to some, this included Bigfoot. I was hoping I might see him on the shore and he might wave.

No such luck.

I remembered reading about some kind of invasive aquatic fern that choked out life in the lake. It grew rapidly and was a nuisance and there was an ongoing battle to kill it. So far, the fern was winning.

In the long run, we humans were the lake's worst enemies. We were the worst of the invasive species.

Leonard and I took seats in the deck chairs under the tarp while Hanson fussed about in the wheelhouse. The rain had started to pick up. The lake was splattered with it and it rattled on the overhead tarp.

Hanson brought out an ice chest. It was full of beer and Coke Zero. I was the Zero drinker, though only if that was all there was to drink. My old-man fears had led me to mostly drink water and, as always, unsweet tea and coffee. Depending on which article you were reading that week, diet soft drinks were bad for you or they weren't. Same went for tea and coffee.

I took a Zero, Hanson a beer. Leonard took neither.

"What do you think, boys?" Hanson said.

Me and Leonard agreed we liked the boat.

"I've named it the *Rachel*. Going to have that painted on the side."

"After your wife?" Leonard said.

"No, after a pet pigeon I once owned," Hanson said. "Of course. How many Rachels do I know?"

"Stupid question," Leonard said.

"I'll say," Hanson said. "Hey, heard Justin came to see you."

"Though it started out rocky, he was pretty nice to us in the long run," I said.

"Heard from my source at the LaBorde cop shop he was trading ideas with you."

"That's right," I said.

"Let me tell you something I don't think you know," Hanson said. "Justin already has most of the DNA information back from the old tuberculosis hospital. I'll tell you how he plays. He's giving you a little of this and that now, but he'll give you way less later. I get that part from cops who know him from Houston. Couple of recently retired cops I worked with when I was there. Justin came along later, but he made an impression. He's a real go-getter."

"Seems it," I said.

"They discovered Minnie's DNA. They were able to get a bit of it from her burnt arm, from the bone marrow, and that's how they made the comparison to what was left of her in the old tuberculosis hospital. They found other DNA that shows someone kin to her died there as well."

"Alice," Leonard said. "I was waiting for that."

"They came to the conclusion that the daughter died before she was stripped for parts. What was left of her was burned up in one of the back rooms with some others. However they figure these things, they determined Alice's body was burned up well before Minnie had her arm cut off and was harvested same as her daughter."

"Brett said she had a feeling that Minnie's arm with the watch on it was a ploy," I said. "That way cops wouldn't be looking for Minnie. Would think she had burned up in her house. Cut her fucking arm off to leave as evidence, then saved her life long enough for the skin and organ theft. That's cold."

"Waste not, want not," Leonard said.

"Looks that way," Hanson said. "These are some scary-ass people. And it gets worse. The lawyer who brokered the will payout, the insurance guy who helped with the fraud, their remains were found too."

"They're cleaning house," Leonard said. "Getting rid of people who can identify them, maybe know too much about them, where they hide out, that kind of thing."

"Seems that way," Hanson said.

"They'll pack up their business and move elsewhere," Leonard said. "Find other assholes who'll help them out for a big payout."

"Course, in the long run," Hanson said, "their payout is death."

We told Hanson some things about the case he didn't know. He was no longer able to help us via the cop shop, but he could maybe offer some advice due to experience.

"This kind of wholesale crime," he said. "It's getting worse. It's like comic-book villains come to life. They're villains for the sake of being villains. It's a lifestyle they're proud of. I liked it when criminals were kind of ashamed of themselves and slinked in the shadows. Not this new lot. Each year they get worse."

"You'd think with all that kind of crime," Leonard said, "cops these days wouldn't have time to shoot innocent civilians."

"The bad cops make time for it," Hanson said. "They should spend that energy on these kinds of motherfuckers, the Johnny Joes of the world. But those kinds of cops, they're scared of real danger, so beating some civilian to death or killing someone over something petty takes the place of real police work. I loved being a cop, and I haven't always done it by the book, but I don't look back on my record and feel ashamed."

While Hanson talked, I was watching a boat moving over the water, skipping over the cold, flat surface between the trees. It was a little smaller than Hanson's boat, one of those you could rent and haul out to the lake by trailer for a day or two of fishing and exploration.

There was no cover over the deck of the boat. I could see as it turned in a wide circle toward us that there were four men on deck and at least one or two more in the wheelhouse was my guess.

"Recognize that boat?" I asked.

"No," Hanson said.

"They got guns," Leonard said.

43

The way the bow of the boat hit the water caused wings to be made of it, and they fanned on either side of the boat as it came toward us. The wings caught the bit of sun that was breaking through the clouds and turned the water wings silver.

Leonard had already hauled the anchor up and Hanson had started the engine. We were quickly moving over the water, and the boat behind us was gaining. When our boat was lined out on a path between the ancient trees, the boat drew in line behind us. Not close, but not far enough away to make me feel comfortable.

A shot picked Leonard's cowboy hat off his head and carried it out in the water.

"That was brand-new," Leonard said.

Me and Leonard hit the deck, tried to lie flat. There was an old-fashioned life ring fastened to the back of the boat, and suddenly parts of it were chewed up, and shots whistled so close over our heads that I saw bits of my hair floating about.

Another shot slammed into the wheelhouse and I heard glass shatter, and then Hanson made a turn in the water that nearly threw me and Leonard out of the boat.

Hanson's boat cut through some hanging moss, ripped away some vines, shot fast toward a shoreline that wasn't all that distant but even though we were traveling at top speed was still too far away.

More shots cut through the air, and then one of our pursuers opened up with an automatic weapon that sounded like a sewing machine if it could sew three times faster than normal.

Bits of Hanson's nice boat jumped out into the water, then I guess we hit a stump, because lots of the boat flew into the water and along with them went me and Leonard.

When I bobbed up out of the cold lake, Leonard not far from me, I realized we were next to a large tree. Moss hung down from it, and though I could see through it, it wasn't bad camouflage.

I saw Hanson's boat stand on one edge like it was doing a boat-show trick, then it turned over and skidded across the surface of the water as if the lake were as flat as a skating rink.

The *Rachel* tipped its stern into the air, did a porpoise dive, and was quickly gone to the bottom of the lake. Moments later, debris from it came floating up, including the tackle box Hanson had given us. Hanson surfaced, grabbed the box, and clung to it like a life preserver.

By this time the other boat was turning around, splitting the water as it did, fanning it higher on either side of the bow than before.

Hanson was injured. I could tell by the way he clung to the tackle box. He carefully opened the box, took something out, closed the box without water sloshing into it.

The boat slowed as it neared Hanson, then came to a stop. The men in the boat leaned over the side of it and looked at Hanson as if he were a rare fish.

I could see now Hanson had pulled the flare pistol from the box. As a thick black guy leaned over the edge with his gun to finish Hanson off, Hanson shot him with the flare gun.

The flare hit the man in the head and the phosphorus exploded. The burning phosphorus from the flare made the man's hair and face catch on fire. He dropped the long gun, stumbled, started screaming. A banshee would have been envious of that wail. The flare burned out. The man fell to his knees and rested his head on the edge of the boat. He must have sucked the flames up his nose, and they had done him in, or mostly. He was moving a little, but I didn't envision him having a long future.

One of the men on board pulled a flat, dark pistol out of a holster and shot him in the head, then boosted him over the side and into the water.

The killer was a little man, and I recognized him. I guess the money had been too good for him to stay gone. It was Kung Fu Bobby. He had warned me.

Kung Fu Bobby looked out at Hanson, lifted the pistol, and shot him through the head. It was a perfect shot. I saw the back of Hanson's skull jump away and splash bloody in the water. Hanson drifted under the lake. The tackle box bounced a little.

Kung Fu Bobby looked out over the water, but the moss and the shadows did me and Leonard good. Beside me, Leonard said, "He's mine."

"Not if I get to him first," I said.

For now, we had nothing to fight with. We drifted against the tree, trying not to make ripples. We eased into the moss and let it hang around us. We could see through it, but we were hard to see unless you knew where we were. They didn't.

I was glad it was cold. Otherwise, this was a great spot for water moccasins. A few minutes more of that cold, and I'd want the water moccasins.

The boat rode around awhile, circled our tree, but no one could see us inside our envelope of hanging moss and vines. The boat turned and went past where Hanson and the *Rachel* had gone down, causing the tackle box to hop around in the water.

I guess they rode around in that area for about twenty minutes before they gave up and started back the way they had come from.

44

It might not have been freezing, but it was damn cold. I could hardly feel my legs or my nuts, and my asshole had closed to keep the water out. We clung to the tree for a while, just in case they planned to circle back.

Kung Fu Bobby would want to know if we survived. If he didn't see us for a while, he might think we had gone under.

Hanson was dead.

I was having a hard time processing that. Hanson was dead. Dead. He'd always seemed damn near indestructible.

Leonard said, "We don't get out of this water, we're going to stove up."

"Hypothermia is not our friend," I said.

About that time, the boat did come back. I guess it had made a wide circle hoping to catch us out in the open trying to swim for shore. Let me tell you, that would be a hard swim. It was too cold, and though I could see the shore, it was too far away to feel happy about.

The boat made a couple of passes and went away again.

We waited some more. I was really starting to feel bad. The cold, the shock, all of it, was getting to me.

"We can't stay here," Leonard said. "We have to try for it."

"Long ways."

"Soon as we get started, it'll be closer. I say we swim to the tackle box, use that as a float, kick our way to where we can stop at trees and stumps, and take a rest if need be. It'll be easier to get up close to the trees than hang for long in the water."

"Neither will do us much good," I said.

But I knew what Leonard meant. On our current tree, I was able to rest my feet against it where it was crooked beneath the water. Not all trees would be as handy, but they were most likely better than open water clinging to a floating tackle box.

Leonard took off his fine but waterlogged coat and let go of it. I kept my blue-jean jacket on. We swam toward the box, and I won't lie to you, I didn't think I could make it there. I couldn't tell if I was kicking my legs or not. I told myself I was, but I couldn't feel them well enough to know for sure. I had to turn my head and look.

I was kicking, but it was a bit like floundering.

Leonard was snapping along a little better. He got to the box first, pushed it toward me, and then we were both hanging.

"We could take turns, one kicking toward shore, the other hanging on to rest," Leonard said.

"Think we need to keep moving. We stop to rest, we get colder, stiffer, and then dead."

"Right," he said, and we started kicking.

The box floated well and it was good to have it, but time clicked on and on and the shore seemed to be moving away from us instead of coming closer. I could see someone walking across the water toward us. It was Hanson. His head wasn't blown off. His black face was shiny. He smiled. It was that great, wicked smile he had. He was waving us to come on. He turned and walked toward shore.

It was inspiring. I tried to kick harder. We went pretty far, and then we stopped at one of the trees, under the cover of its limbs, moss, and gathered shadows. I wanted to let go of the box I was holding with one hand, let go of the tree with my other. I wanted to go under and visit Hanson because he was no longer walking on the water.

Maybe down there in his wrecked boat we could make some coffee. Hot, hot coffee. I'd like that. I looked at Leonard.

"Would you like some coffee?" I said. "I think we should go see Hanson and have him make us some."

"Hap," Leonard said. "I'm about to slap you. I want you to know, from the bottom of my heart, I do it with love."

"What?" I said, and Leonard slapped me.

It was hard enough it hurt, but it was too cold to hurt much. But it did what it was meant to do. Woke me up a little.

"Thank you," I said.

"Would you like another?"

"No, thank you. Did you see Hanson walking on water?"

"No. And neither did you. We rested long enough, we have to go on."

"I know," I said, and away we went, but by now my blue-jean coat was weighing me down, and of course, it wasn't doing anything to make me warmer. I abandoned it to Caddo Lake.

I have to say, when you look out at a shoreline, it can seem a lot closer than it is, and it turned out what I thought was the shore was a long thin island covered in trees.

We climbed on the little island, pulled out the tackle box, and sat on it. Doing all that was only a little less hard than pushing Sisyphus's rock up a hill.

The wind had picked up and it was colder. The rain was little more than a drizzle. We found a place among the trees that offered some barrier and slowed it down. While we were sitting there, I watched shadows like ill-shaped fingers crawling and extending across the water. In the west the sun was exploding red through the clouds and going down.

"I think I'm colder here," Leonard said.

"It's being wet, the wind blowing on us," I said.

"Think? Well, shit, Hap. I hadn't thought of that."

"We got to go the rest of the way before it gets completely dark. Tired as we are, cold as it's about to get, and with the wind picking up, we won't make it through the night."

"I don't want to go," he said.

"Can I slap you?"

"Totally different situation. So no."

We each took a handle on either side of the big tackle box and carried it to the far side of the island. That didn't take long. From that side we could see the actual shoreline and the trees that grew not far back from it.

We placed the box in the water, went in with it, started swimming. The wind picked up and the water began to heave. I threw up what little was in my stomach.

"We're going to make it," Leonard said.

"I know that," I said. "We always make it."

"I would have said the same about Hanson, had you asked me earlier today," he said.

"I know," I said. "But we are different."

"I'm going to take that thought to my heart and hold it," Leonard said.

I think we were kicking harder now, inspired by the relative closeness of the shore. Both of us, by this time, had lost our shoes.

The wind broke heavy and the sky and the lake were so dark, it was as if we were inside a box, closed tight, with no entrance for light. We couldn't see the shore anymore, but we kept swimming.

My hand that wasn't holding the box hit something, and for a moment I thought of a great catfish, thought that I had touched its back, but it didn't swim away.

I was touching land. I pulled myself ashore and dragged the box up before I realized Leonard wasn't hanging on to it.

"Leonard." I called his name several times.

I heard a voice say, "Hap."

He was still in the water. I went back in. Kept yelling.

Leonard wasn't yelling back as loud as before. He could barely say my name, and sometimes the wind gathered it up and launched it across the water, so I couldn't be sure where he was. His voice could have been coming from anywhere.

"Hap," he said. And this was louder, but not close.

"Leonard. Where are you, man? Where are you?"

"I'm onshore," he said.

He had managed to make it there while I was dying out in the water.

A flashlight beam struck me. I could see a shape behind it, dark and spectral and certainly Leonard. I swam toward it. I didn't think I would make it.

The light went out. Then Leonard had hold of me. He had gone back into the water. We were taking turns being exhausted and having second winds. I was pretty sure I didn't have another in me.

We made land and lay down beside the tackle box.

"I remembered there was a flashlight in the tackle box," Leonard said.

"I went in after you, asshole."

"Did you?" he said. "Well, I went in after you too."

We continued to lie beside the tackle box. The tackle box was our friend. I was going to have our names engraved on it. I was going to have it kept in the bedroom where me and Brett slept. I was going to kiss it good night every night just before I kissed Brett good night. I might divorce Brett and marry the tackle box because it loved me and had saved my life and Leonard's.

45

We didn't lie there long for the reasons we hadn't stayed anywhere long. We were freezing and the wind was picking up, and to top it off, it was starting to rain hard. I could hear the water striking the lake. It pounded on my head. I felt like I had icicles on my bones. My teeth were chattering.

We carried the tackle box, each of us holding one of the side handles. Leonard held the flashlight and we walked barefoot into the woods; our feet were wet and soft, hurt something awful, and slowed us down.

We came out of that patch of woods onto a dirt road. We looked down it. In the not-too-far distance, we could see a light.

"A house," Leonard said.

46

I'd like to tell you how nice the owner was to us when we came to the house and knocked on the door, but that would be a lie.

From behind the door, we were threatened by a barking dog that sounded about the size of a saber-toothed tiger along with an old man's voice threatening to shoot our asses off with a shotgun.

It took some doing, talking through the door and all, but he finally listened to us enough to call some law.

"They're coming," he said. "And I still ain't letting you in."

He was true to his word. We went into his carport and found his truck was unlocked. We left the tackle box on the floor of the carport and climbed inside, out of the wind and the rain. It wasn't perfect, damp as we were, but it was a damn sight better than before.

Leonard said, "Fuck it," stepped out of the truck, took the Swiss Army knife from the tackle box, used it to hot-wire the truck from under the dash, started it up, and turned on the heater.

A few minutes later, it was a lot warmer. I closed my eyes, remembering what happened to Hanson. The warmer I got, the more comfortable I got. I went to sleep.

A bird was tapping on my window, and I wanted it to go away. I was trying to sleep. But when I opened my eyes, there was no bird, just a flashlight with a face behind it.

It turned out to belong to a cop.

We and our tackle box were taken to the cop shop near Caddo Lake in a burg of a town that had one filling station. We were going to be charged with breaking into the truck owned by the gentleman with the pet saber-tooth and maybe some other things that I was uncertain of.

With sat on a bench in the warm police station with blankets draped over our shoulders. There was a large clock with a fish design on it, ticking loudly, on the wall. We explained what had happened, about our friend being killed, the sinking of the boat. We wanted them to do something about it. We said we didn't break into the truck the doors were open and we were freezing. Leonard admitted he hot-wired it.

Chief Reynolds was a muscular young man with an intense stare. I had a feeling what he was hearing from us was blah-blah-blah. He didn't believe our tale about surviving in the water that long. If I hadn't survived it, I might not have believed it either.

I described Kung Fu Bobby to them. Leonard had noted a couple of the other men on the boat with him. He gave their descriptions. We didn't tell them we had a history with Kung Fu Bobby or that we called him that.

A petite young woman with her hair up in knot wearing a loose-fitting uniform and a holstered automatic that on her looked big enough to be an antiaircraft gun was writing it all down. The little metal pin over her pocket said GARCIA.

When we finished, they let us sit in the only jail cell in the station. It didn't look to have been cleaned recently and it smelled faintly of urine, probably from the last drunk who had stayed there. The bunks looked like bedbug nests.

In the corners of the cell, thick swaths of green mold ran from floor to ceiling. There was a kind of dew on the wall with it, which meant there were water leaks and the savage rain was taking advantage of it. The way it ran behind the wall, the mold pulsed as if it had a heartbeat. Each corner of the cell had a little pool of water and it was spreading across the floor in thin sheets of damp. The only way to keep our feet out of it was to sit on the bunks and lift them up.

That jail cell seemed like the place where asthma was born.

They give us some nice dry jail clothes to wear. Placed ours over a chair next to a space heater in the office. I was hoping this wasn't going to be our new home and office uniform, because the accommodations sucked, and the clothes weren't orange. They were a brown T-shirt and loose jail pants that were brown and white striped. The cops provided us with some cheap soft shoes to wear. They gave us a cup of coffee and a granola bar apiece from the vending machine in the interrogation room. The coffee sucked and the granola bars were old enough to have been made from original Egyptian grain.

One thing, though: They didn't lock the cell, and the door was left open. The young Garcia sat at the end of the hallway where she could see us. She looked nervous, kept her hand on her pistol butt in case we made a run for the door, back out into the freezing rain.

Convincing them to call Justin in LaBorde took more effort than I expected. I was pretty sure Chief Reynolds was positive we were drug runners and there had been some kind of shoot-out on the lake over product.

Justin vouched for us, and after we got our walking papers and put on our partially dry clothes, which had a toasty smell, the chief came over and said, "Chief in LaBorde says you're okay. But I don't believe your story."

"When we discovered that flying saucer driven by Bigfoot," Leonard said, "we got the same kind of reaction from the military."

"What?" said the chief.

"Just joking," I said. "He's just joking."

"Joke somewhere else," he said.

"Love to," Leonard said.

Garcia told us we could keep the shoes, then provided us with cheap prisoner coats and, using her personal vehicle, drove us and our tackle box through the rain to Hanson's house to fetch Pookie's truck.

When we pulled up in the yard, Rachel's car was there. The porch light was on. The front door was open. I had been so wrapped up in surviving, I had forgotten all about Rachel, her coming home.

Rachel was lying on the front porch next to a spilled bag of groceries.

The cop told us to wait, but me and Leonard were out of the car and rushing up to the porch before she could stop us.

Rachel lay with the not too bright porch light on her face. Or what was left of it. A shotgun had carried most of it away. In our stupid haste, we had ruined some evidence by stepping in blood and bone on the front porch steps. Most of it was washed away anyway, but I realized now I had felt the sticky blood and the crunchy bone from her face beneath my feet.

The kid cop was calling her chief on her cell phone. We went back to her car and climbed into the back seat and sat there, not speaking, shivering a bit from being wet again.

47

We ended up heading back to the little cop shop. Garcia watched us carefully out of the corner of her eye, clearly afraid we might try and jump her on the ride back.

Back at the jail we gave them the Hanson's next-of-kin information. They sent the justice of the peace out there, an ambulance with a body bag. Said they'd send boats out to look for Hanson's body.

Leonard drew them a map that showed as best he could where the *Rachel* had gone down, where Hanson had been killed.

It still hadn't completely sunk in. A friend like Hanson, you don't think of him dying on a boat during a trip to impress his friends.

We ended up in the cell again, only this time the chief locked the door and said, "I knew you two were sons of bitches."

This hardly seemed fair to our mothers.

The chief called Justin again to tell him what had happened. Then the chief told us Justin was coming to see us personally. He'd be there in the morning.

We slept on our bunks, back in our prison clothes, with blankies provided by the cop shop again. They took our jail shoes.

It was warm, though, and we were so tired from swimming and worrying for hours, we went right to sleep. I awoke with powerful leg cramps from all that swimming. I thought they would never go away. I did that thing where you stand up on the balls of your feet to make the cramps go away. It worked. But by the time I got back in bed, the cramps had returned. After a couple more repeat performances of me standing on the balls of my feet, the cramps finally went away for good, but sleep was hard after that.

Leonard was still asleep, of course. Snoring.

I won't kid you: During the night, I cried a little. Silently, but I cried. I had known Hanson for a long time. I'd respected Rachel, even if she hated mine and Leonard's guts.

And with good reason. We had gotten Hanson in trouble again, even if he had invited us to have some time to reconnect. That reconnection, maybe the information he gave us, had led to him being murdered, and then his wife.

She probably never knew what hit her. Guy waiting in the house, probably. When she stepped on the porch, was going to unlock the door, it was jerked open and someone among that boat crowd that had chased us fired a shotgun into her pretty face.

Even though I was sad and mad and going back to sleep was hard, I finally did. When I did, I slept like the proverbial log. When I woke up, I looked between the bars of the cell and saw the clock on the wall. It was nine thirty a.m. and Justin was coming through the front door, followed by the lady cop who had held the umbrella for him on that wet night that now seemed a hundred years ago.

Leonard was up as well. They gave us back our jailhouse shoes. We sat on the bunks and put them on. Leonard got up, hung on to the bars like a professional convict. He sang a few lines of "Nobody Knows the Trouble I've Seen," and Justin said, "Shut up, Leonard."

After a while, Justin took us into custody, drove us and the tackle box away from there in his personal car. The officer followed in Pookie's pickup.

In the car, Leonard, who was in the front passenger seat, said, "Can we stop for breakfast?"

"No," Justin said.

"A quick coffee?" I said.

"No," Justin said.

"I'd even eat McDonald's," I said. "If there's some kind of toy comes with it, you can have it. Could we go through a drive-through if we pass one?"

"No."

"Can we listen to music?" Leonard asked.

"No."

"Perhaps you have an amusing story, Chief?" I said.

"No."

We rode hungry and without music or amusement on into LaBorde and the police station.

48

"H anson was our good friend," I said. "Known him for years. We didn't kill him. It's exactly as we've said. The gift he gave us, the tackle box, saved our lives."

We were all three seated in the interrogation room when I said that. Muscles jumped in Justin's face. I had no idea what that meant. He might have had a moment of intestinal disturbance. He leaned back in his chair, rocking it onto its back legs. The light danced on his slick hair.

We had been telling and retelling our story into a recorder for a few hours, including the part where Hanson said Justin wasn't going to reveal the results of the DNA tests to us.

When Leonard brought that up, Justin said, "I don't have to tell you that kind of thing."

"Liar, liar, pants on fire," Leonard said. "You told us you would."

"You're fucking up our beautiful friendship," I said.

"Damn straight," Leonard said.

"I lied," Justin said. "My pants are on fire."

"That's not very nice," I said.

"I don't care," Justin said.

Justin lowered his chair. The light changed positions in his hair. He tapped a pencil with a chewed eraser on the table for a long while. No one spoke. It was like living in a birdhouse with a woodpecker.

Justin got up and went out. We sat there waiting. I looked at the camera high in one corner of the room and waved at it.

The predicted heat death of the universe was nigh when Justin came back. He had a laptop with him. He put it on the table and tapped the keys, turned it so we could see it. It was an image of a fingerprint.

"You needed to leave the room and get a laptop just to show us this?" Leonard said.

"This fellow I know as Johnny Joe, he's a clever one. Never leaves anything that can fix him up. But in going through the debris, the bodies at the old hospital, we found a partial fingerprint on a gas can. That was a moment of excitement. We ran it. It went with a fellow who had spent some time in juvie and then prison. Lawrence Kuttner.

"I was so happy to have a print of anyone that had been in that god-awful abandoned hospital, I almost went out and bought some party balloons, a stripper, and a dog act. Thing is, the guy belongs to the print has been dead about five years. Found in the woods with his hands and pecker cut off. No one knows who killed him, and back then no one was surprised. At the prison I figure if they'd had a high-school annual, Lawrence would have been voted Most Likely to End Up in the Woods with His Hands and His Pecker Cut Off.

"This sick fuck, Johnny Joe, puts Kuttner's hand on the can on purpose, knowing we'd find the print it made. Must have had Kuttner's hands, maybe the pecker, bagged and frozen somewhere, waiting for just that kind of moment."

"Be happy he didn't leave a pecker print," Leonard said. "That won't be on file."

"Man, that's thinking ahead a long time for a practical joke," I said.

"He most likely had a falling-out with the guy and killed him or had him killed," Justin said. "Took his hands and tallywhacker as some kind of revenge. It was concluded that most likely Kuttner had been alive when he lost his paws and his honey dipper. Johnny Joe knew finding that fingerprint would excite us and that tracing it would deflate us."

"You're telling us stuff again," Leonard said. "You don't really think we killed the Hansons, do you?"

"No. And I been thinking it over. Maybe I still need you two and Brett as aides. Let me walk you out to your truck."

It was no longer raining, but the sky had the texture of a mohair suit. We stood by Pookie's truck, which was parked by Justin's car. Justin opened the car's trunk. I took out the tackle box and set it in the back of the truck.

Justin said, "There's something that I'm going to tell you that's just between us. This is me spreading some trust around. Hanson had a mole in the department."

"He told us," I said.

"I know who it is," he said. "Olivia."

"Olivia who?" I said.

"She's the cop who drove your truck."

"Your right-hand woman?" I said.

"Olivia slipped through to Hanson only what I wanted to get out. Me and her even discussed it. I knew in turn it would get to you. My plan was to let more and more slip through. Again, there's things you can do with the information that we can't. But some things are getting out I don't want to get out. I don't think that's Olivia."

"Another mole?" Leonard said.

"Been thinking how things have gone with me reopening this old case and tying it to newer ones. I get a lead, I follow it, there's a knot at the end. Always a step ahead of us. But you fellows being able to get away with more than we can has a downside for you."

"You coming here, his mole will know," Leonard said. "Johnny Joe will know we didn't drown. You didn't think of that?"

"I didn't until just now," he said. "I had this idea Johnny Joe had a mole in the joint, but it wasn't solid. All of a sudden, it seems solid. You being here, word gets around quick."

"You're letting us be bait," Leonard said. "Them knowing, that plays their hand, and we have to play ours."

"I never said that," Justin said.

"No, you didn't," Leonard said. "But I bet you thought it."

Hanson had warned us that Justin was a crafty son of a bitch. We got killed, that was some sad shit in the neighborhood. We killed Johnny Joe and his gang, that was some happy shit for Justin. He really had a hard-on for Johnny Joe. His personal white whale. That was all right with me, as I wanted Kung Fu Bobby for killing Hanson. I wanted that entire group to pay.

"My advice," Justin said, "is keep your eyes open and your powder dry."

49

We stopped at my place and put the tackle box in the garage.

Leonard said, "I'm going home, Hap. Going to get some sleep. Then I might see if Pookie wants some sweet, sweet loving."

"Who you hiring for that?"

"Ha. Listen, brother, I know guns aren't your preferred thing, but you might want to keep one next to you. Kung Fu comes back, he won't be there to warn you this time."

"When Brett gets home, I'll tell her what's happened. For now, I'm going to let her enjoy herself. After she returns, we may be leaving this place for a while. Most certainly will be."

"Here is harder to defend than my place," Leonard said. "It's like a little Alamo there. They got two ways they can come in. Both are murder holes, way we're set up."

"No matter where you are, someone can get to you," I said. "Trick is them not knowing where you are."

"Right about that," Leonard said. "Tell you how serious all this business is to me. After we get reasonably rested, I say we call Jim Bob. And Vanilla."

"You know Brett doesn't like her."

"I ain't all that fond of Jim Bob neither, but a job like this, I can learn to like him better. He's a deadly motherfucker. As for Vanilla, she gets in motion, she'd make a lion shit its pants. We need people like that, if just for backup until this all passes or it comes down. Brett will understand that. They don't need to do no nails together, braid each other's hair. Brett needs to like Vanilla just enough."

50

I went upstairs, grabbed a pillow, a blanket, the gun from the nightstand, a book I wanted to read, and a flashlight. I placed the blanket and pillow by the door, dropped the pistol in my coat pocket. I opened the door to the bedroom closet, pulled down a short length of attic stairs, and climbed up there.

I had things neatly laid out on shelves and in dresser drawers. Wasn't a lot of room, but the ceiling was high enough, I could move about easily without banging my head.

Christmas lights and decorations, odds and ends were strewn about. Among the odds and ends was a dark leather sheath on a shelf. I unzipped it and pulled out a Remington twelve-gauge pump. The inside of the sheath and the gun smelled heavily of gun oil.

I looked the shotgun over. There were some shells in a pocket on the outside of the bag. Most of them were slugs. I pumped the shotgun to make sure it was still in working order, not that I expected otherwise. It was unloaded, and the action was smooth. I put the Remington back in the sheath.

In a drawer, I had a Smith and Wesson pistol in a quick-draw holster. I gathered up the boxes of ammunition that went with it and some extra shotgun shells, and after examining the pistol, I stuck it and the ammo inside the sheath with the shotgun and zipped it up.

In a cardboard box, I had some postcards from Vanilla. We had an arrangement where she would have the cards sent from a variety of places, European and domestic. I would look at the cards in the order of the dates written on them. There was a small number written on the bottom of each card. When there were enough cards, I put those numbers together, and it was a phone number. I would call and leave a message. I had no idea where Vanilla was in the world, but I knew she would get the message and, if possible, would show up.

She didn't send cards regularly, only if the number changed. Sometimes it did. Postcards were beginning to be obsolete and they were slow to arrive.

She didn't like communication by internet, as she said there were certain people who closely monitored her and might find a way to access her computer. I suppose that was true, but I couldn't say for sure. Anyway, she told me a new method would have to be arranged for the future, but at this point, as far as I knew, the number was workable.

Once upon a time Vanilla had been a very bad woman with a will to be a better one. Certain events and revelations flipped her from the dark side to the gray side. There is not a bright side in our line of work, but at least she was no longer a gun that could be hired for any job, as was the case with Kung Fu Bobby.

Vanilla liked her new status. You might even say, at least to some degree, her old status wasn't her fault. She had been trained from childhood to be an assassin. She was damn good at her job, but her alignment had wobbled, then changed.

I put the cards in my coat pocket and climbed out of the attic with the shotgun sheath. I closed the closet stairs, grabbed my pillow and blanket, and, carrying them and the sheath, went downstairs.

There's a wide hall closet downstairs, just off the living room. It is designed to hold a lot of clothes, shoes, and so on. It has a sliding wall at the back behind a rack of jackets and shirts. It slides easy and reveals a compartment. There isn't a lot of room in there, just enough to sleep. The inner closet location has a small safe in the wall, and that's the purpose of the secret door. The compartment is also a good place to hide. I had installed a sliding lock so that when I was inside, no one could open the door by accident.

I stretched out with the pillow under my head, then put the phone on vibrate, stuck it under the pillow. I pulled the blanket over me, slid the door closed, threw the lock.

Adrenaline was still pumping through me. It overrode my exhaustion for a while. I saw over and over Kung Fu Bobby standing on the deck of that boat pointing his pistol at Hanson, and Hanson knowing what was about to happen and not losing his game face until a bullet tore through his head and tossed pieces of it into the lake.

I thought of that water, that long, horrible swim with the tackle box between me and Leonard. I thought how easily I could have let go of the box and ended it all. But that wasn't in me, was it? Was it?

Well, I hadn't let go, had I?

I wondered what Leonard thought during those moments. I had an idea. And letting go of that box would have never come to his mind.

I tried to read by flashlight, but my mind wasn't right for that. Even adrenaline and dark memories weren't enough to defeat absolute exhaustion. Sleep eventually kicked in, and I slept deeply.

51

I awoke to the sound of a door gently closing. The back door, the one that led out to the garage — I could tell that even in my cubby in the closet. I had to take a moment to truly become awake; had to push myself awake. My whole body hurt like hell from the night before. I could hardly move. But I needed to.

I slowly slipped the latch on the sliding door and, taking hold of the Smith and Wesson, slid the door back a crack and looked at the shadowy forms of hanging coats.

The light in the closet clicked on.

I carefully pushed back the clothes and pointed the revolver at a shape in the light.

It was Brett, hanging up her raincoat.

52

I sure appreciate not being shot," Brett said.

"Sorry."

"You could have killed me, jackass."

"But I didn't. And I think from that angle, I might have missed."

"You rarely miss."

We had moved to the kitchen by this point, and I had told her what happened to me and Leonard, Hanson and Rachel.

"I'm beginning to think we ought to find another line of work," I said.

"You always think that, but that's all you do, think about it. You don't want another line of work, not really. And neither do I."

"I'm less certain these days."

Brett used the coffee machine to fix us another cup.

"I know what you want to do," Brett said. "But should we do it?"

"You said 'we.'"

"Because I want to kill them too," she said. "I want to kill them and grind up their bones. I really do. But should we? We been lucky a lot, and part of that luck was Hanson, and now we don't have him. We have Justin."

"Might not be as bad a guy as we thought," I said. "On the other hand, he might be worse."

"He's manipulated us. It might have got Hanson killed."

"I think Hanson taking the information from Olivia got him killed. Johnny Joe and his crew knew he had it, and even before they knew we had it, they'd made up their minds to take him out. It wasn't that great a piece of information, but next time it could be. Cops they would have a chance of dealing with. But we don't follow rules. We're their biggest threat. Kung Fu Bobby had to have told them what happened with the other crew he was involved with. Right before I foolishly chose to miss a shot at him."

"A bad choice," Brett said.

"I know. But there's no doubt in my mind we need to leave here. Probably already should have. And I know you're no fan of Vanilla, hon, but I think we should contact her. Jim Bob too."

"I can tolerate Jim Bob, but Vanilla seems to be shaking her tail at you."

"She might be."

"We know she is."

"I'm way too old for her."

"She has daddy issues, no doubt," Brett said. "I know her life was horrible and all that, and she's sort of reformed. Sort of. But in the end, I don't give a shit."

"Just because she flirts doesn't mean she will get me."

"I don't like the idea she thinks she might. Keep in mind, you went off with her, it would be adios and kiss my ass. But her doing that business in front of me, it irks me."

"I'm not sure she's doing any business," I said.

"You may not know it on the surface, but someplace just about the height of your testicles, there's awareness."

"But the testicles are not talking to me," I said.

"They whisper. Again, it's just the idea of it that irks me. You wanted her, I'd let you have her. But don't disrespect my highly attractive older self like that. That's my law."

"I'm not."

"I'm talking about her."

"We need her," I said.

"Shit. I know that. Call her. And Jim Bob."

"Jim Bob flirts with you, you know, and I don't worry about it," I said.

"You're you, and I'm me, and you're right, he does. And I admit I kind of like it. Now you admit you kind of like it when Vanilla does."

"Okay."

"I knew it. Your testicles are talking to you."

"Not loud enough for me to really understand. It's like a foreign language. Besides, I'm sure she's over that flirty nonsense by now. It's just a crush of some sort for some reason I can't figure."

"Because she can't have you," Brett said.

"That's right," I said. "She can't."

Brett smiled at me and put toast in the toaster.

53

When Jim Bob answered the phone, he said, "What the hell do you want this time?"

"A favor," I said.

"You always want a favor."

"This one's kind of special."

"For you, maybe."

"Hanson and his wife were murdered, and there's some terrible business going on that is going to require more than me and Leonard and Brett. The cops got their hands tied more than we do."

"Damn. Hanson and his wife?"

"Afraid so."

"You're not dragging Chance into this, are you? Her doing the private-eye thing and all. From what I've seen, she's got her hands full."

"No, I'm not. I haven't even told her yet what happened to Hanson."

"I been helping her a little," he said.

"She said as much."

"She's smarter than you, prettier, and has a lot of potential to be good at what she does. But she doesn't need something like this. Not yet, anyway."

"Never, far as I'm concerned."

"We'll need a point of operation."

"Remember where we met up that time Vanilla was with us? And Booger?"

"Yep. Good grief, you aren't going to yank Booger out from under his damp rock, are you?"

"At this point, no. We're not in need of a psychopath. Just stone killers."

"Yeah, Booger's too crazy. He's a loose cannon and he's ready to shoot if a sparrow farts."

"I did think I might ask Veil if he would help."

"He's a creepy son of a bitch."

"He's silent and efficient and is always down to business, but I doubt I can turn him up," I said. "We're not in contact much anymore, and he doesn't owe me shit."

"Like I do? Like Vanilla does?"

"You owe me your friendship," I said.

"Oh, man, really? You're going for that old chestnut?"

"All I got."

There was silence on the line for a long time. It was broken when Jim Bob said, "You get set, you call me. I'll be there."

When that was done, I called Vanilla. There was no message, just a beep. I left my message. I made it simple.

"This is Hap, Vanilla. We have a problem. Would be glad for you to help us with it. The pay is our best wishes."

That was done. Now I could only wait.

I thought about how to contact Veil, but I didn't have anything solid, bad as I wanted him. I left messages in places where people might get hold of him for me and might not. One of the best places was a pool hall in New York City.

I called there. He wasn't around. No one had seen him in years, and no one knew how to contact him.

I wasn't sure that was true. But the only thing I could do was leave a message for him saying I might have something big he would be interested in and move on.

He was one of those who liked to set injustices right, but he was picky. He wasn't worried much about my personal problems unless they were problems that overlapped with his interests—mainly child protection, but not exclusively.

There's a house out in the country where a bunch of us stayed some years ago. It's a kind of safehouse. It is down a long asphalt road that bleeds off Highway 7. It was once a safe house the cops sometimes used, but some years back, Marvin bought the house and had it redone, had the old log barn across the way that was falling apart replaced with a large red one that could hold a good-size aircraft and at least a dozen paper airplanes if they were placed close together. He kept the old farm equipment that was there out of some kind of sentimentality for the past.

Hanson had plans to flip the place for more retirement money, something to buy a lot of worms with, but he hadn't had the time to do so. Now he was out of time. There would be no flipping by him and no bait shop and no worms.

Brett and I drove out there in the Prius. Leonard came behind us in Pookie's pickup. It was an interesting place that had once been way out in the country. There was plenty of pasture and woods around it, forty acres or so, but the town had muscled its way out there to such an extent that it was near town. The asphalt road that ran to the house was narrow, and you had to be looking for it to know it was there. It was almost concealed on both ends by trees.

I had a key, thanks to Hanson, and thinking about him, remembering Kung Fu Bobby shooting him in the head, made me grit my teeth.

You'll get yours, motherfucker.

The house had new shingles and white paint. The interior was much better than before. It had some different, if not new, furniture. The kitchen had been worked over, and it served as the dining room as well, had a round table with six cheap wooden chairs circling it.

SUGAR ON THE BONES

The bathroom had new tile and a new commode and sink. There was a bigger shower, but not so big you could use it to wash your pet elephant.

There was a hallway off the living room. It led shotgun-style to the back door. On one side of the hall was a closet and the bathroom. On the other side, next to each other, there were two bedrooms with beds dressed in cheap sheets and thin blankets. The pillows were almost flat. You could damn near have slipped them under the door.

Brett and I claimed the bedroom across from the bathroom right away. That bedroom had its own bathroom in it.

Leonard thought Vanilla should have the other bedroom, and he would sleep on the couch. I think what he was really thinking was he would be in a position to keep reasonable tabs on the front and back door.

"For all I care," Leonard said, "Jim Bob can sleep in the tub."

"There is no tub in either bathroom, just a shower," I said.

"I know."

It was stuffy inside, and from having been locked up tight, it was hot, though the day was cool. I turned on the central air and set it at sixty-nine degrees with no thought of it being a sexual reference. No thought at all.

The garage had been worked on as well. It had been enlarged and it connected to the house with a short, narrow screened-in porch. There was a screen door about halfway down it. It led out to the backyard, which was full of long but dead brown grass.

Back there was a redwood picnic table glazed in what I assumed was some kind of waterproof coating. When the light shifted you could see the coating more clearly.

The light wasn't shifting a whole lot that day. We had a break in the rain, but according to the weather report, it was coming back just after sunset. Right now, all we had were threatening clouds and cool air.

"Okay, we got neat Fortress of Solitude digs," Leonard said. "What's next?"

"We may have to create what's next."

"I got an idea," Leonard said, "but I want to think on it a bit."

We went back to the car and the truck, took out our luggage, groceries, and laptop. There was internet, but I was becoming so paranoid about Johnny Joe and Purple Eyes, I could imagine them having a vast network of spies tapping into our connection.

I doubted that was true, but I was considering everything.

The place had a coffee machine that used pods, and after letting the water run and clear the pipes of red rust, we filled the coffee machine's plastic container with it, made us each a cup of coffee. We had some sandwich goods, a few odds and ends. A couple of those items belonged in the refrigerator, which was off. I turned it on and we put the items in it, waited for it to cool down.

I felt a little safer now, and I felt a little goofier as well; treating this thug like he was the mastermind behind a vast criminal network felt foolish.

Only I really did believe Johnny Joe had a mass of operators, because he had a mass of things going on. The idea of being the man in control, if he was the one in control, would be highly appealing to a person like him. He probably jacked off to Lex Luthor in the DC comics, dressed himself as the Joker come nighttime.

I didn't think they could find us here, but I didn't take our safety for granted.

Me and Leonard went out to the vehicles and brought in the tackle box Hanson had given us and the guns. We had quite a few of those, mostly courtesy of Leonard. They were old-style guns. Shotguns and revolvers, couple of automatic pistols, a .22 rifle, the packed shotgun sheath I had pulled from my attic.

We put a loaded shotgun in the hall closet. The one I'd brought in the sheath went under mine and Brett's bed. Leonard placed a revolver on the floor next to the couch, just under the skirting where it touched the floor. He duct-taped a small flat automatic under the kitchen table, dead center. It wasn't a far reach. It wasn't a big table.

On me I had the Smith and Wesson in its holster. It was clipped to my belt, under my coat. I had one of the little .22 automatics in my coat pocket. The .22 rifle was propped in a corner in mine and Brett's bedroom.

Brett had a small Colt automatic strapped to her waistband, under her coat. In her large purse she had a small .22 pistol along with pepper spray, a blackjack, and a stun gun—one shot from that would make you cross your legs and shit your pants.

She also had her wallet in there, a compact, some earrings, perfume, and makeup. She had a motto: "Even if you are going out to kill someone, always carry your girlie items; you never know when you might want to dress to impress."

We put the tackle box in the corner of the living room next to the window that looked out on the front yard and the blacktop that ended pretty much right in front of the house. We had the box as a kind of totem. We also had a couple of .25-caliber pistols in there. I wasn't sure where Leonard had gotten all those guns. Wasn't sure I wanted to know.

After the warm stuffiness was gone, I kicked the air up to seventy-four degrees.

We sat in the living room. Brett said to Leonard, "So, you explained all this to Pookie?"

"Did," Leonard said, "and told him to keep out of it. He's got a grown-up job and grown-up responsibilities, and I'd rather him not get involved. He'd be good to have, but I don't think he should be part of this, being a cop."

"He's been part of it before," I said.

"He may be again, but trying not to go there."

"Wise thoughts," I said. "You were formulating an idea. Did it ever show up fully loaded?"

"It's not much of an idea, really," Leonard said. "But, brother mine, I've always liked simple answers. What I got in mind may be too simple. But we know this: If we'd stayed home, they'd have come for us. You and Brett first, I think. Easier to get to you where you live. Another reason I wanted to get out of my place was to make Pookie safer. I got him living in a Motel Six out on the loop. I don't think they care about him at this point. I don't think they care about the police all that much. What they care about is a bunch of freelancers that aren't beholden to the law and can do what they want to do. They think we are three, but what they don't know, where we'll have them by the short hairs, is we'll have help from

Jim Bob. Maybe Vanilla and Veil. Jim Bob for sure. Having him on our side is like having three men on our side. Having Vanilla is like three women, two men, and an angry dog."

"Okay," Brett said. "But what's the idea you have that might draw them out?"

"We give them some bait. Some rat cheese for the trap. Goes well, trap bar comes down on their heads, not ours. What we do, Hap, is you lead them into your house. They'll think they got you wrapped up like a Christmas present. But we'll be prepared and waiting. And then we kill them."

54

A word like "kill" does not rest lightly on me. I carry it around like a boulder. I try and push the boulder away, but it rolls back.

Even those that deserve killing — that's damn final.

Final can be good. Sometimes it makes sense, dealing with the kind of people we deal with.

But unlike Brett and Leonard, I can't just sweep it into a back closet of my mind and close the door.

It's murder. It's unlawful. It's vigilante.

And I didn't like it and didn't want to do it.

But I knew I would.

I am now far away from my long-ago days of peace and love. And the thing is, you can't uncross that line. You can't go back to Go and collect two hundred dollars and make it so there were never any murders.

Once it's done, it's done. And once it's done the first time, it's easier to do the second.

55

Where Brett and I live, there is a low attic in our garage and it is filled with dust, rat turds, and spiderwebs full of captured insects.

At the front of the attic, facing the street, there is a louvered vent about two foot wide and two foot tall. The louvers are well spaced. I suppose it is there for ventilation. Not a job it properly fulfills.

Old painted signs make up the interior walls. They advertise oil and Coca-Cola. It makes for something to look at in the poor light from the louvered vent. Probably those old signs are worth something now.

I had forgotten the vent was there, but Leonard, who once helped me store some things up there, hadn't.

The attic was part of his plan.

I made my camp near the vent. I pushed down on the louvers until they moved and stirred a little cloud of dust that made me snort, then cough.

I lay on my stomach with pillows propped under my chest and a .22 rifle next to me. It was loaded and I had a box of shells for it. Also, for insurance, I had my pistol and my shotgun with me. I was all set to be a sniper.

Of course, they pretty much had to come from one direction. There were other elements to the plan, however.

I had a few snacks and an old army canteen full of water. I was dressed in black, and even with it cold outside and no heat up there, it was warm enough I found it necessary to remove my jacket.

I studied my position. Through the louvers, I could see the street and the driveway that led into the garage. I could see the edge of our front yard. It really wasn't that good a position, but the end of the rifle would fit through the louvers, could be pointed down and moved from left to right.

What we had done before I ended up in the attic was wait for Jim Bob to arrive. He wasn't driving his red Cadillac with the RED BITCH license plate. Jim Bob drove the Cadillac when he didn't care if he was noticed. He didn't want to be noticed this time. He was instead driving a sedan ten years old. It was a less-than-delightful gray color. You could park that car in an empty parking lot, and most people would walk by it and not remember it.

Jim Bob was wearing a straw cowboy hat and red cowboy boots with the Texas flag painted on the toes. He was carrying his goods, which included a sawed-off double-barreled shotgun, a pistol on his hip. If he was true to form, there was probably a derringer holstered at the top of one boot, a knife in the other.

Once Jim Bob had settled in and told us a couple of fart jokes and one dick joke, he had a cup of coffee while Leonard laid out his plan. Such as it was.

What we knew was they would come for us if we didn't come for them.

So, come a pearl-gray afternoon punctuated by distant thunder and an occasional rip of lightning, we went to my and Brett's house.

How I got there was I laid in the floorboard of Jim Bob's ugly gray car under a dark blanket. It was tight and uncomfortable and too warm. Leonard drove. Jim Bob hid in the trunk.

Brett stayed at the safe house—I hoped that was a correct description— near her phone and handgun.

I think Johnny Joe's bunch were hip to a lot of things, but that safe house had been chosen out of the blue, and even Justin didn't know about it.

We drove up to our garage, and Leonard used our garage device to open it. Once inside, he used the device to drop the sliding door back in place. I got out from under the blanket. By then Leonard had the trunk open, and Jim Bob was out.

"Damn," Jim Bob said. "Felt like a baby squirrel in a snake's belly."

We had our goods back there, and we got those out.

I went up in the attic. Jim Bob would stay in the garage until nightfall, then he would slide out the back door, slip into our house, and go to the hiding spot in the downstairs walk-in hall closet.

Leonard entered the house through the side door, in plain sight. He was to mess around in there for about thirty minutes to make it look like he had stopped by to pick up something for his friends. Innocent business. He was to bring out a paper bag stuffed with provisions from our cabinets.

I could hear Leonard letting the side door close heavy. He was to lock it up and reenter the garage with his bag. When he drove away, he was to watch carefully to determine if he was being followed. He'd ride around a bit until he was certain he was without a tail, or he would lose it. Eventually, he would find somewhere close by to park and eat his sack lunch and wait for us to call him as soon as we knew the bad guys were moving on the house.

Surprise, motherfuckers, we're waiting on you.

I heard the sliding door rise and the gray bomb back out. I heard the door close, and then I saw through the louvers the car backing into the street, straightening out. Leonard drove away.

If they showed up to kill us, we would be prepared, waiting. If they thought to arrive first and surprise us, well, Leonard and Jim Bob had already cleared the house. That was a brave thing to do. They could have been waiting on anyone to come through that door, and whoever it was would have died of lead poisoning or at the hands of Kung Fu Bobby, maybe slapped to death.

And when they came, because we felt certain they would, if we weren't there, it seemed logical they would take positions in our house and wait for us to arrive and then kill us. If Leonard wasn't with us, they would hit him somewhere else. But the house seemed like a good spot for them to wait because they might not have thought we felt threatened there. We did.

These were the scenarios we considered. We were prepared for their sneaky-ass ways.

It seemed like two days before night fell. From my position, I could see the same spots as before, and they were lit up now by the streetlight. Unless our foes were invisible, they'd hit those spots, I'd see them. I'd text Jim Bob and Leonard, let them know. Brett would get the text as well and would call the cops.

Leonard would come, park down the street, enter through the back on foot.

Next thing those assholes would know, they'd have a bunch of us and a bunch of cops up their asses. If we were lucky, there would be arrests and no killing. Leonard had worked that part in for me.

If there was killing, I was hopeful it would be the bad guys and not us the cops shot.

I thought more about what we planned, about how the bad guys might come. They could come over the back fence to the back door. That was all right; Jim Bob, hiding in the closet, would hear them in the hall. He could slip out and pick some of them off.

They came in the front door, he'd hear them there too. They couldn't come from the front and get to the side door, one that led to the short walk from house to garage, without me seeing them. A quick text report from me and he'd be prepared. I would bring up the rear then or, from the louver opening, sniper one or two down. Leonard and the cops would not be far behind.

Of course, they could come across the rear yard, down the path between house and garage, and go in our side door, and I wouldn't be able to see them. Still, Jim Bob could hear them. If they came from all directions at once, which seemed like a plan they would figure, things might be considerably more tense.

That was a big hole in Leonard's plan, and soon there might be holes in us.

Damn, Hap, I told myself. No more inner dialogue. Keep your mind on your part of the plan. You're wandering all over the place.

I lifted the .22 a few times to see how much room I had. It wasn't bad. I could prop the rifle through the wide louvers and shoot. If I saw them and I shot, they were dead. That's how certain I was of my shooting.

Don't worry, man. You're a certified badass. You got the scars, physical and emotional, to prove it. Anyone else had the experiences you've had, they'd be in some kind of facility with a nurse giving them evening pills.

Me, I was all right.

Mostly.

I sent Brett a text.

VANILLA?

She wrote back: NOT YET.

LOVE YOU.

YOU TOO. PAY ATTENTION.

I put the phone down and thought I saw something move at the edge of the street, near the great oak in our yard that grew close to the curb. I could only partially see the trunk of the oak from there. In the glow of the street-light, the tree appeared to be made of shimmering plastic.

And then what I had seen moving came into view.

A cat walked out from behind the tree and went on down the street. A big, pretty black cat that didn't give a damn about humans and their jive.

I watched it do that amazing cat walk on out of view.

A maroon '64 Impala eased by. The windows were dark. I watched it move away, leaving a faint trace of red taillights shimmering on the wet street, and then it was gone.

I heard a bit of movement below. The side door of the garage opening; Jim Bob slipping inside the house. The plan was coming together.

I ate one of my snacks. Peanut butter crackers. I drank some water. I needed it after the crackers. I should have brought less salty treats.

Then I thought I heard something move among the Christmas decorations.

Shit. Rats.

Okay. "Don't bother them and they won't bother you"—that was my motto for the night. Hap and rats coexisting. If Al Polson could live with mice, I could live with a few rats for a night.

Why was my dick hard? Did I want to fuck a rat? I could safely rule that out. Damn, I needed to pee. I eased over to one corner of the garage on hands and knees, sat myself up enough to unzip my pants, and sent a spray of urine into the corner.

Going to smell less than good in here soon.

Hell, I hoped I didn't end up needing to take a dump.

I pulled up my zipper, closed the barn so the mule couldn't get out, palmed and kneed my way back into position.

I picked up the rifle. My hands were sweaty.

I heard the noise in the decorations again.

How many rats were there? And how big were they?

And then I had a feeling of cold fear wash over my body like the devil's baptism.

We weren't smart. We weren't even partially smart.

I let go of the rifle, grabbed the handgun, rolled over on my back, and lifted the pistol.

There was a face. It was a rat, all right. A big one. The light from outside revealed enough of that face for me to know it was Kung Fu Bobby.

He took the gun away from me like I was a kid with a peppermint stick. It was so fast I wasn't sure how he did it.

Oh, yeah, Hap, you're a certified badass. You didn't even know he had beat you up here and was hiding behind a plastic snowman, a couple of reindeer.

Yeah. Badass. That's you.

A hypodermic needle went into my neck.

191

56

I felt comfortable, but my mouth was as thick and bloody-tasting as a used tampon. It was bright, and I had a hard time opening my eyes because of it. I slit them slightly and could see shadows moving across the bright light. I could hear a low rumble of voices, like a radio with bad reception.

Slowly a dark face in front of me lightened and features were added to it. It was Kung Fu Bobby.

"I warned you," he said. "Got offered more money. I'm back on the clock."

I tried to say something, but all I could do was lick my lips with my thick tongue.

"You had a plan," he said. "So did we. When night came, I was going to sneak in the house and drug or kill anyone there so their bodies could be harvested right away. We'd have done it in your living room. Then you showed up in the garage. Can't believe you survived that boat business. You guys must be part catfish."

I wanted to say something, mostly curse words, but my mouth wasn't working right. I was starting to be able to move my body a little more. Whatever drug he had stuck in my neck was wearing off.

"Just so you go out knowing you weren't so smart," he said, and he patted me on the chest, "I knew the other one was in the house, whoever he is, but it was just too delicious having you in my grasp. Carried your fat ass down the attic stairs, all the way across the back lot, down the street to my car. A guy came out on his porch, saw me carrying you. I waved. He waved back. People these days."

"Fug ew," I said.

"Doctor?"

Another face hovered in view. It belonged to a man with silver hair and good cheekbones. He looked at me, said, "Let's get this over with."

The man began to adjust the light shining on me. It was on some kind of high gooseneck and it was so, so bright. Behind it was the less bright ceiling light. I could tell all the blinds were drawn.

Kung Fu Bobby said, "I warned you. You tossed that warning away, Collins. The doctor is going to give you another injection, then you'll sleep and won't wake up. It'll be painless. You can take some consolation in the fact that your pirated organs will be going to good homes, people who pay a lot of money for them. I'm what you could call a shareholder in this business now. That was part of my deal. I'll be living off your internal organs, eyes, and skin for quite a while. The doctor, he'll do all right too. So will the bosses. Everyone gets a share of your hide and innards. Never knew I could be chatty, did you?"

In fact, I didn't. A stocky woman in scrubs came into view. She had short, brown, curly hair, a face as bland as a metal desk. "We're ready," she said.

Kung Fu Bobby leaned close to my ear. "Wish you had dropped this business, Collins. I like your spunk. Your wife and friends are destined for the same fate, though cutting up that wife of yours — what a waste."

The nurse went away and came back with a needle. I could move a little now, but I wasn't fooling myself into thinking that I'd be able to do much. A crippled turtle could outmaneuver me. I might be able to sit up with time and some help. I had that going for me.

The nurse leaned toward me with the needle in hand. The doctor leaned in close to her.

I almost cried a tear, but I didn't want them to see that.

Goodbye, I said to myself. Goodbye, sweet Brett, brother Leonard, and daughter Chance.

Goodbye.

57

The gooseneck lamp exploded, and the nurse's hand exploded with it. She went to the floor so fast it was as if she had dropped through a trapdoor.

The doctor turned and his head jumped apart. He tumbled over me and the back of the couch and hit the floor like a sack of bricks.

I could feel broken glass and blood sticking to me. Some of that blood was rolling down my face.

I managed to sit up without the assistance of a crane and grappling hooks.

I was on the couch in our office. I could see over the back of the couch. The doctor lay there, minus a head. The nurse, on the other side, though still alive, was whimpering and bleeding out fast from the stump of her wrist. She was on her knees. She started to moan, then fell over, done for.

Vanilla Ride tossed aside a sawed-off double-barreled shotgun and kicked mucho doodie-pie out of Kung Fu Bobby. It was a side kick for the record books. It was fast as a hummingbird and hit him in the gullet like a runaway train. He went skidding back into the table where we kept our coffee maker. It was knocked spinning to the floor and exploded plastic in all directions.

I'll give him this: Kung Fu Bobby got up. I wouldn't have been able to. I wouldn't have wanted to.

He didn't reach for a gun. He took position, hands up, body turned slightly. He came at Vanilla with a front kick, just something to cover distance, and then he threw a series of punches, jabs, crosses, and hooks. He was so goddamn fast, it looked like those scenes with the Tasmanian Devil in Warner Brothers cartoons.

Vanilla was faster. She took one of the punches, but it mostly slid off her shoulder. She ducked under his arms and hit him in the balls with an upswung ridge hand. There was a noise like air being let out of a tire.

Vanilla came up under his chin with an uppercut that might as well have been shot from an artillery weapon. Kung Fu Bobby stumbled back, his feet slipping in the nurse's blood. He nearly fell over a red ice chest on the floor. The chest that had been destined to be my new home had Vanilla not come through the door.

There was a look on Kung Fu Bobby's face that I doubt showed up there much: Surprise. Maybe even fear.

I was surprised too. No one handled Kung Fu Bobby like that. No one. Unless your name was Vanilla Ride.

He recovered quickly. He dropped and spun to sweep Vanilla's legs, causing the blood on the floor to fan around him. Mostly a show-off move, but Kung Fu Bobby could pull it off. On someone else, that is.

But not Vanilla.

Graceful as a cat, Vanilla coiled her legs together, leaped over his sweeping leg, and came down on his knee with both feet. The knee cracked. Boy howdy, did it. It was one of those sounds that make you clench your teeth and tuck your asshole under a kidney. I felt like I was going to throw up.

Kung Fu Bobby screamed. He lay on the floor on his side, broken. Weirdly, Vanilla squatted and duckwalked to him and when she was close to his ear, she said, "Hurts, don't it?" She sounded as melodious as a songbird.

Kung Fu Bobby shook his head, still defiant.

Lying there, not able to get up, he tried to draw his gun from under his coat. By this point he was weak and slow, and when he pulled it, it was about as much a threat to her as a pudding pop. She took it away from him with her left hand and hit him in the throat with her right, using a Y-hand.

Kung Fu Bobby clawed at his throat as if he could pull that strike out of it. Vanilla hit him on the side of the neck, just under the jaw, with the butt of the gun. He went unconscious.

Vanilla rose to her feet and stuck Kung Fu Bobby's pistol in her waistband. She stood there in all her magnificent beauty, her long blond hair hanging down her back, her eyes sparkling in the overhead light. She was wearing black yoga pants, a torn black sweatshirt, and hard leather shoes. She looked as if she were about to attend a spin class. She smiled a multi-watt smile, said, "Hi, Hap. How's it hanging, honey?"

Right then, I couldn't have told her if it was hanging at all. I couldn't feel my body, for the most part. I could move, but it felt as if someone else was doing the moving, and I couldn't move much.

Vanilla came to stand over me. She bent down and kissed me on the forehead. Her breath was sweet.

"We're going to make them pay for what they tried to do to you," she said.

She pulled a switchblade from somewhere, flicked it open, and the overhead light danced on the blade.

"Right now, I'm going to cut this guy's throat, just to make sure."

I wanted to say thank you. I wanted to explain it wasn't just about me. I wanted to tell her about Hanson and Rachel, how me and Leonard had been left for dead in Caddo Lake. I wanted to explain I didn't normally like killing, but with these cocksuckers I was glad to make an exception. I was a happy-as-shit hypocrite. Cut on, sweet lady, cut on.

My mouth moved, but I couldn't form clear words.

I fell back on the couch, not able to hold myself up anymore. I heard Kung Fu Bobby gurgling blood.

I felt sleepy again. Real sleepy.

I closed my eyes against the bright lights.

58

When I woke up, I was in the safe house. I had been cleaned up and dressed in sweatpants and a sweatshirt. My feet were bare. I was lying on the bed with my head on pillows.

Brett was sitting on the edge of the bed, looking at me.

"The baby boy awakes," she said, and smiled my favorite smile in the world.

I found I could talk, but my mouth still tasted like a used sanitary napkin. I smacked my lips, said, "Water."

Brett took a glass off the night table. It had a metal straw in it.

I sat up as best I could and sucked at the straw. The water tasted good. I couldn't understand in that moment why I or anyone would drink anything else ever.

"How long have I been out?"

"Since last night through this morning. It's late morning." Brett looked at her watch. "Ten o'clock. Those were some major drugs they gave you. You came in and out, said a Valkyrie rescued you."

"Vanilla. I thought I dreamed it."

"Nope. She's in the living room beguiling Jim Bob. She wanted to help me dress you in your undershorts and sweatshirt, but I declined the offer. I added sweatpants to your ensemble, by the way."

I slowly sat up some more. Brett put the water glass on the table and rearranged the pillows behind me.

"How did she know where I was?"

"She's a smart one," Brett said. "Which, considering her looks, isn't fair to the rest of us. Smart and beautiful. Apparently, she's also deadly. But how exactly did she know? Have to ask her. I been in here taking care of your sorry ass."

"She took out Kung Fu Bobby like he was a one-legged bum off the street. Me and Leonard together couldn't take him down, but she handled him like a plush toy, seemed to be thinking about getting it over with so she could order pizza."

"Vegan is my guess. And the guy you call Kung Fu Bobby, he's dead," Brett said.

"That much I was awake for," I said.

"Vanilla said she cut his throat, put her foot on his neck, and stood on it until she heard something crack."

"That's cold-blooded," I said.

"He was in our house, remember? If I had her skills, I'd have done the same."

"I'm not complaining," I said. "I was happy as a pig in shit to see her."

"I don't much like Vanilla, but I must admit, when it comes to throwing a turd in the soup, she knows how to do it. By the way, Leonard's plan didn't work."

"No kidding."

"Jim Bob didn't even know you were gone until he texted your phone and you didn't answer. Found your phone and guns still in the garage. We thought they had done you in for sure."

At the end, her voice shook a little, and she cried a little. "Goddamn you, Hap Collins. You scared me to death."

"Consider the situation from my end," I said, and I cried a little too.

Brett laughed, wiped away a tear with the back of her hand.

"Everyone is out there," she said. "Well, not Veil. But Vanilla and Jim Bob and, of course, Leonard. He feels like a major shit for his plan not working."

"It was at least a plan," I said.

I got up and got dressed and went out with Brett to see the others.

In the living room, Vanilla was sitting in a chair near the door, looking like a magazine model, still wearing what she'd had on before. She could wear chain mail and make it look like a party dress.

Jim Bob was on the couch near her, leaning forward, trying to chat her up. His big cowboy hat was pushed back on his head and he had on his cowboy duds with the black boots with the Texas flags on the toes. She seemed about as interested in him as she'd be in an article on feeding dung beetles.

"Ah, honey," he said, "you and me, we're gonna work together, we ought to be more friendly."

"I don't think so," she said.

Leonard looked at me and stood up, said, "Damn, Hap. I'm sorry."

He looked really upset.

"That's all right," I said. "I'm not dead, thanks to Vanilla. But just so you know, it was a shitty plan to begin with."

"I've had shittier," he said.

"This is true."

"So have you," Leonard said.

"Also correct," I said. "I should have told you how shitty your plan was before we did it."

"It seemed pretty good at the time," Jim Bob said. "They just showed up before we did."

"Vanilla," I said, "how'd you know I was at the office? That they'd taken me?"

Still sitting in the chair, Vanilla repositioned herself. The way she moved was raw sexuality seasoned with hot sauce and pepper.

Brett gave me the side-eye, and I tried to think about cats, but that didn't lead to a good place either, so I thought about tacos, but that wasn't working for sure, and so I thought about a nice quiet place by the beach with me under a tree and the wind blowing and Brett holding a gun to my head, and that almost worked.

"You didn't say to meet you here at the safe house, so I assumed your house was the meeting point," Vanilla said. "I went there earlier yesterday."

"Were you driving a maroon '64 Impala?"

"You know I like old muscle cars."

"I saw you go by."

"That had to be my second time," she said. "I had been there earlier. No one was there. I left, drove around, stopped, had dinner, drove back, didn't see any lights. I had no idea where you wanted me to go. A third time by, and what do I see, faintly? A man carrying a body over his shoulder like it was a sack of laundry. That would be you. He was going down that path between your house and the garage, along the side of your backyard fence.

"I saw the direction he was going. I drove around the block, lights out. There was enough light from streetlamps and houses for me to see clearly enough without turning my headlights on. I stopped behind a parked car and watched. The man carrying you waved at a man on a porch, then carried you a little farther and put you in the trunk of his car. I followed. Stealthily, of course."

"Of course," I said. "So, no great mystery?"

"Luck. But since I came by to help you, it wasn't all luck. I had a reason to be here. I was at the wrong place at the right time, lucky for you."

"I'm glad I didn't tell you to meet us here," I said.

"I bet you are," she said.

"The question is, what's next?" Leonard said. "The doctor, a woman, and Kung Fu Bobby are lying bloody and dead in our office. That can't be good."

"Oh, they're not there anymore," Jim Bob said.

"Come again?" Leonard said.

"The cleaners have been there," Jim Bob said. "Three sisters I know, one quite intimately at one time, another is a bowling buddy, the third is mean as a snake and prefers a snake's company."

"Sounds like to me," Brett said, "you ought to be a shoo-in with her."

Jim Bob grinned. "The sisters have no morals but they can keep a secret and can clean up a battlefield and make it look as if the most violent thing happened there was a rivalry between ant clans. Hap, you owe me twenty thousand dollars, by the way."

"Damn, man," I said.

"It was leave the bodies there or have the folks from Houston, the sisters, drive down in their so-called janitor van, sometimes two vans, and take care of business. Vanilla told me what happened; I called them. They were here within two and a half hours. Had the place clean as the queen's china in another two hours. I went over for a look. They work quick and efficiently. The bodies and blood were gone almost immediately. Then they went about cleaning the rest of it up. The couch had to go, so you'll need a new one. The walls were spackled and repainted after they dug some buckshot out of the drywall. You no longer have a table and a coffeepot. The desk and chairs are fine. And once again, you owe me twenty thousand dollars. I'll take a check."

"I'll figure it out," I said.

"I'll hold you to it," Jim Bob said.

"The Trixies," Vanilla said to Jim Bob. "They're your cleaners."

"You know them?" Jim Bob said.

"Remember, once upon a time, I was in the assassin business."

"Aren't you still in the assassin business?" Brett said.

"I know bad from good now, thanks to Hap," Vanilla said.

Thanks, Vanilla. Her compliment was causing Brett to measure the width and depth of my grave in her head. Everything Vanilla said sounded like a blow job. She had been raised like that. To use herself in all manner, shape, and form to achieve what she was meant to achieve. It's not a good way, but it has its powers. Al could vouch for that.

Vanilla's change from being an assassin for hire who would kill whoever she was paid to kill to being the person she was now was dramatic, and perhaps a little shaky. It was a natural progression, not some word or two I'd given her.

Me and Vanilla had never been intimate, and I planned to keep it that way. Old man like me, not sure what she saw in me, but I want to admit right here and now, without any grandstanding, it was nice a woman like that saw something in me. Then again, she seemed to enjoy her work a little too much. Standing on Kung Fu Bobby's throat was intense. However, considering my position last night, three cheers for the cruel and merciless.

For that matter, I was also surprised a woman like Brett loved me. She was everything I had ever dreamed about. I was solidly on Team Brett.

Yay, team!

59

Me, Leonard, and Jim Bob went into LaBorde in Jim Bob's nondescript car. We dropped in at Kroger and bought more supplies, keeping an eye out for anyone following us.

As it turned out, nobody seemed to be lurking in the aisles next to the green bean endcaps giving us the side-eye. When we came out and Jim Bob drove us off, we didn't notice a car following us. No monkey on a tricycle.

To make sure that was the case, Jim Bob drove around awhile, and we talked.

"I like to think how wonderful it is with your lovely wife and Vanilla back at the safe house," Jim Bob said. "Bonding, sharing big-girl stories, doing each other's nails."

Leonard laughed.

"You know that's not happening," I said.

As for Vanilla and Brett, despite their differences, I felt good with Vanilla there. She was as deadly as Jim Bob, maybe more so. She was surely as confident as he was, and not many people were, though Leonard came close. And Brett, well, she was no shrinking violet either. Me, I was perpetually nervous.

We told Jim Bob in more detail about Al Polson, what he had told us, what he had experienced. Told him what little we knew about Purple Eyes.

Jim Bob said, "So this here Polson fella was fucking the same gal his daughter was fucking?"

"Appears that way," Leonard said. "But not at the same time."

"Motherfucker must have had a big truckload of stupid driven up his ass."

"I like to think of him as one of life's naive innocents," I said. "He doesn't strike me as stupid, just gullible."

"I don't know," Leonard said. "Let's not slice and dice it. He's got to be kind of stupid."

"Just because some gal can do more tricks with a six-inch dick than a monkey can with a hundred feet of grapevine don't mean she's your soulmate," Jim Bob said.

"How could Al know?" I said. "He's a kind of skewed romantic."

"She had him buy a big rubber dick," Leonard said.

"Now that's getting over into the soulmate arena," Jim Bob said, "so what do I know?"

"Way he described it, it was long enough to reach his soul," Leonard said.

"Here's something else you could say that hasn't been said," Jim Bob said. "Surely if she did all we know she did, she most likely got Polson's name on some insurance, so something happens to him, money goes to her. That fits her MO."

"But nothing's happened," I said.

"Not yet," Jim Bob said. "Maybe she's waiting for the right time. If she handed Polson a pen right after giving him a pony ride, he might have signed anything. More likely, though, this Purple Eyes forged his name. That would be the easiest way. Fits better if she waits, kills him later, and collects. Right now, there's too much smoke around him. Know one goddamn thing, these stringy pieces of dog shit will do anything to anybody. And another thing: I wasn't friends with Hanson, not like you guys, but I respected him. What they did to him and his wife, they ought to pay for that in a serious manner."

"Kung Fu Bobby done paid," Leonard said. "And it disappoints me. I wanted to be the one to kill him."

60

We decided to see Al again. Jim Bob had floated the idea there might be a life policy on him, one that went to Purple Eyes in one of her guises should Al suddenly get run over by a runaway truck, and the idea was now front and center.

Me and Leonard hadn't considered that possibility at all. It might be good to make sure Al was still okay and, if he was, to at least warn him of the likelihood of his being insurance-targeted.

When we got to his place, a new gate had been installed just past the cattle guard, and beside the massive white yurt was an equally massive white enclosed garage that looked to be made of stone blocks the size of those in the Pyramids. You could have landed a jet in there. Rich people could get things built fast.

On a flagpole, the Jolly Roger was flying. Out back, the mobile home was still visible.

"That mobile home," Leonard said. "That's for his mice."

"Be damned," Jim Bob said. "What I'm thinking, just looking at it, is them poor mice don't have a shoebox garage for their windup cars. That's inconsiderate."

I got out and opened the gate, got back in, and Jim Bob drove us through, rattling over the cattle guard. The path to the yurt had been scraped wider and was down to the clay. My guess was a topping of some kind was forthcoming.

We walked up to the yurt door and rang a bell. Inside, instead of an actual bell, it played a heavy metal song that I couldn't have identified if the musician were with me.

The door opened, and there was Al, looking a lot better that before. He was dressed in white sweatpants, a sweatshirt, and house shoes. His shaved head was damp. He looked to have recently gotten out from the shower. The dogs yapped at his heels.

"Y'all shut up," Al said. "Dogs, not you folks."

The dogs shut up.

"Go to your room, goddamn it," Al said.

Ending with a couple of protest barks, they trotted off.

"Tell you what, they like their room pretty damn well now, way it's set up for them. Ain't just the back of a mobile home that was once dunked in water. They go to their new room quick-like. Sometimes they don't even bark. They got their own TV tuned to the dog channel. You know about that?"

"No," Leonard said. "I don't watch dog TV."

"Me neither, but they do. Okay, now and again I watch. It's kind of hypnotic. I think if I was going to send some sort of subliminal message, that would be the way. You know, aliens wanted to hypnotize us into walking off cliffs or drowning ourselves, that would be the way to go. Who you got with you?"

"Jim Bob Luke," Jim Bob said, stuck out his hand and Al shook it. "Sometimes I go by my stripper name, Long Dong Larry."

"You remind me of that country singer Jerry Reed," Al said. "He's dead, by the way."

"So that can't be me, can it?" Jim Bob said, pushing back his hat with two fingers. The two men laughed together like someone had tickled their buttholes with a feather.

"Get your asses on in here," Al said.

We slipped inside and eased the door shut. We were in a living room about the size of my and Brett's house. There was a set of open doors on each side. The interior was painted a soft blue color that made me kind of drowsy.

"Let's go in the kitchen and have a drink. I also got Pop-Tarts and Hot Pockets. Ate both cold a few days before I found a good toaster and a good microwave. You get one of those cheap microwaves, damn thing will blow up."

"Was what you put in it wrapped in aluminum foil?" Jim Bob said as we strolled to the kitchen, which was painted a light mint green.

"Now that you mention it."

"There's your problem," Jim Bob said. "It can't handle that stuff and will blow up on you. Start a fire. No aluminum foil or metal or cats can go into it. It don't work that way. That kind of shit is its kryptonite. Kidding about the cat. I don't know if they'd cause it to blow up or not."

"Now I know," Al said.

"Knowledge gives one power," Jim Bob said.

"You know that's right," Al said. "Also, think I'll hire some kitchen help to put stuff in the microwave for me. I'm not much of a cook."

"Well, sir," Jim Bob said, "they don't really call toasting Pop-Tarts and warming up shit in the microwave cooking."

"Got me there," Al said. "Truthfully, I'm a little scared of those damn things. Not Pop-Tarts, but an exploding microwave."

We sat on stools at a bar in the kitchen while Al prowled through the cabinets. "Johnnie Walker okay?"

"How can you call Johnnie Walker only okay?" Jim Bob said. "Get me a fruit jar for that shit."

"None for me," I said.

"Me either," Leonard said.

"A beer, then?" Al said.

"I'll take one, yeah," Leonard said.

"I'm good," I said.

"I know," Al said. "How about some juice? Hell, you can be just as manly as we are if I put it in a dirty glass."

"I wouldn't mind the juice, minus the dirty glass."

"I was just fucking with you," Al said.

I certainly hoped so.

He actually found a fruit jar and poured it half full of whiskey for Jim Bob. There was enough whiskey there to pickle a good-size herring. Leonard had a Lone Star in the bottle, and I had apple juice in a small jar with blue and red stripes on it. I recognized it as belonging to a brand of peanut butter.

Jim Bob took a sip. "Well, shit in my face and call me Mildred, that tastes like Johnnie Walker on steroids. I felt my liver go to the back of my spine. I think it wants me to crap it out."

"I like to put a bit of wood alcohol in it," Al said.

Jim Bob gave him a look.

"Just fucking with you. There's some Wild Turkey mixed in."

Jim Bob and Al did the feather-on-the-butthole laugh again.

"Sure do give it a love bite, don't it," Jim Bob said.

"Don't it," Al said.

I glanced at Leonard. He was glancing at me. Jim Bob was pulling off his folksy magic. He knew how to play people. He could be whatever they wanted until he wasn't anything they wanted.

That said, Jim Bob and Al reminded me of one another in many ways. The difference was I thought Al might be crazy. To be generous, maybe he was just grandly eccentric.

"I see you got some more of your stocks sold," I said.

"That's right. A good lawyer helped me out, and in record time. I got my money. Had this big yurt and the garage put up fast."

"How are the mice?" Leonard asked.

"Multiplying. I bought some mouse food for them. Ironically, I keep it in a cat feeder. You know, one of those things that contains food, drops it into a bowl as they eat. Sometimes at night, I like to go up there and toss them bread pieces. They come right out of that couch, look me in the eye, and go to work on that bread. I like to listen to them squeak."

"Al, show Jim Bob that photo of the woman you knew as Earline," I said.

Jim Bob looked at her photo. "Oh, double hell. She could get the pope to knock over a filling station and shoot the attendant."

"Yep," Al said. "I hate her now. What she did. But you know, and this is the part that chaps my ass a little raw, at times I remember her fondly. Not just the sex, though that was fabulous. She knew how to play me. Handed me a lot of confidence I was lacking right then. Wouldn't seem it, but yeah, I got some gaps in the confidence department. I think she could be anyone she wanted to be. And I figure it's the same with this Johnny Joe fellow you told me about. He's probably not hiding out in the bushes or in some secret fucking lair but is right amongst us."

"Mind if I freshen my drink?" Jim Bob said, and poured from the mixed-liquor bottle. It was a small dose this time.

"I've come across all kinds," Jim Bob said after taking a bracing sip of the whiskey. "Same as you, I figure he's right amongst us, tight up in our ass like a dog tick. He plays normal. I mean, lots of professional thieves and serial killers have jobs. Even families. This guy is a serial power broker, and that includes theft, fraud, murder, and who knows what all.

"My guess is no one except a few close confidants know who he is. I think Purple Eyes is his sock puppet. But its Johnny Joe's fingers moving the sock."

"Seems so damn elaborate," I said.

"Most of the time, criminal masterminds don't exist. Most criminals can't get out of a grocery store with a stolen Twinkie. Even the best of them have generally served more than a few stretches in prison. This guy, maybe when he was young, he got stung by the law. But he learned from his mistakes. He didn't keep doing the same thing over and over, expecting a different outcome. He diversified."

Jim Bob threw the rest of the whiskey down his throat, said, "But we'll get him."

61

Jim Bob didn't seem loaded, but he was smart enough to ask Leonard to drive, get us rolling.

We managed to talk Al into coming with us, staying with us until it was all sorted, as the British say. He grabbed a few things, shoved them into a tote bag, then locked up the yurt using a button-punching code. He didn't ask to say goodbye to the mice.

He brought a pistol with him. Stuffed it in his coat pocket. He said he was a good shot. You could never really tell what was solidly true when talking with Al, so I took it with a grain of salt. I don't like carrying a pistol on me, even though, as I'd nearly been murdered, it was a logical choice, considering who we were dealing with. I damn sure don't like people I don't know having one, just in case they want to play Wild Bill Hickok. Hell, even people I do know having guns can make me nervous if I don't know their gun training, because these days you don't need any — just a desire to shoot something and the money to buy a gun and ammunition, maybe a cute holster with your name stamped on it.

I know some guys in town who, due to the open-carry law, like to strut around with their holstered guns highly visible. It's sad seeing grown men playing at being Roy Rogers.

As we drove along, Al, who was moderately drunk, made a few calls to find out about the insurance business, see if there was a policy out there on him that he was unacquainted with.

When he finished his calls, Al gave us the scoop. He had fired his old lawyer during a court appearance, was left with no one to represent him. A lawyer showed up with a smile and a business card, said he could fix Al's problems. Al, with his usual lack of impulse control, hired him on the spot, now had him on retainer.

The court business had been about how some of Al's money was tied up in certain stocks and investments like a hostage victim. He said the lawyer had helped him unlock some financial barriers, got his complicated stocks and investments loose, which supplied the funds for the yurt, garage, a new car, and general maintenance of a continual mouse colony in the mobile home.

It was decided we should all visit the lawyer so Al could talk to him in person. I think Al was drunk enough that all kinds of things seemed like good ideas. Al called him, and he and the lawyer made plans.

Leonard drove us to a café for coffee. It was good coffee. When it was time for us to meet the lawyer, Leonard tooled us over there. We went into a big building, rode a smooth gliding elevator up to a second-floor office to meet Graham Ray.

We were let into the office by Graham himself. The place looked empty enough to cause an echo if you spoke too loudly. There was a new-looking couch and two chairs in the waiting room. There was no receptionist unless the receptionist was a ghost.

We were led into the lawyer's conference room. No one offered us coffee. Graham Ray was the only one on duty, it seemed. He didn't look or act like a man that was used to waiting on people. He looked like someone used to being waited on.

The conference room was sizable and not all that clean. The corners had spiderwebs and things in the webs that were probably the remains of flies.

On one windowsill there were several enormous dead moths, possibly suicide victims. They lay with their wings full of holes.

We were seated at a long wooden table with a shiny surface. Unlike the windowsill, it was clean and smelled of some kind of lemony table polish. The smell was intense enough, I pushed back from the table to clear my head.

Graham Ray sat at the head of the table. He had a pleasant, bony pink face and a near bald head with strands of what looked to me like poorly dyed hair, black and waxy like shoe polish. I noted that from the way he wore his blue suit that he worked out, lifted weights. His shoulders, chest, and thin waist showed that. The body didn't seem to go along with the face. If he had looked any more pleasant, he would have been a tropical island.

"I see you've brought some friends," Graham said to Al. Graham looked us over with his catlike green eyes, smiled at us. It was one of those shyster-lawyer smiles that was about as sincere as a one-night stand.

"They're working for me," Al said. "They're private eyes. You can say what you need to say in front of them."

Graham looked at Al, said, "You sound as if you might have been imbibing, Al."

"Just a touch," Al said.

Al asked us to introduce ourselves, my guess being he couldn't remember our names.

We did that. Except Jim Bob. He said, "I'm only giving out my stripper name right now. Long Dong Larry."

That was, to put it mildly, strange.

Jim Bob looked at Al. Something about that look kept Al from correcting him, giving out his real name. If he even remembered it.

"That's interesting, Mr. Long Dong Larry," Graham said.

"Some days I just feel cautious." Jim Bob smiled his very good smile and Graham smiled a pretty nice one back. Two bullshitters bullshitting each other.

"Sometime you'll have to demonstrate to us your stripper skills," Graham said.

"Those skills are well honed. I swing a big dick, and this room won't work for me. Too small. And seeing me strut my stuff costs," Jim Bob said.

"That's fair," Graham said. "Everything in life costs, doesn't it?"

"Pretty much," Long Dong Larry said.

"Damn, man," Al said, looking at Jim Bob, "that's some weird shit, and I'm pretty fucking weird myself, and on top of that, I'm drunk as Cooter Brown."

I eyeballed Leonard. He wrinkled his forehead slightly.

Without missing a beat, Graham Ray changed gears. "Just so you know, Al, I'm on this situation with your money. I think I can have the rest of it free of foreign investments in a reasonably short time. And then there are those other things. I'll take care of those as well. You can count on it. I'll treat it like it's my money."

"But you won't spend it like it's yours," Al said.

"Only the part of it that I earn," Graham said.

I assumed those "other things" the lawyer referred to were some sketchy offshore investments. I had begun to think Al was a lot better off than he'd said he was, and I already thought he had plenty of loot, despite all his poor-mouthing. Had to. For a lawyer to do all that, to find out if he was falsely insured somewhere, rescue what I presumed was illegal investments, that was time-tedious and would cost more than a smile and a handkerchief.

Al and Graham talked a bit. Business still. That went on for some time before they turned to talking about football, why the Broncos weren't doing good and didn't they know that so-and-so stunk in the halfback position. Al talked with enthusiasm, and though Graham had opinions, they were dry as yesterday's toast. It was more like he was trying to be polite and engage. He seemed to know the subject, but his interest might have been borrowed from a TV sports show.

I tuned out. Sports talk interests me only a little less than discussions about calculus. Well, talk about boxing or martial arts, and my ears will perk up, but I never got into team sports like football, what an old friend of mine called Run, Bump, and Mill.

I could see Leonard's eyes were glazing over as well. Jim Bob was watching the two of them talk business. He was that kind of guy. He paid attention to everything. I was like him in my dreams, but the truth was, I was easily distracted.

Oh, look. A kitty.

This football talking between them went on awhile, then they wrapped up with Al saying something about the Dallas Cowboys that made Jim Bob say, "Now, wait just a goddamn minute. You have done quit opinionating and have done gone to preaching. Ain't you got no Texas pride?"

Well, now, that went on for a while before a truce was called.

With the coffee, talk, and time, Al seemed to have sobered up a little. Jim Bob seemed exactly the same before and after that fruit jar of whiskey.

Moments later we were out in the hall, stepping into the elevator.

Riding down, I said, "What the hell was that all about, Jim Bob? Your stripper name?"

"I don't like lawyers," he said. "Even the good ones."

Al said, "Believe me, as a personality, Graham is friendly but still stiff as a Viagra dick. But he's smart. Damn sure got me out of some messes and managed to get my money out of places I thought the only way of getting it back was armed robbery. He's got some skills."

"So did Jack the Ripper," Jim Bob said. "Glad you got your money, but I still don't like lawyers."

62

Ending up at the safe house, we told Al that if he wanted to be protected, he had to work at protecting himself first.

No calls that told where we were. And in fact, the fewer calls, the better. We weren't thinking anyone was tracking our phones, but caution was expected.

He was still taken with Brett, and now he was taken with Vanilla as well. Neither was overly taken with him.

In a private moment in the hallway, Brett said, "Maybe we could drug him and put him in the closet with a plastic bag over his head."

"It's an idea."

We then retired to the bedroom and stretched out for a rest. I told her all that we had learned about the lawyer and the insurance being checked on.

After talking we both slipped off to sleep. I didn't realize how tired I was from stress, how bad I needed a nap, until the buzz of my cell phone woke me up.

Brett slept through it. I picked up the phone, slipped out of the bedroom and out the back door. I answered the phone.

It was Olivia from the cop shop.

"I know you don't really know me, but I wanted to tell you something because you were friends with Hanson."

"Still am, even if he's gone."

"Of course. Hanson said if anything went haywire for any kind of odd reason, I should tell you or Leonard or your wife, Brett. It may be nothing, and I've tried to be a good little soldier, but Chief Justin makes me nervous."

I wasn't expecting that.

"How so?"

"I was pretty free with information with him about Hanson. I wanted to help Hanson, but I wanted to keep my job, so I told him I was slipping a few things to Hanson so they would get to you and Leonard. Justin made it clear to me that he didn't mind me telling Hanson things so it would get to you guys because you could do what we couldn't do."

"What's changed?"

I could hear her suck on her teeth. "I think Chief might have been the one to tell this Johnny Joe where to find you and Hanson."

"That doesn't sound right," I said. "Justin gave us the dope on Johnny Joe. The guy seems to be his personal nemesis."

"I know. But I think that might be a front. I think he might be working with them. And I think it might be even truer that he's working both sides of the street. He has this son, very sick boy, and the money needed for his treatment is devastating."

"I didn't know that," I said.

"That's the case."

"You think that makes him vulnerable to payoffs?"

"I think it could. I may be talking out of school and talking about the wrong school, but lately, we get a lead, and the guy's gone. I tell you this not because I'm certain but because I get bad vibes from mine and Chief Justin's conversations."

"Okay," I said. "I'll take note."

"Keep in mind, I'm fully aware I may be wrong. My thought is Johnny Joe pays Chief Justin for certain information. Chief did get his son into an expensive treatment in Houston at the Methodist Hospital. Insurance only covers part of that, so how's he managing?"

"Trying to have his cake and eat it too."

"If you and Leonard take Johnny Joe off the board, there's no one to turn on him and say he was taking money."

"Except you."

"Yeah. Except me. And that worries me."

"I'm going to complicate things for you. Get information that might help, don't discuss it with Justin."

"I stopped that anyway, soon as I started to suspect."

"Call me, let me know. If you find out something that will lead to us taking down Johnny Joe, that's good for all of us."

"Agreed. Where are you?"

"Let's just say someplace safe."

"All right."

"Watch your back," I said.

63

I called a meeting, and we all gathered in the living room. I told them what Olivia had told me.

"Grief," Jim Bob said. "That don't sound good. Think there's anything to it?"

"I don't know what to think," I said. "Could be paranoia. Justin may have made some other kind of deal to get money for his son's treatment. Olivia giving Hanson information and then him getting killed, that could have made her nervous. If you want that to fit into some kind of conspiracy, you can make it fit."

Brett said, "Sounds unlikely to me. I didn't get those feelings from Justin, that he was insincere. Quite the opposite."

"Sick kid can make you act like a fool," Al said.

"It could be the snitch isn't Justin," Vanilla said. "It might well be Olivia herself."

"You didn't tell her where we are, did you?" Jim Bob said.

"No."

"Okay," Jim Bob said, "that's good. What we're going to do is ditch all our phones. I got a shitload of burners in a bag in my car. I'll pass them out. We can put a few necessary numbers in them, but our regular phones, they got to be decommissioned."

"I only use burners," Vanilla said.

"Figures," Brett said.

"There go my porn links," Al said.

"What's next?" Brett said.

"First, you stay with us, Al. And don't be chatty with anyone, even on the burner."

"I will need to talk to my lawyer," Al said. "I got money hanging."

"Use the burner," Jim Bob said. "And you might need to toss it after a bit, get another. Just to be extra sure. You know, like wearing clean underwear if you go clubbing. You never know who you might meet and who might want a peek. I'll go get the phones."

We spent some time putting into the new phones numbers we would need, then Jim Bob took all our old phones and drove away with them.

Leonard looked out the kitchen window as Jim Bob departed.

He said, "There he goes. Motherfucker probably gonna sell our goddamn phones."

64

Early in the morning, a heavy mist was on the grass in the field in front of the log barn. There was a drizzle to go with it. I looked at the barn through the kitchen window while I sipped a cup of coffee. It was barely light and I was the only one up, though I knew everyone else, like me, slept light and would be ready to spring into action should there be any action.

Another hour, if that, and everyone would be up anyway, having slept on ideas, hopefully some good ones.

I heard Leonard cough, clearing his throat, but he didn't get off the couch. He rolled over.

I suppose one can take only so much of a bad thing before he needs some kind of good thing, so I poured another cup and slipped outside into the gentle rain, wearing my raincoat, the hood pulled up. I walked across the road and the field to the big red barn. The wet grass blades made my pants legs wet and dampened my ankles and shoes. The mist floated about my knees.

I slid the barn's big red door back with one hand, maintaining a death grip on my coffee cup with the other. I went in.

Inside it was quiet like an empty church. Hay dust drifted up from the floor, and there was enough of it to make that sweet smell it can make and not enough of it to plug the nose and make it hard to breathe. The hay had long ago been carried off. There was an old, rusted horse-drawn hay raker in one corner of the barn, and it looked to have been last used about the time Jefferson Davis was president of the Confederacy.

There was a bench made of old wood and faded varnish near the back wall. I sat on it and it felt solid as the Rock of Gibraltar.

I sipped and watched the rising light fill the doorway. The drizzle drizzled out. The sun touched its warm tongue to the mist, and like cotton candy, it melted.

A wider strip of sunlight came through the open barn door carrying a small bit of heat with it. It felt good. I sipped the last of my coffee, sat the cup on the bench, leaned back against the wall, and closed my eyes for a moment. I tried to think back on all the things that Justin had told us, looking for some reason to believe he was setting us up in such a way that if we won out, he was okay, and if not, he still won out.

I couldn't really put that idea together.

Instead, I remembered the cold look of Kung Fu Bobby, the nurse, the doctor, the bright light, and the weak feeling, like a calf just born. To be melodramatic, I had tasted my own doom, and it was bitter.

Now I was here, given another chance to leave this stuff alone but knowing I wouldn't. I was bound to continue because I was me. It was like reading those old Gold Medal novels where the main character, nearly always a man, was on a path of destruction and the reader could see it, and the protagonist could frequently see it himself, but onward he went, striding toward a sour inevitability. Like standing on a railroad track threatening an oncoming train.

I opened my eyes and there was a shape in the doorway.

Leonard.

He came across the barn, moved my coffee cup to the end of the bench, and sat down beside me. "I got up for a cup, looked out the kitchen window, saw you walking out here, figured you wanted to be alone, so I thought I'd fuck that up."

"Thank you."

"You all right, brother?"

"Yeah. You?"

"Yeah."

"Are we scared?" I said.

"Not that we'd admit to anyone else, but hell yeah."

"It's a lot."

"It's a lot and we don't even know how big the lot is. That's what gets me. Stand me up in a straight-on fight, and I'll wade into it. But this kind of shit, me being away from Pookie, wandering around in the middle of nothing and not really knowing nothing, that ain't no way to do things."

"What about Olivia being the ears and eyeballs for the bad guys?" I asked. "About her maybe leading us down the garden path? And at the end of the path will be a big monster. You think that's true?"

"I think that's a maybe. We don't know her. Justin, he's not my fucking buddy either, but we know him a little. Seems like a guy that in the end is out for himself. Likes to throw his dick around. He's using us and we're letting ourselves be used because we want the same thing he does. As for his son and needing money, I don't know. He didn't give me no reason to think he's sneaking on us. Then again, we been fooled before. Especially you."

I laughed a little. It felt good.

"Of course, I guess that plan I came up with of you being in the garage attic wasn't so good."

"You think?"

"I think about them having you, that Kung Fu Bobby piece of shit, and I get sick to my stomach. That was my fault."

"Wasn't your fault. They just outsmarted us. It wasn't a great plan, but it wasn't a bad plan if we had been there first. They were ahead of us."

"I think I may have stretched my string too tight and too far," Leonard said. "I think about leaving this business, but somehow, I can't."

"There will come a time, I suppose, when we both will step away," I said. "We're not getting any younger. I always think about quitting when things get like this, but I can't."

"We are such numb-nuts," Leonard said.

"No, we are foolish and of the belief that we are the Lone Ranger and Tonto."

"Just to get it straight," Leonard said, "I'm the Lone Ranger. You're Tonto. If we do Batman and Robin, you're Robin, though you ain't got the legs for it, wearing them little tights and all."

"We were plastered with too much of the heroic stuff growing up," I said. "Us thinking we could be heroes. That's our problem. That's on us."

Leonard was quiet for longer than I expected. He said, "No, Hap. The problem is that not that many folks want to be the Lone Ranger. We stand up. Give us that. Life shouldn't be about flowing downriver with the leaves. We don't just turn our backs. There aren't many heroes left, and I don't just mean the ones that use their fists or guns. Standing up, that's us. Falling down on purpose, that's not us. I think of Hanson. He knew he was done out there in the water, knew what was about to happen, but he didn't flinch."

"Right now, I'm thinking I don't want to stand up or fall down. I want to crawl in a hole and hide."

"But you won't," he said, "because you know what needs to be done before that lawyer bullshit in a courtroom, and somehow deals are made, and people walk that ought not to. And they just start it all over again."

There was truth in what Leonard said, and there was also justification.

"Hap, I been thinking I might hang up the private-investigation business, and the other day, when I got to the gym before you, I was offered a job training folks in boxing and martial arts."

"You didn't say."

"I'm saying now. I was quiet on it because I was thinking that shit over. I think I'd like that, training people. Young folks."

"You'd be good at it," I said.

"I know that. You would too, but I know you're tied in with Brett. But I also know you're feeling the weight. I mean, ain't we just now talking about that?"

"We are. Can you make a living teaching at a gym?"

"I got money packed back, dude. I get paper cuts from counting it."

"You didn't put it in the bank?"

"Figure of speech, Hap."

"Right."

"I told the gym guy I'd think on it. I've thought on it. Get all this done, I don't lose a leg or a nutsack, I'm going to do just that. He wanted you too. I told him I'd ask."

"I can't," I said.

"I know. But I did ask."

"You did indeed."

"We ain't gonna tell nobody about this, okay? Not yet. I want to break it to Brett at a better time. Like when and if I survive all this crap."

"Of course," I said. "It's a big decision, though."

"You and Brett ain't wrong. Thinking about having a life with Pookie, I feel I got to change my ways of doing shit. Never thought I'd say that. But I never been in love this way before."

"I'm happy for you," I said. "You know what a decision like this calls for, don't you?"

"Vanilla ice cream, of course. Or banana pudding. Or just vanilla cookies with a Dr Pepper."

"I was thinking a cup of coffee, but yeah, that sounds good too."

65

When we got back to the house, everyone was up and sitting at the kitchen table eating toaster waffles with butter but no syrup. We had forgotten the syrup. And by this point, me and Leonard had forgotten ice cream for breakfast as well.

Brett, barefoot, wearing a faded sundress, smiled at me, said, "Morning."

I leaned down and gave Brett a kiss, stood by her chair with my hand on her shoulder. It was warm and soft and satisfying to me.

I caught Vanilla's eyes on us. They were narrowed and she was no longer eating. I don't know what she was thinking, but whatever it was, it made me uncomfortable. One time Vanilla climbed into my shower with me, and that made me uncomfortable too. I sent her packing. It was the right thing to do, but it was like spitting out a favorite food instead of enjoying it.

Leonard decided to toast himself a couple waffles and tuck in, but coffee was all I wanted. I made myself another cup, putting some milk in it this time.

I sat on the couch in the living room, sipping the coffee, and waited for them to finish.

Jim Bob came into the living room first, carrying a big mug of coffee, looking like the cat that had just eaten the canary and had a rat in its pocket for later.

I knew he had some ideas about what was going on. I didn't push him, though. I waited for the others to finish and join us. He'd say what he had to say in his own time.

Me, I had some ideas myself. They had gathered together out there in the barn, and something about my conversation with Leonard had solidified them. I was still racing them through my mind when everyone came in and sat down.

I said, "I have an idea or two about things. I bet we all have ideas. But do you mind if I go first?"

No one thought I shouldn't.

"Not long ago, when me and Leonard had our first contact with Kung Fu Bobby, we got caught up in something not too unlike this. I won't mess you around with all the details, but we learned there was quite an East Texas crime syndicate, like we're talking about now. It was run by a man named Keith. Last name being Keith. He was into all manner of business, like we're seeing here, and he ran it all as efficiently. I think there's a connection."

"He's dead," Leonard said. "And now Kung Fu Bobby is too."

"I know. But what got me thinking was how broad this business is and how Kung Fu Bobby was involved in both. We got Keith — killed him, in fact. But it occurred to me, when we got him, even though a lot of their business fell apart, there were still a lot of ants at the picnic."

"I get you," Brett said. "You think someone else stepped in and took over."

"I do. This is more of the same with a new leader. Someone probably part of it back then, but a worker bee, not the leader. Someone who might have started with things like driveway-asphalt fraud. Small cons. Someone ruthless who played with power and murder like a hobby. Someone like that could easily have become part of Keith's operation.

"Maybe this operator had plans to move up all along, usurp Keith. And without being aware, we helped him do it. Reason Kung Fu Bobby was back was that the old syndicate of greed and murder never went away, not completely. It just limped off and licked its wounds. No telling what went on behind the scenes, but finally Johnny Joe and Purple Eyes rose to the top of the sewer water, like turds. I don't think I'm guessing too hard to think it's the same business with new top operators."

"That's the Kung Fu Bobby connection," Leonard said. "But how do we connect the old leader with the new one? This Johnny Joe is as elusive as a water snake."

"I'm not sure," I said. "If I'm right and they are connected, then we may be able to think about it now in such a way we can see connections."

"Al," Jim Bob said. "How well do you know your lawyer?"

"I just know that he's quite the wiz," Al said. "Got me a lot of tied-up money and such."

"But what do you know about him? Said you met him in court, right?"

Al nodded.

"You ever been to his office before yesterday?"

"No."

"What kind of big-ass lawyer has an office that looks like it's just been emptied out? Has a brand-new couch and chairs but still has a vacant look. There wasn't a diploma on the wall. No receptionist. And that football talk. Talked like he had memorized some things off a sports channel, not like it was a real passion."

"I have met him several times, though," Al said.

"He got you your money back, but if I was you, I'd check and see how that's playing out in your bank account," Jim Bob said.

"I built a new home, garage and got a new car with some of that money," Al said. "Paid him a fee. He must be a good lawyer. It turned out well for me."

"For most of us, what you spent on your house and car is a lot of money," Jim Bob said. "But is it a lot of money for you? Meaning, is it just a piece of a larger pile?"

"I suppose it is," Al said. "I've done well in business without knowing anything about business."

"You have lawyers other than Graham, right?"

Al nodded.

"But they don't work the bad end of the street too well, do they?" Jim Bob asked. "They could hide your money, but they couldn't get it back when you wanted it. Legal complications, right?"

"Yes."

"You got taken to the cleaners by Earline, so you need the money faster than your lawyers could get it, and Graham approaches and offers you his card, and you have him go to work for you. Is that right?"

"Yes."

"But you didn't research him?"

"Not really."

"Damn, Al," Jim Bob said, "you been drinking too much mixed whiskey. Someone you've never seen knows you have illegal money and comes out of nowhere to help you get it, you got to have at least wondered how he might know about it."

"Suppose that should have occurred to me," Al said.

"I'm going to guess you gave him all your information, confided in him that some of your money might be in tax dodges," Jim Bob said. "Offshore. Wherever. Gave him information you'd only give a lawyer. A crooked one."

"That's right," Al said. He was starting to grow smaller. It was like he was melting.

"I was you," Jim Bob said, "I'd look at my bank account. Even if last time you checked was yesterday and it looked good. You got accountants?"

"Yes. And more than one bank."

"Have you had the accountants for a long time?" Jim Bob asked.

"Most of them."

"Check with them and see how the numbers are floating. What your investments look like now. You got other stocks you haven't cashed in, other assets, check on those too. Graham may not actually be a lawyer, but I'm sure he has some sketchy but good computer guys. Based on the information you gave Graham, they were able to break into where your money was and move as much of it as could be moved. Maybe all of it. Next step, Graham gives you a taste of your own money, charges you for his time, a healthy fee, no doubt. Then he, with aid from his assistants, start siphoning off your rescued money, slowly but steadily. Earline sucked your obvious money dry. And I bet you told her about your other money. The sneaky money."

"I might have," Al said. "I thought we were going to get married when my divorce went through. I wouldn't buy a big ol' knotted rubber dick for someone I was just going to hang out with. That's not my style."

"Good to hear," Jim Bob said. "But Earline got you twice. She got your money and your wife's insurance money, and she and her partner are stripping you of what's left. You and dozens like you. All manner of conniving and thieving goes into their everyday life. It's their job. It's what they do."

"Damn," Al said.

"Yeah. Damn. Looked this Graham up, and there's a website, but there's just a number to call. That website and number were built just for you, in case you looked. You'd see he was listed, and that would be enough for you."

"I didn't look."

"Not surprised. Know what? That website, it's still there, but I called that number this morning, and it's no longer working. I should have put it together faster. Graham made me suspicious with his office and the way he talked. He's soulless. Of course, most lawyers are, so that wasn't as big a tip-off as it should have been. I kept thinking about that office and him and the kind of money you had, and this morning, after visiting his website and calling that number, I felt like I had figured it. Yesterday, in that office, I bet we met the man that was part of Keith's operation before it was his. An operation that has a toe in everything and is run like a business. And this guy who was a cog in Keith's operation is now the one who pulls the gears. Yesterday, I think we met Johnny Joe."

"Ruh-roh," Leonard said in a Scooby-Doo voice.

66

I sat there thinking: You got them wheels within wheels, baby. All manner of this and that coming together in some kind of plan bigger than the planners themselves.

The ones you're after got this crime machine started, and now it's rolling downhill fast, and it's got an ass-end full of bricks and explosives.

Worse, you are now a passenger on that downhill ride, and behind you the fuse is lit and hissing in your ear. For them or you, or you and them, there's going to be a tumultuous Armageddon.

Bones will break. Blood will fly.

You know this, yes, you do, but onward you go with the others, whistling in the dark, the hiss of those explosives loud in your ear, a knight on a white charger of sorts, rolling hell-bent for leather, lance extended, and tied to it, dangling, Lady Death's veil, a token of her favor.

Ride on, idiot. Ride on.

67

I wasn't sure if we were waiting or planning. Our next move was hard to figure. Who was who, and where did you go to find them?

An answer of sorts was forthcoming. My cell rang.

I stepped outside on the porch to answer it.

It was Olivia.

"I may have something for you."

"Yeah?"

"Justin, he's got a move on. He's meeting this Johnny Joe fellow."

"Yeah?"

"That's right. I think it's a payoff and an information swap."

"Justin has some helpful information for Johnny Joe or what?"

"Can't say. Only know what I overheard on the phone. I'm out taking a chewing-gum break behind the cop shop, and I hear him talking around the corner, not knowing I'm there. Just heard one side of the conversation, but I learned the when and the where. I can't really do much, being bound by the rule book. But you don't have that book."

"Not the one you're talking about, no. But you can arrest them if they're working together to do nefarious stuff. No rule-breaking there."

"True. But they might not say anything I can hear that leads to an arrest. You know and I know they're dirty. But I got to show all the dirt and justify it. You don't."

I considered that. "How do you know it's just the two of them?"

"Guess I don't, but that's the idea I got from what I heard. You should come with Leonard, and that's it. Just the two of you for the two of them. Come with anyone else, it'll be too many and go sour pretty damn quick."

"How do you figure?"

"It's easier for two to put the sneak on them than for a battalion clattering harness and rattling swords."

"Nice way to put it."

"It's up to you. I'm just passing on what I know, not all that it's about. You get Johnny Joe, rack up Justin for being dirty, you've nipped the head off the snake."

"Where?"

"Old roller rink out at Scully."

"When?"

"Dark thirty," she said. "Sky fades, you might want to truck that way. There's an old blacktop road behind a stretch of trees growing along a little creek. Beyond the creek is the skating rink."

"I know the road."

"Creek is wide enough to jump over if you've had a good dinner. Go that way, and you'll see the back of the rink. There's a stretch of unmowed grass between the creek and the rink. Use the back door."

"Just waltz on in?"

"How you dance through the door is up to you," Olivia said. "They're meeting come dark, but who knows, one or both of them might come a tad early. That's all I got. You have to decide if you want to do it. I've given you what I know, and you can do with it what you want. Got to go."

And go she went.
I stood there with the phone in my hand, thinking things over.
I looked at my watch.
Two thirty.

68

Me, Leonard, Jim Bob, and Al drove over to Graham's office. We rode the elevator upstairs. The door was locked, but there was glass on either side of the doors, and we peeked in. That place was as lonely as an execution chamber.

Jim Bob picked the lock. No one was inside. We went through all the rooms. Wasn't anything to find but a stray paper clip. In the room with the big table, the spiderwebs were still there, along with the dead moths. A dead roach on its back had been added to the mix.

"I'm going to venture Graham never even rented this office," Jim Bob said. "Just boldly picked the lock and offered it to himself for use for our visit. Played a role and borrowed a space to play it in."

"That seems chancy," Al said.

"Not in this building," Leonard said. "If this place was any deader, someone would need to bury it."

"I feel like a big ol' donkey's ass," Al said.

We shuffled around in there for a bit more, then went out.

We drove Al back to the safe house, where Brett and Vanilla were sitting at the table laughing. They seemed to have buried the hatchet, and not in each other's heads. They both had on sweatshirts and sweatpants, running shoes.

After we told them what we'd found, they said they were going for a run. Carrying handguns, of course. They planned to stay on the road in front of the house, so I figured that would be all right. Still, it made me nervous.

I followed them out on the porch, trailed by Leonard, Jim Bob, and Al. We watched them trot away. Yes, I look at women's asses. You have to have some vices. Those fine asses went on down the road and out of sight.

"That one you call Vanilla," Al said. "She taken?"

"Good luck with that, buddy," Jim Bob said. "I've used all my bullshit and some truth too; none of it warms her up. Only person she seems to like is Hap, and for the life of me, with me standing here looking at the motherfucker, I can't figure it out. And Brett, she's taken. And I can't figure that out either."

"Why I didn't mention her," Al said. "I know she's taken. Come to think of it, I ought to give up on women and take up with donkeys. I'm not doing too well on any of my choices, for that matter, and not just my romantic partners. My lawyer is a shyster, and maybe he's also this sinister Johnny Joe, and he's connected to that conniving bitch Earline. It comes to being a good judge of character, it ain't me."

"About the size of it," Leonard said.

"Want me to run down the road so you'll have something to look at?" Jim Bob asked Leonard.

"I can do without seeing your old saggy old ass wiggling along," Leonard said.

"I know better than that," Jim Bob said, and slapped himself on the ass. "That there, boys, is USDA prime."

69

Scully is a little community that was once a town back in the old days. It slowly diminished over time, and then LaBorde grew out that way.

Now I suppose you could call Scully a kind of suburb of LaBorde, though it's mostly rural with pastures and cattle, a few spotty businesses like the Dollar Store and a Circle K. It's biggest claim to fame, up until the eighties, was its roller-skating rink. Lot of people went there. They had numerous birthday parties and even sleepovers for the kids. Parent chaperones. Ice cream and cake. Considerable puking.

Well before dark, I had Brett drop me and Leonard off at the stretch of trees next to the little blacktop road near the creek. No one seemed to be watching.

I had a shotgun with me and a pistol under my coat. Leonard was carrying the same setup. I also feel obligated to mention that he was wearing what I call a train engineer's hat, bought obviously at Stupid Hats Are Us. It was black and he wore it cocked at an angle.

Brett drove away. We edged through the trees, found a place where we could jump across the creek, more of a brook, really. We eased into the cover of the trees on the other side of it.

We lay down on the damp leaves and waited.

"This is crazy," Leonard said.

"That's why I asked Vanilla and Jim Bob to get here early. My guess is Vanilla is in one of the trees with that weird plastic rifle. Girl can climb like a monkey and shoot good as or better than me. Hell, she might be perched above us."

"I've yet to see a shooter better than you," Leonard said. "And the rub is you don't know one kind of weapon from another unless it's a club you're carrying. Ain't fair, man. I've spent a lot of time at the shooting range trying to be decent, and you can get up in the morning, blow a fart, and shoot better than Billy Dixon. Naturally good eyesight, hand-eye coordination, I guess. Goddamn genetics."

"I don't think much about it. I just shoot."

"That's what I mean. That's the part annoys me. And you mostly hit what you're aiming at."

"With shotguns, both of us will hit what we aim at."

We lay there awhile. Some shadows were mixing with the pink of the falling sun.

"Ground is damp and cold, Hap. I want to go home."

"You want to be here more than me."

"Truth," he said. "But I like to complain."

"I know that."

"Did you bring any gum?"

"I hardly ever chew gum. And since when do you want gum?"

"Since I got bored."

"Gum will cure boredom?"

"Gives me something to do."

"Do the times tables in your head."

"Didn't want to do that shit when I was in school, so why would I do it for fun?"

"I didn't say it was fun. It's something to do."

"I get over times ten, I kind of get lost. Could pull a Louis C.K. Ask permission to take my dick out and beat it until it screams for mercy and spits mayonnaise."

"I do not give you permission. And that's not mayonnaise, no matter what your mama told you."

"Hell, and I been putting it on my bread, using it to mix tuna fish."

"You are nasty, Leonard."

"How about I Spy? I spy something white in dark clothes."

"A preacher."

"No."

"Leonard, I know you're going to say it's me. White guy in dark clothes, but that's too silly and too easy."

"I didn't want to strain your brain."

"Let's just shut our little mouths and keep our little eyes open and see how Olivia's information shakes out."

"Crazy she'd ask just me and you to come. That's like saying 'Come on out, we're going to strip you naked, cover your balls in pork-chop grease, tie you up, and let you visit a pride of lions that haven't eaten in a week.'"

"That's what I thought. Though not with the whole lion idea and all. Why I didn't follow her instructions."

"How about movie trivia?" Leonard said.

"No."

"Book trivia?"

"Again, shut your little mouth and keep your little eyes open."

"Me and Pookie are definitely getting married, by the way. If I don't get killed tonight, you'll be my best dude."

"Dude?"

"You get killed, I'm thinking about pulling someone off the street. Both of us get killed, you'll save on buying a suit and I'll save on a deposit for a venue."

"Congratulations. Let's don't get killed tonight if a wedding's truly in the offing."

"It is."

"When?"

"Still kicking it around, but it's agreed."

"Who's going to walk you down the aisle?"

"Nobody. And nobody is going to walk Pookie either."

"Will you be wearing that hat when you get married?"

"Maybe," Leonard said.

"Are you going to go 'choo-choo' all the way up the aisle? Will you call yourself Thomas the Tank Engine?"

"I'll be Casey Jones."

"He ran his steam engine off a ditch, got scalded to death by the steam."

"No."

"How it turned out. Well, I mixed 'Wreck of the Old Ninety-Seven' into 'Casey Jones.'"

"I'll be someone else, then, but a train theme might be in the making."

"I know it won't be a church wedding, so what's the scoop on who's officiating?" I asked.

"Not sure yet. Like I said, don't even know where. I was thinking a boxing referee. They can marry you, right?"

"I don't think so."

"Ah, a train engineer. They got to be like a ship's captain, right?"

"I don't think so. But for a venue, bet you could rent this old skating rink cheap."

"That's a thought. Hope we don't shoot the place up the too bad."

70

It was a clear night. Starlight and moonlight. No rain for a change.

We were braced for things to go down ugly, to have been betrayed by Olivia.

It sounded to me that the reason it was out of the way was that it was a trap, and she had set it. If it was a trap, we wouldn't be walking into it blind, and not with just the two of us. It sounded strange to me that Olivia was insistent that we not bring anyone with us; from her perspective we were the ones in charge. Taking us out would be a good start if she was trying to make high marks with Johnny Joe. We had rocked his boat a little, and killing us before we really became a problem might set it right.

Jim Bob had convinced us that Al's lawyer was the man we were actually looking for, Johnny Joe. My guess was Johnny Joe had some idea that Jim Bob had his number. I remembered how they had looked at each other. Two old badgers feeling something was wrong, that there was a stench in the air.

Al had one of his accountants checking on his money and was putting a stop on the lawyer doing anything with his funds. That still might not keep it all from ending up in Johnny Joe's hands. The foreign money, the illegal money, wasn't exactly FDIC-insured.

I was thinking on all that when on the far left where the creek turned between a thinner stretch of trees, I saw a small light in the woods. Could that be Jim Bob or Vanilla?

"See it?" Leonard said.

"Yeah."

The light hopped a little and went out.

The light didn't come back on. We waited.

And waited.

Then there was a sound like someone trying to stifle a cough in church. There was a rattling in the trees behind us, a stray shot.

"A silencer," Leonard said.

Another cough, and the dirt kicked up in front of us. It was so close, some of the dirt went into my mouth. I spat it out and we crawled back into the deeper cover of the woods.

There was yet another cough, but this one didn't sound the same. It sounded more like how a puppy sounds when it has kennel cough.

Had I also heard a kind of moan from the woods? I couldn't be sure.

No more shots were fired at us, but whoever had fired that shot had seen us. Which meant the shooter had a nightscope and had been peering through it and located us. After all, we were expected.

The second sound, the kennel-cough bark, must have been Vanilla firing her weapon.

We waited some more, trying to figure what was next. Fearing the shooter might be changing directions in such a way he could see us with his nightscope. We eased even farther back, each of us behind a tree in deeper shadow.

Another muffled shot, this time from the opposite direction. It whistled over our heads and smacked into a tree, spraying pine bark. There was another shooter, and somehow, they were at an angle where they could see us, even if only a little bit.

There was that other coughing sound again, the puppy with kennel cough. To our right, a shadow fell out of a tree and landed on the ground so hard, it made my soul hurt.

A minute passed.

Then another.

We heard someone behind us.

It was Jim Bob. He was crossing the creek.

"Don't get your panties in a bunch," he said.

"Better get down," I said. "Someone's shooting."

"I got a feeling it's done," he said. "Might be another asshole in a tree or among them, but I doubt it. I can guarantee you without looking, Vanilla got them both, and that's all she wrote."

"Unless someone's in the rink," Leonard said.

"Nope," Jim Bob said. "Just came from there, snuck in and looked, trailed back around along the creek, came out here. You know the plumbing in the rink still works, maybe the electricity. Must still use the building for something."

We waited quite a while longer, then crawled up toward the front of the trees. Jim Bob walked forward as we crawled. He didn't so much as slouch.

Out to the left we could see Vanilla carrying the black plastic rifle, which was little more than a tube. It had a nightscope on it that was also simple and streamlined. She was walking across the grassy clearing toward us like maybe she had been to the powder room and was strolling back.

71

Turns out Olivia is not a good person," Jim Bob said.

"I feared as much," I said.

"She had a stupid plan," Vanilla said.

"You two seem confident that's all the shooters there are," Leonard said.

We were all standing at the edge of the trees, perfect targets if there were others hiding in or amongst the trees. Leonard and I were brushing damp dirt, pine needles, and leaves off the front of our clothes.

"I assume they felt they would get you two in a cross fire, snipe you out before you even got to the rink," Vanilla said. "They must have thought you were pretty dumb and would come without backup."

"Sort of hurts my feelings," Leonard said.

We walked into the woods where the last shooter had fallen out of a tree. Looking up, in the beam of Jim Bob's flashlight, we could see one of those climbing deer stands, kind that you could use to scramble up with, then position against the tree. The deer needed to up their game.

Jim Bob pooled the light beam around the head of the dead man on the ground. He was dressed in black and had a black cap that had partially slipped off. He was one of the men that had been on the boat when we were swamped and Hanson was shot.

Good.

Jim Bob bent down and looked him over, went through his pockets. He found a wallet, but he didn't find any identification in it. What he did find, he put in his coat pocket. It looked like some receipts. "Got him through the heart, Vanilla. That was some shooting."

"I'm some shooter," she said. "Also, the nightscope helped."

"Still, at that distance, and that being low caliber, that was some shot," he said.

We walked across the clearing to the other side of the woods. There was another body there lying under a tree. A lean woman dressed in black. Most of her head was missing. Vanilla searched her, found nothing.

"She came and sat right under the tree I'd climbed," Vanilla said. "And I would like to report that I didn't use any kind of device to climb that tree. Strapped the rifle on my back and climbed up."

"Not a lot of low limbs," I said. "So that's impressive."

"Use your arms and feet right and you're in shape, you can climb easily enough."

No. I couldn't do that even if I were in prime shape. Vanilla must have been part squirrel.

"I'll give her this," Vanilla said. "She had stealth. I was sitting in the tree and didn't hear her come up under it until she fired a shot. If she had been a little farther away, I wouldn't have heard the silencer. Looked down, there she was."

"That was lucky for us," Leonard said.

"No," Vanilla said. "Luck was not involved. I would have got her anyway."

Must be wonderful to have that kind of confidence. And must be wonderful to deserve it.

I pulled out my cell and called Brett to pick me and Leonard up where she had dropped us off. She was waiting not far down the road.

Jim Bob and Vanilla went deeper into the woods and across to his car, wherever he had parked it.

"All we did tonight was lie down in the goddamn dirt," Leonard said.

"I'm okay with that," I said.

72

"Olivia, Olivia, Olivia," Leonard said. "You are a very bad girl."

All five us were inside Olivia's house. Me, Leonard, Jim Bob, Vanilla, and Brett. Olivia was wearing pajamas and her feet were bare. She had green-painted toenails. They matched her fingernails.

"You broke in," Olivia said. "That's against the law."

"So is setting someone up to be killed," Leonard said. "And technically we didn't break into anything. Jim Bob picked the lock."

"You need better security," he said.

"So this is your help," Olivia said, eyeing everyone.

"Uh-huh," I said.

We were standing. She was sitting on her couch. She looked small and sad in her oversize brown and white pajamas.

"I didn't have any choice," she said. "I wanted to warn you after I did it. I been sick about it, but I couldn't say anything. I couldn't."

"Laryngitis?" Brett said.

"They kidnapped my son and killed my ex-husband," she said. "They did their research. They knew all about me. Now they'll kill Berry."

I had noticed pictures of her and a child in several photos framed on the wall. Some showed the child as a baby, others as a toddler, a couple of him as a preteen.

"From where did they kidnap him?" Jim Bob asked.

"Wells," she said. "My ex-husband lives there. It was his time to have our son for a while. They took my ex-husband too, but they killed him. I've seen the photos. They showed me that my son is still alive."

"Do you have those photos?" Leonard asked.

She nodded. "And a video."

"Let's see them," Vanilla said.

Olivia went to get them, and Brett went with her. Olivia tried anything funny, Brett would certainly knock the hell out of her. She was big-time worked up over Olivia trying to have me killed.

Olivia and Brett came back, and Olivia pulled up the photos and the video. We took turns looking at them. The first shots were of a man lying on the ground in a ditch. His head was covered in blood.

Other photos showed the boy. He was close to the camera and he looked frightened. If you could wipe that fear off his face, he would be a good-looking kid. No one looks terrific when terrified.

There was a video where the boy asked his mommy to do what they'd told her to so they wouldn't hurt him anymore. Which meant, of course, they had hurt him or had convinced him they would if he didn't say what they wanted. After all, they had killed Berry's father.

"They contacted me, told me they had Berry, had killed Earl. They told me what I needed to do. I didn't feel like I had a choice."

"Justin?" Leonard said.

"What I said about him wasn't true," she said. "I had to come up with a story, for Berry's sake."

"You made up the part about his sick son?" Leonard said.

"He's sick, but it's not that bad," she said. "They think they got it on the run, and he'll be fine. I don't know exactly what it is, but it's curable. I picked that up through scuttlebutt. I don't know the real details, but it's what I could come up with."

"Where's your ex-husband's body?" Jim Bob asked. "Has it been found?"

Olivia shook her head. "Not that I know of. My guess, they shot him, then took the organs, like the others."

"This is like being in an *Alice in Wonderland* universe," Brett said. "Olivia, I ought to take that lamp and beat your teeth out."

"Hold on," I said. "That lamp looks expensive."

"No," Brett said. "I'm not as forgiving as you are. It's her, the lamp, and me."

"I did what I had to do," Olivia said. "And now they'll kill Berry, harvest his organs. They will, you know. They are ruthless."

"We know," I said.

Vanilla took some plastic gloves from her coat pocket and pulled them on. She went into Olivia's bedroom. We could hear her clattering around in there.

"What's she doing?" Olivia said.

"Looking for lies," Jim Bob said.

73

Justin was in Olivia's living room with us. We had called him over. When Brett let him in the front door, a cold wind like death's breath came in with him. Even after the door was shut, it took a few moments for the room to warm.

Justin said, "I'm sick to my stomach learning this."

Olivia didn't say anything, just hung her head.

"Think how we feel," I said. "Those henchmen were trying to kill me and Leonard, and she set us up."

Brett, Jim Bob, and Vanilla had all found seats in the living room. Me and Leonard and Justin stood.

"But you killed them," Justin said.

"We didn't kill anyone," Leonard said. "Imagine our disappointment."

"You're saying the snipers hid in the woods and shot themselves so they could get out of the weather and you could go home," Justin said.

"I killed them both," Vanilla said.

"Don't yank me," Justin said.

"I killed them," she said. "Had I not, they would have killed Hap and Leonard. Or tried."

"Who are you?" Justin asked her.

"Cosmetology school didn't work out," Vanilla said. "So I became an assassin. Call me Vanilla."

"Now you'll be called a prisoner," Justin said.

"That won't happen," Vanilla said. She didn't raise her voice or look mad or worried. She looked certain.

Jim Bob said, "Olivia, if she's telling the whole truth, may not have had much choice."

"I'm telling the truth," Olivia said.

"If so," Jim Bob said, "she did what she thought she had to do. I'm not saying she should get a wink and a pat on the back, but I don't think she's the stone-cold mastermind in all this. I think they played her. Remember, they have her son, and her ex-husband is dead."

"I still don't like her," Brett said.

Justin took a deep breath and let it out. "This is getting somewhat complicated."

"Tell us about it," Leonard said. "Look here, man, you wanted us to kill these guys off the books, and we did. In self-defense, so don't turn all self-righteous on us now. The rest of them are still out there, the master-mind, whatever the fuck his true name is, and Purple Eyes. And they have Olivia's son."

"Yeah," I said. "I'm not in love with what Olivia did, but I get it."

Justin pursed his lips and thought on things.

"Best we don't say you two aren't dead," Justin said. "I think we get out in the news that two bodies were found at the roller rink, and that will be true. But we don't say which bodies."

"Bad guys see it, they'll think it's Hap and Leonard," Jim Bob said.

"Right," Justin said. "Hap and Leonard are thought dead. And if they were going to spare your child, Olivia, he'll be spared. But you can bet on this: they'll want more before they let him go."

"If they let him go," she said.

"I don't mean to be a party pooper," Brett said, "but he could already be gone. I think it needs to be said."

"Until we know otherwise," Justin said, "we consider him alive."

"You know what happens next, don't you?" Vanilla said. "They used Olivia. They don't need her anymore. They'll come for her."

Olivia didn't burst out crying. She lifted her head and said, "We have to stop them. Chief, I know I fucked up, but I have to think my son could be alive. I want to help catch them. No matter which way it is."

"I wouldn't trust her to wipe her own ass," Brett said. "I think she's a conniving, lying bitch."

Brett was beginning to vibrate a bit, and I thought for a moment she might vibrate into another dimension.

"Hold on that decision a moment," Jim Bob said. He pulled the papers he had taken off one of the dead assassins out of his coat pocket. "I looked these over. I been thinking about what's here, and it gives me an idea."

74

Chief Justin called it an informal arrest, and that meant, for the moment, Olivia was traveling to the safe house with us.

Brett blindfolded her and made the blindfold extra-tight. Olivia was put in the back seat of Justin's car, told to lie down and stay down. Brett rode with Justin to make sure she stayed down. My lady was looking for any reason to smack her.

I thought about my daughter, Chance. Would I have done what Olivia did? I think I would have found another way, but had another way not presented itself, I might have done the same thing.

When we got to the safe house, Al met us at the door. He said, "There's this one-eyed guy that showed up."

I was the first on the doorstep, and as soon as he said it, I said, "Veil."

Veil was waiting inside. He was standing by the sink, his back against it, sipping a cup of coffee. He had on a black eye patch. His skin was thin and colorless, his hair was gray, and the suit he wore was gray. If he had been wearing a tie against his gray shirt, he would have looked like a Mafia boss on his way to a formal sit-down. He looked thinner than usual and had aged significantly. The good eye still had a sparkle to it.

"Veil, old friend," I said.

"Hillbilly, how are you?" He had a sharp New York accent.

"Been better," I said as he put down his coffee so we could shake hands.

"Al here has been telling me your woes."

"He doesn't know the all of it," I said.

The others were filing in.

"Where's your car, and how did you find us?" I said.

"Really, Hillbilly, you have to ask? I can find anyone anywhere."

"Means who we're hiding from can do the same," I said.

"Maybe, but then, I'm not like them."

He certainly wasn't.

Leonard came over, said, "Been a while."

Veil nodded.

They didn't care much for each other, but Veil had once defended Leonard in a court of law, and it had worked out well for Leonard. It was a wild case, and Veil had used a novel defense, but it worked.

"You still a lawyer?" Leonard asked.

"I am, but I don't practice much. Not law, anyway."

I introduced Veil to those that didn't know him. I didn't try and explain him to Justin or Olivia. Even Al, who had been talking to him nonstop, didn't really know that much about him. I knew that because Veil rarely revealed much beyond his surface.

For that matter, even though I considered him a friend, I didn't know that much about him outside of our interactions. I saw him rarely, but now and again I got a handwritten note from him. I thought warmly of him. We had a bit of history, and it was hardcase history.

Now we were all seated except Veil. He stood against the living-room wall near the door.

Justin looked around, said, "So you've gathered a team."

"Olivia is not on that team," Brett said.

"I'm aware," Justin said.

Jim Bob took a few minutes to give Veil and Al the dope, all that had happened. When he finished, Veil said, "What's next? Get to the point."

"You're a bit tense there, gray man," Jim Bob said.

"You don't want to see me tenser," Veil said.

"Don't look at me like I'm a turd you could roll uphill with a stick," Jim Bob said.

Veil's coat fanned open. A gun was suddenly in his hand. He wasn't pointing it at anyone.

"I don't roll turds uphill," Veil said. "But I can shoot one."

Jim Bob slowly grinned.

Vanilla let out a little laugh.

"Now that you boys have shown your dicks," Brett said, looking at Jim Bob, "what exactly is the plan you got?"

"Saved it until we were all together," he said. "What do we do with Olivia?"

Olivia had been sitting quietly. Back at her place, we had allowed her to change out of her pajamas. She had on jeans, tennis shoes, a sweatshirt, and a leather jacket.

"I'm sorry," Olivia said. "I was scared for Berry. I'm even more scared now. Would I do it again? Probably. But I didn't know what to do. They killed my ex, and they threatened my child."

Jim Bob said, "Olivia, you want to have some redemption, let me ask a question of you. Were you supposed to report to your boss, Johnny Joe or whoever, when the job was done?"

"No," Olivia said. "The ones they sent to kill Leonard and Hap were supposed to report."

"That's out of the question now," I said.

"Yeah," Jim Bob said. "But we can move on them."

"First we got to know where they are," Leonard said.

"I have some idea," Jim Bob said. "But Chief, I'm thinking you might not ought to know this. Things go bad, you can deny you know anything."

"You're right," Justin said. "And Olivia, I'm going to place you under house arrest with an ankle bracelet. It won't be an official arrest, but I can't take you to jail. Johnny Joe already knows too much, and just in case there's someone else on his payroll, on the inside, I'd prefer they not know you've been arrested."

"I truly am sorry," Olivia said.

"Just don't try and fuck us anymore than you have," Justin said. "Stay in the house."

"Nothing matters to me except Berry," Olivia said. "Please save him."

She and Justin left in his car.

Jim Bob reached into his coat pocket, took out the receipts he had removed from the dead shooter, put them on the coffee table, began to smooth them out.

75

All these receipts are for coffee from the filling station on the highway, same side as the roller rink," Jim Bob said. "Station is just down the way from the roller rink. The receipts date several days in a row. That means to me they were posted somewhere near the station and the roller rink."

Veil, pale-faced and sweat-popped, said, "They came there by car, or they walked. Did you find a car key on them?"

"No," Jim Bob said.

"Means they probably parked the car nearby and walked down to the shooter spot," Veil said. "Key is probably with it. Find the car, you might find out more about them. Car has to be within walking distance of that roller rink."

"Someone could have dropped them off," Vanilla said.

"True," Veil said. "Here's another thought. The boy must have been with them. Which means he's most likely nearby. If he's alive."

"Then we need to go now," Brett said.

"Too many of us and it's a mess," Veil said. "Me and Hillbilly will go."

"I'm not leaving Hap dangling," Leonard said. "Where he goes I go."

"Me and the girls are gonna hang," Jim Bob said.

"We can talk about boys," Brett said.

Jim Bob said, "Me, I want to talk about makeup and such. Listen here, guys. You got your burner phones. If you need to make a call, toss the burners afterward. I got a bagful. Veil, you need one?"

"Got my own," he said.

We walked outside. Veil said, "Let's take my car. I have my things there."

We followed him over to the barn. His black SUV was parked inside.

We climbed into the SUV, Veil behind the wheel, me shotgun, Leonard in the back. Moments later, we were on the highway.

"Putting me in the back of the bus," Leonard said. "You know that shit ain't right."

Wires were leaking out of a large tote bag that Leonard was lifting. "Heavy," he said.

Veil turned in his seat a little. "Push the wires into the bag, gently, and put that aside. It's best you don't play with it. Don't make me turn this car around, Leonard."

"You're always so mean to me," Leonard said.

76

As we drove in the direction of the roller rink, Veil said, "I'm going to say this now, and then we won't speak of it again, going to get it out of the way."

"Get what out of the way?" Leonard asked.

"I have a cancer and it's well advanced and I don't have much time left," Veil said. "I'm glad you asked me to help. It's my last worthy moment."

"What do the doctors say?" I asked.

"That I have some very black lungs and I shouldn't plan on a tour of Europe or, for that matter, plan to do much of anything except choose a crematorium."

"Sorry, Veil," I said.

"Yeah," Leonard said. "That sucks."

"No one gets out of this alive," Veil said. "I embrace death to be rid of the discomfort and the pain. I take a pharmacy of pills just to walk around a bit from day to day. The sweat you see has nothing to do with the weather."

"Yep," Leonard said. "It's a little chilly for that."

"Okay," Veil said. "It's been discussed."

We rode in silence. When we got to the roller rink, Veil drove us out to the filling station where the would-be assassin's coffee had been purchased. It was closed this late, but when we got there, Veil said, "We'll cruise back from here, look for a side road. That's where they would leave their car."

"There's one," Leonard said, leaning over the seat, pointing to a side road.

"Not close enough," Veil said. "They had to walk carrying rifles. They'd have been seen, because going through that patch of woods would take some work. They'd want to start as close to where they needed to be as possible."

We were almost to the roller rink. We saw a narrow road that went up through the trees. It was mostly grown over and had probably never been prominent. It was little more than a trail. Veil drove down it, the limbs slapping the windshield, gently scraping the side of the SUV.

And there it was. A black SUV not unlike the one we were in, a later model, maybe. It was parked on the side of the road.

We got out and walked to the car. You could stand there and look over the roof and see the roller rink through the trees.

"They started here," Veil said. "One stayed on this side, the other went behind the rink and into the trees over there, if I understand your stories right."

"You do," I said. "The woman was in the trees, the man in this patch here."

"That Vanilla can shoot, if she shot across that gap between trees and hit her target," Veil said.

"Oh, yeah, she can shoot," Leonard said.

Veil took a pair of blue plastic gloves from his coat pocket and then pulled out a device made of folded metal slides that linked together. He folded them out and they locked in place. He used it to lock-jock the goons' SUV, and within instants he had the door open.

He bent inside and looked around. We stood back, making sure we were out of the way. After a few minutes, he pulled something out of the SUV and held it up.

We drew close to have a look.

It was a piece of paper with some numbers on it.

"One of them wrote down an address, or at least the house numbers," he said. "Probably trying to find the place set up for them to stay."

"We have numbers, but they could be to anyplace," Leonard said.

"I think it's not that far away," Veil said. "They could have put it on their phone, so we're lucky they were the sort that used pen and paper."

He closed up the SUV, and, with us back in his ride, he turned around and pointed us toward the highway and drove us out there. We came to the station and parked momentarily in front of it.

"They could have been anywhere," Leonard said. "Far out somewhere. Stopped here in the mornings to get their juice."

"No," Veil said. "These numbers fit the across-the-highway numbers."

What he meant was the station number was an even one; the odd ones would be on the other side of the highway.

Veil drove us across the highway. There was a house there. We could read its address painted on the curb. The numbers were the same as on the paper. We pulled up the drive and around back of it.

No one came out of the house and took a shot at us. No one unleashed a dog on us. No lights went on in the house.

In the glow of the dash lights, Veil said, "We either have the right number and no one's home or we have the right number and there are others in there. I doubt the latter. Figured you guys would be easy to pop, that's my guess, so they just sent the two. But, be wise, because I could be wrong."

"They were certainly wrong about us being easy to pop," Leonard said.

"Thanks to Vanilla," I said, "we're still here."

We got out of the SUV.

Veil said, "Caution."

77

Veil used a penlight to guide us.

There were vines on a trellis and they grew bravely against the cold and were actually quite green in the glow from the penlight. They ran up that latticework in thick lines and wrapped around the covered back porch. Veil, his gloves on again, opened the screen door and we stopped onto the enclosed porch. There were two rusty metal chairs there and a round metal table.

We stood there a moment and listened. Not even a mouse fart.

Veil gave us plastic gloves, used his lockpick to get us in. It was so fast, it was as if he had a key.

Inside it was dark, and the house felt strange. It's hard to describe that, and I'm not one to believe in supernatural things, but I've come across it before. When you could feel something wrong inside a house without seeing anything. You just knew.

Of course, that may have had to do with the fact we were inside the house formerly occupied by two people who had tried to kill us, so it was hard to think of the previous owners living here before they put it on the rental market. Hard to imagine them having Thanksgiving and Christmas, making love in the bedroom, maybe having kids and dogs running about. But some of that must have happened at one point in time.

Now whoever had lived there in the past was gone and there was a feeling of dread about the place, real or imagined. With Veil using his penlight, we moved through the kitchen. He floated the light about. There were some dirty dishes in the sink and a trash can full of Styrofoam coffee cups from the station across the highway. There were also some fast-food wrappers. For all I knew, they hadn't rented the place at all but had found an unoccupied space to move into and rigged the utilities.

There was an open wall that went into a wide living room full of too much unmatching furniture. The house smelled musty, and the furniture having cloth cushions was probably part of that. The place hadn't been aired in ages.

Yeah. The shooters had just taken the house over, no doubt.

I carefully opened a bedroom door. It smelled of urine and defecation in there. I had thought the place was empty, but there was someone lying on the bed. I pulled my pistol and pointed it in that direction. The figure didn't move. I focused the light on the person's face.

It was a kid. His eyes were closed. His legs were wrapped in duct tape. So were his hands. There were strips of it that ran across the bed and pinned him there.

It was Berry.

I rushed over to him. He didn't move. I put my pistol away and touched the side of his neck with my fingers, searching for a pulse.

It was weak but he had one.

He was alive.

78

While we waited on the ambulance and the police, we searched through the house. I had cut the tape loose from Berry, and he made a bit of a noise. It was somewhere between a cough and a throw-up but wasn't quite either.

With the tight tape off him, he was moving slightly. No races would be run, but he was relieved a bit and his body flexed, even though he was mostly unconscious.

He didn't know me from Mother Goose. Didn't know I was there. He was dehydrated and in a bad way, but the EMTs would be there within minutes and they could do more for him than I could.

"Well," Veil said, "when they went for the kill, they left their phones and wallets, and here they are."

We were standing in another bedroom down the hallway. Veil slipped the phones and wallets into his pocket. One of the wallets was actually a small purse.

"They were sleeping together," Veil said.

"I hope they had a good fuck before Vanilla killed them," I said.

"I hope they didn't," Leonard said.

"You boys think about the strangest things," Veil said.

79

Berry wasn't doing so good, and Chief Justin said he wouldn't have lasted much longer in the house. Berry was dehydrated bad, and due to his keepers being killed, he would have died from lack of care. But there was also this: If they hadn't been killed, they would have killed him. No way Olivia would have gotten her son back from them. She was most likely scheduled for termination herself. That way, all roads from Olivia and Berry would have led to nothing.

The way Chief Justin played it was, we had found him and been Good Samaritans. Of course, why we were in the house wasn't something easily explained, but Justin told us he'd figure that part out. We had done good. He didn't ask for any more information than he needed to fake our work, so to speak.

It hadn't been Justin's plan, and Hanson had had some doubts about Justin, but when it came to this, at least, he was on our side.

We didn't mention that Veil had their wallets and phones in his coat pocket.

We had to answer some questions, so it wasn't entirely easy, but we finished that and came dragging into the safe house as the sun came up. Needles of pink shot through the trees and tore the shadows up.

We slept. The wallets and phones needed to be examined, but we had done what we could up to that point. Now our bodies needed rest.

Later that day, I awoke to a hand on my crotch and a kiss on my ear. I hoped it wasn't Jim Bob.

It wasn't.

Brett said, "How do you feel?"

"Which part?"

"Any part."

"There's one part that seems to be doing quite well."

"I can tell. What about the rest of you?"

"The rest of me is less erect, but, you know, I don't mind a bit of pain and sacrifice if it leads to your pleasure."

"And yours."

"True. That's what I was really worried about."

What followed took a while due to the fact I was tired but also due to the fact that neither of us wanted to be in a hurry.

80

After we showered and dressed, we came out into the living room. The sun was bright and warm through the window and it made the room look strange, somehow, as if everything was plastic.

Jim Bob was telling a story that was making everyone but Veil laugh.

Leonard never laughed at any of my stories or jokes.

When Jim Bob finished, Veil, sitting upright in a chair, said, "What's the point?"

"That it's funny, Veil," Jim Bob said.

"Who says it was funny?" Veil said.

"Well, somebody was laughing."

"It wasn't me."

"No," Jim Bob said. "I suppose not."

Jim Bob looked up from his comfy living-room chair, took in me and Brett, then smiled his hundred-watt smile. Me and Brett went into the kitchen, made coffee, dragged some stale cake doughnuts out of the refrigerator. Jim Bob said, "We thought we heard some bedsprings squeaking."

"Do tell," Brett said.

"It sounded like the mice in my couch were having a stroke, there was so much squeaking," Al said.

Veil, tired of bullshit, said, "I looked at the wallets and phones. I think we can find them. Anyone up for a trip to Colorado?"

That got our attention. Brett and I carried our meager breakfasts into the living room.

"The shooters Vanilla whacked are out of Colorado," Veil said.

"Al's daughter and her girlfriend went to Colorado on vacation," I said.

"Yeah," Al said. "And my understanding is Alice was never the same afterward."

"Most likely," Veil said, "your daughter saw something that scared her, and it may have been something to get her to work with them, get insurance money from you and your wife."

"I see," Al said. He looked as if he might turn into a puddle of water.

"My guess is, Alice didn't want to play ball, and that led to her death and everything else that has happened that has to do with you and your wife," Veil said. "Purple Eyes might have thought she had Alice hooked, but Alice wasn't as hooked as she'd thought, and so she had to be disposed of, and Purple Eyes had to pretend to be her. Riskier, but she got away with it."

"And she fucked me into submission," Al said.

"That sweet thing is powerful stuff," Jim Bob said. "I know many a grown man and some not so grown that have been wounded by it, and it doesn't even have any sharp edges."

"I think what deeply attracts me to this group," Vanilla said, "is the class."

"Just listen," Veil said. "Hap, can you hand me my laptop? On the kitchen table."

"Ain't got no bones in your legs, Veil?" Jim Bob said.

"It's all right," I said. I went and got it.

Jim Bob eyed me as I handed the laptop to Veil and sat down.

Veil opened the laptop and downloaded the contents of the assassins' phones to it. He opened files, showed what was there to those of us on the screen side, then moved the laptop around for the others to see.

It was the assassins' video and photo libraries. I thought: Even killers like to take photos of landscapes and nice selfies.

As we went on Veil began to point certain things out, and finally what it all came down to was some geography that wasn't East Texas, or any of Texas, for that matter. It was high, wooded mountains, and there were towns, and one of the towns was split by a highway. Someone was filming while another drove. Eventually there were still photos of what looked like a theme park. There were roller-coaster tracks with roller-coaster cars. There were concession stands. Spinning-wheel rides. But there were wrecked cars and broken machinery as well. It was an enormous scrapy-ard. At the back of the yard was a large house that seemed out place, as if inserted into the property while no one was looking.

It was two stories tall, painted blue and white. The photo of the house was not a good one, and the lemon sunlight bled over the roof and the sides of the house in an unnatural manner. There was a shape at the window, mostly shadow.

Then there was a video of the female assassin Vanilla had killed. All of her head was there. She was alive and had an interesting face and unnaturally large eyes, green as Ireland. She was sitting in a swing that was part of a row of swings, and she was swinging higher and higher, giggling like a little girl. Off camera, I could hear a man laugh, a deep-chested laugh.

She jumped off the swing as it swung toward the phone camera. She leaped so far, she must have landed in her partner's arms, because the camera swung wide and blurred. Then they were facing the camera, and a selfie was taken. The man was the man we had found in the woods, having been shot out of the tree. Close-cropped hair, slight growth of beard, and a tan face. It was crazy to see them having fun, doing what normal people do, and then to think of them in the woods, the man shot through the body, the woman missing part of her head.

There were more videos, and we watched a lot of them. Finally, Veil paused one, said, "This is where they are."

"You can't know that," Jim Bob said. "And besides, where is that place?"

"Your girl Alice went to Colorado with Purple Eyes, right, Al?"

"Right," Al said.

"This is Colorado," Veil said. "I know the topography. I know some of the places. I've been there a few times on various matters. My take is the man sometimes called Johnny Joe, sometimes Graham, works different sections of the country. He wears one section out, he moves on. But in time he comes back. East Texas has had a run, and maybe they are still here. Could be. But I think the assassins were set to take care of you, Hillbilly, and Leonard. Didn't work out. There are a lot of calls on these phones from Colorado, fewer to Colorado. I think Johnny Joe and Purple Eyes are back in Colorado. At least one of them, and the shots are being called from there. When they regroup, they'll come at you again. From what little I know, I can assure you they are vengeful types. Right now, he may have no idea his killers failed, but he's bound to suspect it. He's there safe in Colorado, and maybe he's left some others here, maybe even the girl. But things have been hot, and his attempt to eliminate you two hasn't been so successful. He's trying to get out of your sight. I have another reason to think he is there."

"But you don't know. These two visiting a carnival doesn't prove anything," Leonard said.

"Did anyone note anything unusual about the carnival?" Veil said.

"That house at the back—what an odd location," Brett said.

Veil nodded. "Yeah. That's it. My thought is the house has been moved in recently. The stone supports holding up the porch aren't completely settled. I think the carnival and all the wrecks, the land that holds them, has been purchased as their headquarters."

"It's like our man's lair," Vanilla said.

"Seems that way," Veil said. "And it didn't take much research to find where the place is. I've even seen it from the air with Google Maps. But there is one thing in the videos the assassins made of themselves that is most curious to me, outside of the date on them being a couple days before Vanilla mopped them up."

Veil tapped some keys. The video piece with the house at the back of the carnival was pulled up again. He tapped some more keys and moved the mouse, and now the shot slipped past the swing set and went close on the house and the shape at the window.

"I've never met your man, but tell me if you might recognize this person."

Everyone came around behind Veil and leaned forward for a look.

It wasn't a great shot. Someone standing in shadow at a window that looked out onto the front porch.

But when Veil brought the image closer, adjusted the shot to make it clearer, we could see most of the face. It was the man I had known briefly as Al's lawyer Graham. Aka Johnny Joe.

"Well, shit and fall back in it," Jim Bob said.

81

In the early night the rain came back, and while it rained, plans were made for us to travel to that spot in Colorado that Veil had discovered. We would take the fight to them. Carry it to the dragon's lair.

No one wanted to sit around and wait for the dragon to show up again and maybe surprise us. It was better that we should surprise the dragon.

Leonard said, "Well, Hap. You know what this calls for, don't you?"

"Hell yeah," I said. "The Elephant of Surprise."

"That's the one," he said.

While the others prepared for the trip, which we would take in cars, me and Brett went for a drive. I drove. I didn't worry about being followed because the thugs, if there were still any in town, had no idea where to follow us from.

The rain was gentle. It made little mud trails across the windshield. The wipers messed it up worse, leaving smears.

"You're going to tell me to stay here, like the big man protecting his woman," Brett said. "Am I right?"

"You are. But not for the reasons you think."

"You mean not for the reasons you're going to give."

"They're good reasons."

"You say."

"Our family is you and me and Chance and, if she doesn't ditch us, Reba. Chance takes care of Reba, but she depends on you for advice. You're like a mother to her. You've said yourself you weren't such a good mother to your children and you were glad for this opportunity with Chance. If something happened to me and Leonard, Chance and Reba would be left hanging."

"Chance does fine. She's grown."

"I know. But Chance needs you. Your moral support. Advice. She admires you, and you know it."

"Maybe," Brett said.

"If all of us get rubbed out, well, she's lost all her moral support and her family. One of us needs to stay here, and that should be you. You know me and Leonard have been through the fire more often than you."

"I been through it a few times," she said.

"A few times. I rest my case. Please stay. Stay at the safe house, because they could come back to our place. They may still have people posted in town. Bet you could arrange for Chance and Reba and Buffy the Dog to come stay with you until we get back."

"Al will still be there, won't he?"

"Until we can get back, yes. He's not safe at home either."

"I don't know, Hap. I lose you, that would be pretty hard to take."

"You could lose me if you go with me," I said.

"We could both lose."

"Why I'm asking you to stay here, for our daughter."

"Our daughter," Brett said. "I like the sound of that."

The rain stayed steady. It had washed the windshield sparkling clean by now. I slowed the wipers.

I drove us all the way to Diboll before turning around. We came back through Nacogdoches, then cut over toward LaBorde, took the long black-top back to the safe house, and parked out front.

Brett leaned over and kissed me. It was a great kiss full of sweetness and mystery.

Hoped it wasn't my last.

82

Me and Leonard rode with Jim Bob. Vanilla and Veil rode together in his SUV; they led us on our trip to Colorado. Of course, no one needed a guide. We knew where we were going, and when we didn't, the GPS did. But we tried to stay within a reasonable distance of one another.

The on-and-off rain was off again. The sun was out and the day was clear, a blue sky, no clouds, just lots of dark birds flying in formation.

Jim Bob said, "I offered to let Vanilla ride with me, take your place, Hap, but she rode with the old guy."

"Face it," I said, "your mojo doesn't work on that gal."

"Something wrong somewhere, because yours does."

"Even a blind hog finds an acorn now and again," Leonard said. "That girl needs a daddy, is the thing."

"I can be a daddy," Jim Bob said.

"Not that kind of daddy," Leonard said.

"What kind would Hap be?"

"I see your point," Leonard said.

"You can quit now," I said.

We rode along for a while. Leonard wanted to stop for water and a pee break, but Jim Bob made him hang on until we came to the outskirts of Dallas.

In the convenience-store bathroom, standing at the urinals, relieving ourselves, Leonard said, "Jim Bob is an asshole."

"Just now noticed that?" I said.

"No. But I like to make note of it from time to time."

"I'm right here," Jim Bob called from the bathroom stall behind us.

"We know," I said.

* * *

Out of East Texas, on past Dallas, the area seemed bleak to me, and the area beyond it bleaker yet. I have said many times it's hard to believe pioneers stopped in these places on purpose. I have to assume the wheels came off their wagons and they gave up and decided to live there next to a water hole.

The length of the ride led to an almost hypnotic boredom that seeped from the head down to the toes and crawled back up again.

We stopped only for food and more pee breaks. The food was good barbecue and bad potato salad. Still, the meat was heavy and it seemed tangled and too warm in my colon. Sitting for so long didn't help either.

Veil called, said maybe we should stop near Palo Duro Canyon for the night, arrive tomorrow fresh.

The motel we ended up at was one of the original ones built in the area. A sign said so. Back then it was called a tourist court. Vanilla got her own room, and Veil and Jim Bob shared one, me and Leonard another.

The room was small and seemed dead. The air had to be stirred up by turning on an old-style air conditioner. It moaned like someone with a bellyache. I knew how it felt. That barbecue and potato salad was still with me and in a tight struggle with one another.

That night, in our beds, Leonard said, "Here we go again."

"Yep."

"I never used to think about this shit, but now I worry I'll get killed and leave Pookie alone."

"He'll get over you. I know I would."

"Fuck you. I'm serious."

"I know," I said. "One reason I convinced Brett to stay home. What family we have, I want preserved. Something happened to me and you, someone is there to carry on."

"It's a funny way to think, isn't it?"

"I don't know," I said. "Not so funny."

"Just never occurred to me too often we could be killed. I mean, you're you and I'm me, and we have been through some serious shit. Nearly died but have always come out of things okay. Now I think about what we're doing and think maybe we won't come out okay."

"We're older, Leonard. And we like our nice cozy homes and our nice cozy lives with our loved ones when we can manage it, and we want to manage it more."

"Also, got to where I need my own toilet to shit in, not some other toilet."

"Me too," I said. "Definite sign of old age. Toilet attachment."

"The commode here rocks when you sit on it," he said.

"Noticed that. And the bed's hard. Used to be, I could sleep on a rock and be all right. I'm like the Princess and the Pea now. I can feel anything and everything. I like my mattress at home. I like my sweet, warm wife."

"And I have neither vanilla cookies nor Dr Peppers with me. And no Pookie."

"Sure sign of the apocalypse," I said.

"Good night, Hap. Don't get killed tomorrow."

"Same to you, brother. Good night."

83

Next day Jim Bob drove into the mountains. It was easy going at first, then the roads narrowed and you could see drop-offs and tumbled rocks. Sometimes there were guardrails and sometimes there was only a thin hope and an inch of gravel between you and a long drop that would end with a boulder in your teeth.

There were snowcaps on the mountains, like cotton dunce caps. I had read before leaving home that a heavy snow was in the offing and much desired for this area due to tourists and skiing.

It turned colder as the minutes passed. Jim Bob turned up the car heater. It was mostly a blast of hot air that warmed your front, dried the inside of your nostrils, and kept the back of your neck chilly.

Finally, it turned level in the mountains, and we cruised into a Colorado town lost to time. The youngest buildings looked as if they had been built in the forties and fifties. Quite charming. A goodly number of the men we saw wore cowboy hats, big buckles, and boots. They looked as if they might go *High Noon* on you in the blink of an eye. The women seemed to like

Navajo-style jewelry and patterned shirts, and most had on blue jeans and boots like their male counterparts.

We had caught up with Veil and could see his SUV in front of us. Jim Bob kept us near it, and then the charming town was behind us and there was a wide highway and purple shadows crawling across the mountains. The mountains looked as if they were leaning against the sky.

Another ten miles or so, and Veil slowed. Off to our right, way out in a field, we could see the dead carnival rides, wrecked cars, and discarded machinery that we had seen on Veil's laptop. From where we were, the rides looked like bones that belonged to odd-shaped Martian invaders. Some were practically on top of others, and some had fallen over from wild winds or had collapsed from gnawing rust.

There was an old color-drained sign leaning against a barbwire fence. The sign said FUN RIDES AND STRANGE EXHIBITS. We could see the big house at the back of the carnival junk, cars, and machinery. It looked as out of place as a pig with a pistol. A road ran up to it.

Farther to the left was a long colorful building that was part of the carnival and had probably housed stalls for ball tosses, darts and balloons, and the like; I couldn't tell for sure, being far away. I could see a narrow dirt road leading to it, and I could see a better road coming out of the trees on the right and going right up to the house. Then the road curved around the front of the house and widened into a parking space.

Veil parked at the side of the road and we parked behind him. We sat in the cars and looked at where we intended to be later on.

Veil started the car, crossed the road, turned around, and headed back into town. We followed suit. The purple shadows had darkened and were painting the mountains with night.

Back in town, we found an old but nice hotel. There were plaques in the hotel that dated it back to the late 1800s. There was another that said Butch Cassidy minus the Sundance Kid might have robbed the town bank, but it also said it might have been Kid Curry that done it. The only thing certain was it had been robbed. The safe was in the hotel, because part of the hotel had once been a bank. The safe was about six feet high and about twelve feet deep. The door to it was wide open. There was no money inside. No gold bullion. No silver. Nothing. Just dead air and a thin spiderweb in the back right corner. The spider had either died or gone on vacation.

On the wall, under framed glass, was the stretched skin of a large rattlesnake. The rattles were set off to the side of the frame. On a sign under the frame, it said the hotel owned the largest rattlesnake skin in Colorado. They failed to mention anything about the skin's original owner. They could at least have given it a name: Duke the Rattlesnake. Sonny Serpent. Ronnie Reptile.

We all checked in, hauled our luggage upstairs, then hustled back down and gathered in the dining room. It was warm without being sticky, and it made me feel sleepy.

Vanilla ordered a salad that wouldn't have been enough food for a caterpillar. Jim Bob had a hamburger. Veil's dinner was a beer and French fries.

I ordered a rib eye steak that was about the size of the source beef but without the horns and hooves. It was well marbled and tasted fantastic. There were sides of fried potatoes and grilled mushrooms. There were slabs of toast the dimensions of gravestones and two grilled green onions. I followed this with a hefty slice of chocolate meringue pie that would give my blood glucose a workout, leave me with hypoglycemia, and make me wish I were dead.

I really had to go back to eating better. I was beating my gut up. But in the back of my head, I was thinking like Leonard was thinking: This could be it, and if I was going to die, I wanted to go out with a steak in my belly, not a kale salad with mango dressing.

Leonard had a steak too.

We talked and decided tonight wasn't the night to do anything. We were too tired from the long drive. Only Vanilla wanted to get it over with. Young whippersnapper. She didn't look tired at all.

It was decided tomorrow night was it. We would take a night to rest and mentally prepare. You have to get your head right to kill someone, you know.

I went upstairs and was glad we had all taken separate rooms. I needed the alone time. I called Brett on one of the burners and told her where we were. I didn't discuss killing anyone.

"I love you," she said.

I said the same.

I took the beach-towel-wrapped disassembled shotgun and the pistol out of my luggage. I cleaned and oiled them both, placed the pistol on the nightstand, and placed the pieces of the shotgun back in the luggage with the towel once more wrapped around them.

I had a book with me, but I couldn't read a line. Couldn't concentrate. I was in one way worked up and in another exhausted from the drive and the heavy meal. I made a note to myself to eat light before tomorrow night. Light meal. Shotgun and pistol. Kill people. Then come back for a shower and a nice nap.

Jesus.

I washed my face and brushed my teeth and put on my pajamas. I sat on the bed and looked around the room. It was decorated in quaint-cowboy style. A set of longhorns on the wall. Wallpaper adorned with a variety of pistol images. The nightstand lamp had one of those old-fashioned lampshades with cowboys and Indians on it. They were all on horses, frozen riders from the past.

I felt a bit out of time myself.

That damn pie was making me feel sleepy. Okay, the steak and potatoes and fried and grilled vegetables were part of that as well.

As I sat there on the bed, I wondered if I might be looking at some of the last things I would ever see. Later, if I lay dying and my life flashed before my eyes, I hoped it wouldn't include that shitty lampshade.

I turned off the light and slipped under the covers.

84

When I awoke it was still dark. It was too early for breakfast, and I wasn't really hungry anyway. The steak was hanging in.

I showered and brushed my teeth and did what I would normally do, then went downstairs. There was a big room off to the side of the welcome desk, and it was full of soft chairs, many of them facing a series of high and wide windows that looked out at the back of the town and the mountains. At that time of dark morning, you couldn't see the mountains.

I saw Veil sitting in the darkened room, looking out the windows at nothing at all.

I went over and sat down in a chair next to him. He said, "You've gotten so you walk heavy."

"I have more to move around than I used to."

"You should be sleeping," he said.

"So should you."

"Couldn't sleep."

"Me either."

"I never do," he said. "I don't even try anymore. I catch a catnap now and then, but I haven't slept through a night in years. Can't remember when I used to sleep."

"Insomnia?"

"Life has gotten too heavy. It weighs on me when I lay down. Thought I'd come here and see the sunrise. I haven't seen one for about as long as I haven't slept. You'd think being awake so much, I'd see one, but I haven't. I didn't know I was missing seeing one until lately. I intend to see one this morning. Sun should rise where I'm looking. There's nothing in the way of my view besides memories."

"How are those memories?"

"Some are excellent, others less so. I look in the mirror and see my ghost."

"When I look, I see a tired man moving into old age. Hell, even Leonard is feeling less fresh these days."

"We are what we are, Hillbilly."

"You don't think we have a choice to be otherwise?"

"I do think we have a choice to make our own decisions and become what we want. What I think you don't see about yourself is that you have become what you wanted to be, even when you don't think so. You're a protector, Hillbilly. So am I."

"Leonard says that too. I don't feel that way. I feel like I didn't listen to myself enough."

"Leonard knows who he is and so do Jim Bob and Vanilla. And so do you, but you haven't realized it yet."

"If all the choices I've made are because I wanted to make them, that depresses me," I said.

"Welcome to the club. Though, truth to tell, you've been a long-standing member. These people — Johnny Joe, Purple Eyes, the ones who work for them or follow them — they have made their choice. I don't care if Johnny Joe didn't get to have a puppy when he was little or that a team of Brownies used to beat him up on his way to school. I don't care if Purple Eyes was sold into prostitution. I don't care what any of those people were made from, because they let their cloth be sewed. The outfit they wear, they made for themselves. People can and do rise above all manner of obstacles because they choose to. I see nothing human about those who act inhuman. And nothing human about those who let them continue to act that way."

There was a crack of light, pink as a ripe persimmon. It widened its way over the mountains, and shadows ran down the mountainside like melting chocolate ice cream. It was astonishingly beautiful.

The pink spread and the mountains became clearer. We sat there until the pink sky brightened. Slowly the pink faded and the sky was less bright. It was now gray and looked polished. There was a smattering of white clouds with gray strands streaking through them.

"Snow," Veil said. "It's coming."

"How do you know?"

"Listened to the weather report on my phone."

"Oh."

"It's called preparation."

It wasn't long before there were little flakes of snow. They blew across the windows like tossed confetti. The flakes swelled in size and began to gather on the ground, and the light shining on them made the ground blindingly white.

"That's going to make it tough," Veil said.

"Suggesting we abort?"

"We do, what will those murderous bastards do tomorrow or the next day, a week or a month from now? Whose life will weigh heavy on our bones? I can't carry much more myself. We've got all the rats in one nest, or a lot of them, anyway. I came ready for this even though I didn't know what it was I came for. I knew it was bigger than a bread box if you were calling on me. But as for waiting until later, that's not acceptable, snow or no snow. And in a way, the snow may be to our advantage. They will most likely hunker down, and for us to do what we plan to do, that's a good thing. 'Wet snow. Blood and ash. The end of everything.'"

"Nice poem," I said.

"I just made it up."

We sat there and watched the snow blow and listened to the wind whistle. Eventually we heard the rattling of dishes in the dining room. We went in there and by this time I was slightly hungry and ordered coffee, toast with butter and jelly. Veil had one poached egg and black coffee. We ate in silence. Somehow silence seemed right, even though we were hours away from what we planned to do. In the night. In the snow. So cold and final.

85

Leonard and I spent some of our day walking and looking about. It was a nice little town. I could have lived there during the summer, but living there this time of year would be awful. I liked the idea of snow, but as for being where it was a regular event, beautiful as it was, I'd rather buy a snow globe and sit by the heater.

It was good for it to be just me and Leonard. It gave us a chance to talk the way we always did, with laughs and jokes and some annoyance at one another. In one store, Leonard bought a black ski hat with bear ears on it, put it on immediately, and strolled around outside with it. It was like taking a walk with Yogi Bear.

Later we found a small grocery store where he bought a box of vanilla cookies. He chided the manager for not carrying Dr Pepper. He had to set-tle for a cream soda.

We stopped at a bench beside a ski shop, and Leonard opened his box of cookies. As usual, he grudgingly offered me a couple, but after that I was cut off. He did let me have a swig of his cream soda. Had it been a Dr Pepper, who's to say. He could hold tight to that beverage.

Vanilla and Veil had gone off to reconnoiter. Find the best way for us to go about doing what we were going to do, as if there were a good way.

We were sitting there, Leonard eating his cookies and drinking his pop, when we saw Jim Bob sauntering toward us. With his hat and boots, he looked like he belonged in this little town. All he needed was horse shit on his bootheels.

He sat down between us and, without asking, reached into the box of cookies and took a handful. Leonard's mouth fell open.

"Did you or did you not just take a fistful of my vanillas?"

"I did indeed," Jim Bob said, and ate one of the cookies like a lion having a hedgehog for lunch. One snap and it was gone. "Nice hat you got there. Did a dying polyester bear will it to you?"

"Jealousy," Leonard said, "is an ugly thing. And it's not polyester."

Leonard put the cookie box on the far side of himself.

Jim Bob ate the rest of the cookies he had snatched.

"Vanilla and Veil are back," Jim Bob said. "They've called a meeting. Thought we'd gather up and they'd tell us what they have to tell. I'm supposed to buy some basic mountaineering equipment."

"Oh, hell no," I said.

"It's not like that," Jim Bob said. "We need just enough rope and the like to scale about fifty or sixty feet."

"I can do that," Leonard said.

"I'm not sure I can," I said.

"Yeah, you can, Hap," Jim Bob said. "We'll need the right shoes too. Nothing too mountaineer-style. We're most likely going to have to do some running. I have some work boots I'll wear." Jim Bob eyed Leonard. "Might want to slow down on those cookies. You'll be too full for lunch."

"I'll do all right," Leonard said. "I'll take a dump before lunch."

86

The sunlight shone through the dining-room windows and onto the part of the floor closest to the windows. The bright spot it made looked like a golden drop-off to nowhere.

I was sitting at the table with the others, having finished a lunch of salad and soup, keeping it light. I was sipping a cup of coffee, listening to Vanilla.

"There's a back road that leads to the rear of the house and the carnival rides. It's a good road and goes right up to the front door. But if we were to come in on that, they would know we were coming pretty quick. The woods and rocks on either side of the road clear up, and then there's a big space with the house on it. Easy to see who's coming. But there's a rock face and you can get to it by taking a trail on foot. It's not far from the road, but it drops off back there and there's just the forest in one direction, sloping down so sharp you could lose your footing and slide off into nothing. Other side, there's a not-too-high — fifty- or sixty-foot — rock face. We can climb that. It comes up near the back of the house. Almost its back door. It's not exactly a space anyone would expect someone to use. That gives us a jump."

"Because it's straight up and dangerous and no one in their right mind would come in that way," Veil said.

"Well, that sells me," I said.

"It only takes a few minutes to climb if it's not too slick from snow and we can get traction," Vanilla said.

"Sounding better yet," I said. "So we all go through the back door, guns blazing."

"No," Veil said. "I will come up the road eventually, when they are distracted. I can't make that climb. But you can bet I'll be there for you. When you hear my horn honking, get the hell out of the way, and don't hesitate."

"When I get to the top of the rock wall," Vanilla said, "I'm going to move around beside the house and out to the rides and find myself a sniper position there. I'll be picking off anyone I can, wiping up stragglers."

"Hillbilly, you and Leonard go through that back door like a tank," Veil said. "That's what you do best. Hit hard and fast."

"The Elephant of Surprise," Leonard said.

"Exactly," I said.

"And me?" Jim Bob asked.

"You, my man, you go through the front door," Veil said.

"That's like saying crawl into a lit cannon and wait for it to go off," Jim Bob said.

"Wait until Hap and Leonard come through the back, and when you hear that, give it a couple of beats, then you go through the front door," Veil said. "Frankly, you probably won't get that far. The rats will be coming out of that front door at a run, and you'll be off to the side waiting to pick them off."

"All right," Jim Bob said. "That sounds like shotgun and pistol work."

"What it is," Veil said, "is bloody work."

87

Just before the shadows got long, with snow blowing and the wind howling, we checked out of the hotel and put our suitcases in Jim Bob's car along with the climbing equipment we had bought.

Veil and Vanilla went in his SUV. They knew the back road, so we were to follow them. That would take some work; the way the snow was blowing, you could get lost crossing the street.

I had called Brett after lunch, and we talked awhile. I told her tonight was it, but the rest of the time we talked about other things.

I hated to tell her goodbye.

We came to where the road narrowed and there was a wide spot on the left side, but on the right were the trees, and the boughs of the trees were decorated with snow, and it seemed like ice cream in the moonlight. The snow was turning deep.

Jim Bob parked us behind Veil's SUV. We got out and went around to the trunk and got our guns and climbing gear out. Vanilla was doing the same. Veil was wearing high boots with a heavy coat, standing still and cool as a statue, except for when he touched a cigarette to his mouth. There were smoking puffs and breath puffs in the air around him.

Vanilla was dressed all in black and her hair was under a black wool cap. She had a headband over that with a headlamp on it. She took a broken-down bow out of her case and began putting it together. It was one of those strong ones with arrows with wide heads, and if one went into you, and you pulled it out, a whole lot of you would come out with it.

She finished putting it together rapidly and put her leg against it and bent it so she could string it. She took a sheath out of one of the cases, screwed all the arrows together, put them in a quiver, and fastened it across her back. She slung the bow over her neck and shoulder. She had her plastic rifle with her, and it had a broad strap that she merely hung over one shoulder. She had a large revolver stuck in a holster on her belt. She looked like a modern-day ninja.

Leonard, still wearing his stupid hat with the ears, looked like a cartoon bear. He got his weapons out of the trunk and slung the strap that held the shotgun over his shoulder. Dropped a pistol in his coat pocket.

Jim Bob wore black as well. He had on dark boots that laced up. It seemed strange, seeing him without his cowboy boots. He took off his cowboy hat and placed it on the seat, pulled a dark ski mask on. He hauled a sawed-off shotgun in a holster out of the trunk. It was sawed off at the stock and the barrel. He slipped the holster on his belt, under his coat. On the other side he had a holstered .45 revolver. That thing could knock a hole in a hole.

I was also decked out in black, and the coat I wore was kind of light for the weather, but I was hoping when I got heated up from activity, I would be comfortable enough. Mainly I didn't want to be bulked up and hot if I had to move quick.

I had a pump shotgun strapped across my back and a Smith and Wesson .40-caliber Bulldog five-shot revolver stuck in a holster on my belt. I always feared an automatic would jam.

I pulled a black ski mask over my head but rolled the front up and pushed it on top of my head. A mask over my face made me claustrophobic. I got closer to action, I'd pull it down.

We gathered around Veil. He said, "Vanilla knows the way. She'll lead you. Like I said, I'll meet you. Text me right before. When you see me coming, might want to get out of the way. I'll be honking. You are forewarned, and that's the end of that."

Veil lit another cigarette after dropping the nub of the first into the snow. They were unfiltered. That helped explain his fatal diagnosis.

Following Vanilla, we took a precarious route across the road and down a hill packed with snow, more of it falling. The wind had picked up hard enough to blow a shadow away.

Going down the hill was hard work. The trees were close, though, and we used those to help keep us on our feet as we followed her down. She hardly touched the trees. She moved with the grace of a lynx.

When we were pretty far down the hill, there was a snowy trail beside a gurgling stream. The only light, besides the snow-beleaguered moon, was Vanilla's headlamp. Seeing moonlight through snow was so crazy and beautiful, it made me sad that I might get killed.

As we moved along, the snow crackled under out feet like crackers in cellophane. We came to a rock wall that was wide and high. We were going that way so we could come up to the rear of the house.

"You're certain this leads to the house?" Jim Bob asked.

"Certain as we have to be," Vanilla said.

"So you're not absolutely sure," Leonard said.

"Ah, old black bear of so little faith, you'll see soon enough," Vanilla said.

She started for the wall, unfastened the climbing gear from herself, and set us in motion.

88

It was done pretty much old-school.

Vanilla slung a rope and hook up a few times before she found a hold on a precarious rock projection that looked as if a sack of marbles would cause it to come loose. She went up the rope easy enough, bouncing her feet on the wall, climbing rapidly, snow twirling around her. She paused about halfway for the rest of us to catch up. We needed to go into the big moment together.

Jim Bob started up.

I looked at Leonard in his bear hat, said, "You look like a fucking fool."

"You and me, Boo-Boo," he said.

We cast our hooks and lines a few times, finally got hooked in, and up we all went, the snow blowing, the rock wall slick, our feet slipping. The dead night became a bit bright from time to time when the moon escaped from behind clouds before being sacked over again by more rolling snow clouds.

The air was cold and the snow had made me more than a bit damp, so that wasn't helping. My leg was cramping as well. To make matters worse, Leonard, for whatever reason, was clowning, hanging to his rope by one hand, feet against the rock wall, smiling at me. In that moment, he was a mountaineer bear without a care in the world.

By the time I got to the ledge and lay on my belly, I felt as if I wanted to jump off the cliff and get it over with.

My stomach was full of butterflies. The air was full of snow. And Vanilla and Jim Bob were moving.

Vanilla flicked off her headlamp and lay prone on the ground a moment, then when all of us were over the rock wall, she was up and going again, little more than a running shadow. She slipped along the edge of the house, going down on all fours when she came to a window, running under it like a dog.

When she got to the end of the house, she peeked around to get a glimpse of the porch. I saw her slip the bow off her shoulder and fasten an arrow against the string about as fast as it takes someone to blow a breath out.

The arrow flew and her breath flew out with it. I couldn't see her target, but I had no doubt she had punctured someone's life plans. And then Vanilla was moving again, toward the rides, where she would find a sniper position.

It would be up to Jim Bob, coming around on the other side of the porch, to pull anyone she had killed to where they wouldn't be seen for a while, or at least long enough for us to make our moves.

The snow was really swirling now.

I pulled my burner phone from my pocket. There was a text from Jim Bob.

VANILLA ARROWED A GUY

I texted back.

COMING IN TWO BEATS

I went first, but not to the back door. Leonard and I made a whispered variation to our plan. I got to the first window alongside the house, dropped to a knee, peeked inside. There were two or three people moving about and there was a light on. They were carrying plates and coming out of a room on the other side of the house. An early dinner brought from the kitchen. It might have been dark and cold, but it hadn't been night long. No one had given up the day yet.

I could see a number of those cooling containers for body organs in choo-choo-train order along the wall. Were the parts of humans in them or were they merely there for future storage? It was like peeking into Dr. Frankenstein's house.

Maybe we should wait until they went to bed, kill them in their sleep. Would there be a guard? Perhaps. Right then my temples were pounding and I was fighting tunnel vision. I had learned to keep my thoughts and vision sharp under these kinds of circumstances, but I was cold and a little afraid, so I was faltering.

The damp ground was soaking through the knee of my pants, and I was on the border of miserable, but it was now or never. I thought about it too much longer, I'd be climbing down that wall, heading back to the car.

Me and Leonard met up at the back door. We looked at one another. We were going to hit that door as hard as we could and give them the Elephant of Surprise. We slung our shotguns into position and focused.

That's when there was the booming sound of a big ten-gauge shotgun, and the door flew open and knocked me off the steps, onto my back, into the snow.

89

A guy about the size of a water buffalo in platform shoes but actually dressed in khaki and lace-up boots came staggering out, hands to his chest, blood squirting from between his fingers. The smell of the blood was coppery and some of it sprayed onto my face. It was hot, like drops of acid.

He looked at Leonard, then down at me. His eyes were wide and confused. He tried to say something, but all that came out of his mouth was a gout of blood. Snow spun against his face like little moths to a flame.

Leonard moved aside, put out his foot, and tripped the man off the porch steps. He landed facedown in the snow, making a spray of red and a sudden puddle of the same against the white of the snow under his head.

The back of his shirt was ripped open where the shotgun load had plowed all the way through, and gore was easing out of that. It was a miracle he had been able to stand, make it through the door. The miracle, such as it was, had ended, and Jim Bob's shotgun was the obvious explanation for the dead man's hole.

Jim Bob wouldn't have jumped the gun out of nervousness. I knew he had been put in a position where he couldn't wait. Maybe he had been seen.

We were in for it.

I sat up, slipped a bit in the snow trying to get my feet under me. Leonard had already moved into the house and his shotgun roared and I heard things rattling and falling. As I came up the steps, a shot whizzed so close to my ear, I felt my earlobe vibrate.

Three men were trying to get through the opening of the living room to the foyer and then the front door. Two of them made it. Leonard cut down the other, caught him solid in the back, and down he went. He tried to crawl. As Leonard strode toward the now open front door, he put the shotgun to the head of the man on the floor and finished him.

There were shots outside. One of them was that puffing noise Vanilla's rifle made, the other that soul-dividing sound of Jim Bob's ten-gauge.

I hadn't fired a shot. A moment later, glancing out at the porch, I saw a man just off the steps, lying facedown. On the porch was the one Vanilla had put an arrow through — it had gone into his throat. I saw off to my right, still in the house, a man with his back against the hall wall. The window that was almost in front of him looked out on the porch. The glass was shattered. Jim Bob must have been seen by the man inside and clocked him early, shooting through the glass. That was what had got the ball rolling.

I turned and went back into the living room and through the rest of the house, going cautious, ready to shoot. I found a side door open, and when I stepped outside, I could see six people moving swiftly down the slightly elevated dirt path that led across the long expanse of carnival rides and rusting junk.

As I watched, there was a puff sound, and blood and human matter jumped up from the head of one of the people on the trail, a woman, and she went down. Vanilla on point again.

The rest disappeared amongst the carnival equipment. I noted one of them was Graham and another was a well-built blond woman that I surmised was Purple Eyes. They were trotting swiftly and carrying long guns.

There was another puffing sound, then a ping out amongst the carnival rides. Vanilla had a rare miss and hit metal. The escapees were swallowed by the bends and twists of rusting metal.

Leonard and Jim Bob had come around to my side of the house. Vanilla maintained. I saw she was positioned high up on a dangling bucket ride. She was in one of the buckets with her rifle. She didn't try to climb down. For now, she was more useful to us where she was. She had a better view than we did.

"I don't like it, boys, but I'm going in," Jim Bob said.

Leonard and I grunted agreement. My tongue felt too large in my mouth for comment.

I went down the middle and Leonard went to my right and Jim Bob to my left. As we entered among the machines that had given there last good moments to yelling, puking kids and teenagers who wanted to hold hands, I tried to stay focused, knowing any of the killers could pop out at any time. I took some comfort in the fact that Vanilla was up and behind us, ready to shoot.

We came to the long building at the back of it all. It had push-up fronts and two of them were pushed up. I could see the tip of a rifle poking out.

I yelled, and we all hit the snow as the air was torn with a racket of gun-fire. One of those bullets damn near named me man of the year, but instead burned by me with a whistling sound.

I rolled over behind a mass of collapsed equipment, poked my shotgun around the corner, and decided I was too far away for it to matter enough. I had to get closer.

Jim Bob and Leonard had rolled up behind some broken-down rides as well. Jim Bob said, "Well, unless you two ladies have too much sand in your pussies, we're going to have to go after them."

"Say that to Vanilla," I said. "The sand-in-the-pussy part."

"Nope," Jim Bob said.

In spite of Jim Bob's words, none of us volunteered to jump up and run at them. We would have been nothing but rags before we had gone five feet. The long building where they were housed was over a couple hundred feet away.

Where the gun had fired at us previously, I saw a head raise up slowly, then I saw what looked like a cap flying off the top of his head, but the cap was the upper part of his skull. I hadn't even heard the puff that time, just a sound like someone had dropped a cheap water glass.

Vanilla was on the job.

But the others in the building, they were well embedded. Not as subject to her marksmanship. I was formulating a sneak-around plan, thinking about moving through the equipment, trying to get closer for the shotgun advantage, but the rides didn't really offer that much protection.

I was on my belly on the ground behind a chunk of metal that belonged to an enormous merry-go-round with wooden horses on it. When the guy Vanilla had popped had opened up with his gun earlier, it had taken the heads off a couple horses, nipped a tail off another, and punched through several others like a wet finger through a paper napkin.

Butterflies fluttered in my belly, but I was determined to get closer. Before I could act, I heard a horn honking again and again, turned to see Veil driving up the road in front of the house. I suppose he could see our situation, because he drove off the road and onto the trail among the junk.

My position was slightly elevated near the trail, and looking down I could see the SUV coming up it. Veil had one hand on the wheel. He had a cigarette in is mouth and was lighting it with a lighter. He was wearing something across his chest. It had wires on it.

Last sight of Veil was a haze of cigarette smoke. There was more honking, and then I knew what had been in the bag in his back seat and why he'd wanted Leonard to stay away from it.

Veil had indicated what he planned to do without really saying it.

He hit the gas and the SUV howled and went to the peak of the trail, then down it. It wasn't much of a change of elevation, but it sent the SUV sailing in the air momentarily. It hit on all four tires, bounced, landed hard. Veil didn't slow down one whit.

Bullets flew, striking the windshield and the SUV's body, but it was too late to stop him. When he hit that long, low building, there was an explosion that blew it apart and sent a ball of flame high and wide. The heat of it licked at my face and singed my eyebrows.

"Son of a bitch," Leonard yelled out. "Son of a bitch has done it."

A flaming body came running out of the ball of fire, rushed toward the woods, fell into the snow, rolled over a couple of times, reached out with a blackened hand, and didn't move again.

I saw the woman then. Purple Eyes, I still assumed. Her hair was partly on fire and she was sporting some flames on the back of her shirt, but she wasn't altogether ablaze. She ran back toward the house, then veered, flaming more now, and ran over the small cliff we had scaled, her feet pedaling air.

She might have survived the fire, but the leap off that cliff was going to be a hard recovery.

The SUV was little more than a charred husk. I thought I could see a body behind the wheel, but I didn't want to look. I knew who that was and how he would be: charcoal and smoke. He had gone out the way he had wanted to, and he had saved our asses.

I hated to admit it, but I was glad. I didn't like to think of Veil inching out into the dark fantastic on a morphine drip in a hospice.

We lay where we were briefly, then I stood up, the shotgun in front of me, and wandered toward the remains of the SUV and the building.

The building was so cheaply made, it had blown completely apart, and pieces of it blazed in the snow. There were some twists of darkened meat that were what was left of Johnny Joe's team.

I walked over to the man on the ground. There was enough of his face left for me to determine it was Johnny Joe, aka Graham, the lawyer we had met. He squirmed a little.

Jim Bob and Leonard came over. Leonard looked down on our adversary, said, "I think it's going to be a warm day, shithead. Don't you?"

I thought at first the man said, "Fuck you," but it was really just a coughing noise and a puff of smoke that came out of his mouth.

By this time Vanilla had arrived. She was carrying her bow and rifle. She looked down on the dying man, his body licked by little flames, emitting puffs of smoke, unable to move. She dropped the rifle and bow, pulled her handgun, and shot him through the head.

"Call it charity," she said.

90

The fire was still burning, but lower than before. The building was little more than ash and some tossed smoking lumber. The SUV burned brighter and the wind whipped the flames and they made a snapping sound, like flags on a blustery day.

I finally looked at Veil's body, but there was really nothing left but the blaze crisping his shattered bones. Glass from the SUV lay in the snow, and the fire flicked light on it. The snow came down on that, and even as I watched, the glass was buried by it.

"We have to start moving," Jim Bob said, and move we did. I had a difficult time convincing myself that Veil was gone. I half expected him to come out of some dark spot lighting a cigarette.

We stopped at the place where we had seen Purple Eyes go over in a flash of smoke and flames. Vanilla held her headlamp in her hand, and all of us pulled out our flashes for a look and let our yellow beams flow over the ground below. There was nothing to see but some spots of blood in the snow.

"Damn," Leonard said, "that bitch is Rasputin."

We didn't climb down the wall. All we had to do now was walk along the road, back to the car. We debated going down and then around to the bottom of the wall to look for Purple Eyes, but maybe someone passing by on the highway had seen the explosion or the flames, and the fire department and the police were on their way.

We just didn't have time to search.

"She may have survived that jump," Jim Bob said. "The snow's grown thick. But I can't imagine her not being damaged in the jump. I figure she crawled off like a snake to die in the woods."

"Maybe," Vanilla said.

"I'm telling you," Leonard said, "that bitch is like a cockroach. She can survive anything if she survived that jump. Next thing you know she'll be on a beach somewhere drinking liquor out of someone's skull."

We walked down the road and loaded up the car with our guns and gear. Jim Bob hauled us out of there, through the night and snow, the car heater blowing, making my damp self sleepy and warm.

After what I had done, how could I be sleepy? But I was. I felt like a kitten in a basket full of soft yarn.

I glanced in the back seat. Vanilla sat behind Jim Bob. She was leaning against the door. She looked fast asleep. She had a smile on her face.

Leonard was on the seat beside her, looking at her.

"That bitch jumped," Leonard said, "but this here Vanilla bitch, she's bound to be the goddamn devil."

"This bitch is awake," she said without opening her eyes.

91

We didn't try and stay in town; instead, Jim Bob drove us onward through the snowstorm until it was too bad to see. We found a little burg with a Best Western and got rooms. As with all our purchases since leaving LaBorde, Jim Bob used a charge card with another name on it.

By this point, I had lost my sleepy feeling and was edgy.

Leonard and I shared a room. Leonard was in bed, sitting up, with pillows propped behind his head. He called Pookie with his burner, then looked at me while I used my burner to let Brett know we were okay, that I loved her. Then I called Chief Justin to tell him what we had done. I put the phone on speaker.

When I finished telling Justin, he said, "I didn't hear any of this, but I'll do what I can do to keep you guys unconnected, though that's not my jurisdiction."

"I know."

"You did all you said you did, it'll be all right."

"Not for them," I said.

"No," he said, "not for them."

"Fuck them," Leonard said in the direction of the phone. "Had the time, I'd have salted the fucking earth and pissed on Johnny Joe's corpse and shit down his burned-up mouth."

"Leonard sounds happy," Justin said.

"Oh, yeah," I said. "What about Olivia?"

"What about her?" he said.

"You know what I mean."

"You do some crazy things for your kids. You guys came out okay. At my behest, Olivia will move on and hopefully never speak of it again. She has her boy back, and that's enough."

"But Berry might talk about it," I said. "He's old enough to remember."

"Yeah, but according to Olivia, he's smart enough to forget. Or pretend to. I think we're good. I'm glad those bastards are gone."

I told him about Purple Eyes.

"That's interesting, but if she jumped from the height you say, even with snow on the rocks, she couldn't have come out of that intact and might not have lasted too long with broken legs."

"You wouldn't think so," I said. I talked to Justin some more as I sat on the bed, seeing the parking-lot lights through a window with the curtains pulled back. The snow was churning in the light like soapsuds in a washing machine.

I told Justin about Veil, explained who he was and what happened.

"I don't know there's anything I can say or do about him," Justin said. "Authorities will mix him into the mix any way they want."

"I don't think he'd care," I said. "He completed his mission."

When I hung up, I glanced at Leonard. He had his bear hat pushed back and was fast asleep, the pillows still propped behind his head.

I went over and eased his head down by removing one of the pillows. That way he wouldn't wake up with a stiff neck.

I pulled a cover over him. I went and drew the curtains closed, cutting off the light.

I lay down on my bed, pulled the covers over me. The heating unit rattled a little, then turned to a satisfying hum.

My arms were outside the covers. My hands trembled a little. I smelled of smoke.

I wondered if we had really killed that organization. We'd thought we had before, and then another had risen up from it: Johnny Joe and Purple Eyes. I didn't really know what Purple Eyes' connection was. Was she a prominent hired hand or the mastermind of the whole operation?

Perhaps we had put a big enough dent in it this time there wouldn't be any coming back. Perhaps with the head of the snake gone, the rest of the body would die.

Impossible to know. At least at this point.

I finally began to drift off. My last thoughts were of a woman, her clothes smoking, crawling through a snowy forest with vengeance on her mind.

92

Sometime after all of it, I got a call from Al to come out to his patch of land and see him. On a warm day that was an interruption in a series of cold days, me and Brett and Leonard drove out there in the used car me and Brett had bought. A hybrid Chevrolet. We had given the old Prius to Chance.

I was surprised to see the mobile home was nothing but smoking bones, so to speak, and the white yurt was now a blackened yurt or, rather, a pile of burned lumber. The carport and Al's old car looked fine.

Beside the carport was a large tent. The flap was up and I could see camp furniture in there, and Al himself. He came walking out, wearing khaki shorts, shoes without socks, and a Hawaiian shirt with palm trees and hula girls on it.

He lifted a hand as we arrived.

We parked and walked over to the tent. Before we were inside, Al said, "One beauty and two ugly beasts."

"Usually," Leonard said, "I wouldn't tolerate anyone talking about Brett and Hap like that."

Al laughed his big laugh and we went into the tent and sat down in the camp chairs.

"What happened to the yurt and the mobile home?" Brett asked.

"Damn chicken snakes got into my mice, so I set the couch on fire. Well, snakes got out anyway, crawling everywhere. The couch fire got out of hand, and you can see the results. A spark got to the yurt. Who knew the damn thing would burn like paper? I accidently burned up some mice, but most of them made it out."

"Hope you had insurance," Leonard said.

"Did. Got the money already. Even though I started the fire. I thought that might be a problem, me starting the fire, but the yurt burning down was an act of the wind. The mobile home is on me. I'm rebuilding soon. No yurt this time. Going for a two-story."

"Feeling more traditional," I said.

"Seems that way. So, you never heard if Earline, or whatever her real name was, survived?"

"No idea," I said. "The Colorado authorities didn't know to look for a body near the cliff, and we weren't in a position to tell them about her."

"She's probably nothing but some animal-picked bones by now," Leonard said.

"I guess so," Al said. "Damn, she was awful, but what bones she had and what flesh she had stretched over them so nice. But here's the reason I asked you to come out."

Al got up and went to a dresser that was set in there, opened the top drawer, scrounged around, came back with a large cardboard box. He handed it to Brett.

"Damn, that's heavy," she said.

"Jim Bob and that stunning woman with the scary eyes each get one too," Al said.

"If you can find her," I said. "What is it we have here?"

Brett placed the box on the floor and opened it. There were lots of green bills in it. Large denominations.

"That's a lot of money," Brett said.

"And all honest as the day is long," Al said. "Nothing dodgy there. That's your fee for services."

Brett went through it. After quite a while, she said, "This is two million dollars."

"I know," Al said. "Divide it by three."

"We can't take this," Brett said.

"Man's offering," Leonard said.

"I don't mean to sound like an elite asshole," Al said, "but it's nothing for me. Now that I got all my money loose, I'm a rich mother. So on top of your fee, that's a gift."

"That's damn generous," I said.

"You saved this old fool and took care of someone who I think in time might have taken care of me. That's worth two million dollars."

"Out of curiosity," Leonard said, "how much do Jim Bob and Vanilla get?"

"Five hundred thousand apiece. They weren't in on it from the start."

"I'll try and contact Vanilla for you," I said. "Jim Bob is easy to find."

Al brought out liquor then. I passed. So did Brett. Leonard had a drink.

"Got any vanilla cookies?" Leonard said. "Goes good with a whiskey like this, I kid you not."

"Afraid not," Al said. "I have some crackers."

"That's okay," Leonard said, lifting his glass. "All right, then, here's to your happy ass, Al, and to the sad absence of vanilla cookies. May all your snake-eaten mice go to a mousy heaven full of cheese and no reptiles."

"Good enough," Al said, and tipped his glass.

ACKNOWLEDGMENTS

ABOUT THE AUTHOR

Joe R. Lansdale is the author of nearly four dozen novels, including *Rusty Puppy*, the Edgar Award–winning *The Bottoms, Sunset and Sawdust*, and *Leather Maiden*. He has received eleven Bram Stoker Awards, the Edgar Award, the British Fantasy Award, the Grinzane Cavour Prize, and the Spur Award. He lives with his family in Nacogdoches, Texas.